**Quintin touched his**

He laid his mouth gently against the slight rise of an almost-healed blister. It felt so warm, and was ridiculously like some heady perfume. When he kissed it, he heard Riley drag in a deep breath of her own.

"Quintin..."

"I know," he said in a slow, husky voice. He lifted his head to catch her gaze. Her mouth was parted, and she was frowning. "Insane, isn't it?"

"I—" The word was a trembling sigh, barely more than a whisper. She wet her lips. When she tugged her hand away, he released it immediately. "I think I should get back to the men."

He watched her walk away from the shadows and back into the soft light where the cowboys stood. Watched her, and thought how much he had liked what happened. How he had enjoyed it more than he had anything in a long, long time.

But what he'd done had made a difficult situation even more so, and he couldn't help but realize how foolish he'd been.

Dear Reader,

By the time I finished writing *That Last Night in Texas,* I had developed quite a fondness for Ethan's business partner and best friend, Quintin Avenaco. As the story evolved, I grew more and more interested in exploring his tragic past and what had brought him to this point in his life. So when my editor asked if I might like to write about Quintin, I was ready.

Unfortunately, that's where my muse deserted me. I knew what Quintin's goals for himself were. But for the life of me, I couldn't imagine the kind of woman who could bring him out of his painful past and make him willing to face the world again. Weeks went by, and I began to wonder if I'd ever find her.

Then I came across a magazine article about a group of people who had lost their jobs as a result of the economy. They had been brought to the lowest point in their lives, but instead of giving up, they reevaluated the talents they had developed, the strengths they could tap into, the dreams they had left behind as too impractical. Instead of trying to find a new position in their chosen fields, they channeled their efforts into creating new careers for themselves. Some of them succeeded on a grand scale. Others had to adjust to earning a bit less money, but they were far happier than they'd ever been in their old jobs.

I thought a woman with that kind of brave, single-minded purpose might work well as my heroine and make an excellent match for a loner like Quintin. So that's how Riley Palmer came to life—a divorced mother of twins who is desperately determined to make a good life for her children, even if she has to persuade a lonely, no-nonsense cowboy like Quintin that she will make an excellent ranch manager for him.

I hope you enjoy Quintin and Riley's journey. Please don't hesitate to contact me at eannbair@gmail.com or visit my Facebook page. I love to hear from readers.

All the best,

Ann Evans

# Temporary Rancher
## *Ann Evans*

TORONTO NEW YORK LONDON
AMSTERDAM PARIS SYDNEY HAMBURG
STOCKHOLM ATHENS TOKYO MILAN MADRID
PRAGUE WARSAW BUDAPEST AUCKLAND

Recycling programs
for this product may
not exist in your area.

ISBN-13: 978-0-373-78486-8

TEMPORARY RANCHER

# ABOUT THE AUTHOR

Ann Evans has been writing since she was a teenager, but it wasn't until she joined Romance Writers of America that she actually sent anything to a publisher. Eventually, with the help of a very good critique group, she honed her skills and won a Golden Heart from Romance Writers of America for Best Short Contemporary Romance of 1989. Since then, she's happy to have found a home writing for the Harlequin Superromance line. A native Floridian, Ann enjoys traveling, hot-fudge sundaes and collecting antique postcards.

## Books by Ann Evans

Don't miss any of our special offers. Write to us at the following address for information on our newest releases.

Harlequin Reader Service
U.S.: 3010 Walden Ave., P.O. Box 1325, Buffalo, NY 14269
Canadian: P.O. Box 609, Fort Erie, Ont. L2A 5X3

# CHAPTER ONE

THE COMPUTER SCREEN glowed in the darkened shadows of the living room. Riley Palmer stared at it, wondering why she couldn't seem to hit the email send button.

"Do it, Riley," she muttered softly. "Nothing ventured, nothing gained. Do it for Wendy and Roxanna and yourself. Do it for the National Organization for Women. Just do it!"

Her fingers hovered over the mouse as she tried to find courage.

Tonight her sister's small apartment felt cozy, but foreign somehow. Both the girls were sound asleep in Jillian's spare bedroom—as they should be this close to two in the morning. Her sister had gone to bed after the late news. The place was so quiet Riley thought she could hear her wristwatch ticking.

It was the perfect time to think about making life-changing decisions, the perfect time to work through her thoughts in peace and quiet, and she'd spent the past two hours doing just that. So why couldn't she send this email?

She knew that some of her reluctance was because her email wasn't completely honest. She hadn't lied, exactly. Just embroidered a little. Considering the current job market, who *didn't* do that when they applied for work these days?

Desperation made a powerful motivator. She'd been divorced from Brad for almost a year, but she was still sleeping on the couch in her sister's apartment while the twins took the second bedroom. Jillian had been an angel about all of them sharing such tight quarters, but it wasn't right.

Riley needed a job. She needed decent money coming in. Most of all, she needed a home for her eight-year-olds, Wendy and Roxanna. The decision to leave their father had been hard enough on the girls. They deserved stability. Security. Faith that their mother could provide for them. So if that meant adding a few embellishments to her résumé and omitting one big, stupid drawback that shouldn't even be an issue… Well, so be it.

And really, would Charlie Bigelow ever steer her wrong intentionally? He'd been friends with her family for nearly forty years. He'd helped Riley and Jillian plan their parents' funeral after the accident, guided them through probate, even walked Riley down the aisle. All those times when Brad had left her on the ranch to figure out things for herself, hadn't Charlie been the one she'd turned to for advice?

If he thought this Quintin Avenaco guy would make a fair boss, and she'd be a great ranch manager for him, then who was she to disagree? Charlie didn't just know livestock. He knew people.

Riley had always been a little impulsive, and in the past had made a few foolish decisions she'd been forced to live with. But this was a chance she *had* to take. She couldn't stand the idea of spending another week searching for a job and coming up empty-handed. With that thought, she surrendered to impulse and clicked the send button before she could change her mind. The email zipped into cyberspace. "There you go, Quintin Avenaco of Beaumont, Texas. You've got mail, cowboy."

Almost immediately she had second thoughts. She should have checked her résumé one more time, tried to find a way to honestly address the only problem she could see that might get her a big fat no right off the bat.

She placed her hands on either side of the screen. "I take it back! Give me a do over, darn it."

"So now you're talking to yourself?"

Riley nearly yelped out loud. She turned to

find her sister at her shoulder, yawning. "Geez. You scared the life out of me."

Jillian frowned down at her. "Why are you still up?"

"The usual. Job hunting. Charlie Bigelow called me yesterday afternoon with a lead. I'm following up on it before it hits the classifieds."

"Great," her sister replied, though she sounded too sleepy to care much.

"I hope it will be great. I hope it pays a ridiculous amount of money, though right now, I'd settle for a place to live."

"You have that here."

"I know, but you're family. You have to pretend you like living in a two-bedroom apartment with four people. And when *two* of those people are rambunctious eight-year-olds…"

Jillian gave a grumpy growl. "Don't say a word about my nieces! They're angels. You're the one I just tolerate."

Riley smiled up at her. Really, how would she have managed without Jilly's help this past year? Her life had been torn to shreds by Brad's infidelity, Wendy's stay in the hospital and that bitter court battle for custody. Through it all, Jillian had been a rock.

"I know my kids," Riley told her. "Somehow they've reverted to the terrible twos without my permission. Wendy starts bawling if you just look at her the wrong way. And Rox…Rox's answer to everything I say is 'Why?' I checked her scalp yesterday to see if 666 had been branded there."

"They're just…unsettled right now. But I think we're managing."

"I have to do more than just manage, Jilly. We can't continue to impose on you this way. I know Doug wants to take your relationship to the next level, as they say. But he can't do that with the three of us underfoot. So that means I need a decent paying job and a place to call home."

Jillian conceded that point with a grimace, then stared down at the computer screen. "Anything else encouraging out there? I heard Wegman's is thinking about opening up a third store. They might need accounting help."

Before the girls were born, Riley had been a pretty competent bookkeeper. "I'm not going after any more accounting jobs. Every bean counter in the country seems to be looking for work in Texas." She put a big smile on her face, ready to go into sales mode for Jillian's sake. "I'm reinventing myself. All the magazines say that in this job market you need to review the talents you have and find work that fits them. So I did."

Jillian looked at her askance. "What talent do you have besides accounting?"

"You don't have to sound so incredulous. There are lots of things I can do. And I just took the first step."

She tapped the computer screen and clicked into her sent mail so Jillian could see her latest message.

"'Dear Mr. Avenaco,'" Jillian read over Riley's shoulder. "'I understand from a mutual friend of ours, Charlie Bigelow, that you'll soon be in the market for a ranch manager…'" She straightened and scowled. "You're applying to be his ranch manager? When have you done that kind of work?"

Riley frowned back. "Who do you think managed Hollow Creek? While Brad was playing footsie with his boss's daughter, I kept our place up and running. I might not have the *official* credentials, but I can do that job, and pretty well, I think."

"Really?" Her sister looked very skeptical now. "You know everything about running a ranch."

Riley felt her cheeks grow hot. All right. Admittedly, there were a few holes in her résumé that she'd glossed over. But she didn't see her shortcomings as a serious problem. "Well, maybe not *everything*. But close enough. Charlie's been out to this guy's place in Beaumont. He says Avenaco's only going to run about one-hundred head. Strictly horses." She lifted her eye-brows. "He's probably a Sunday cowboy who's in love with the idea of the Old West. Which means he'll be open to someone else's direction."

"Or he'll second-guess every move you make, and watch every dollar you spend to be sure he's getting his money's worth. He could drive you nuts, micromanaging. And what about…what about the other thing? The fact that you're…"

"A woman?" Riley finished, wishing her sister hadn't gone there. It had taken Riley two hours to convince herself she could overcome the gender problem. "I keep reminding myself that this is the twenty-first century. Texas State had thirty students in their ranch management class last year. Four of them were women. I checked. That has to be a good sign, doesn't it?"

"Did any of those women get jobs? This is Texas. You know the men here can be…kind of chauvinistic."

"Some of them. That's why I'm not telling this guy I'm a female." She lifted her chin, prepared to argue if her ultraconventional sister found fault. Which she did. Immediately.

"You *lied* to him?"

"No!"

Riley pointed to the bottom of the message, where she had signed off. "I used my real name.

It's not my fault Dad wanted a boy, and I ended up with a name that could work either way."

"But Avenaco will probably think you're a man."

"Then that's *his* foolish mistake," she said, determined to be positive. "If he flat out asks me, I'll tell him, but otherwise…"

"Did you tell him you have two little girls?"

"No. What difference does that make, as long as I can do the job?" Seeing her sister's face, Riley called up some of the same reasoning she'd used on herself only hours ago. "Look, it's not like I'm going to dress up as a guy and lower my voice to try to fool anyone."

"I'm relieved to hear that."

"Stop staring at me like I'm one of the trespassers who sneaked into the White House. I just want to establish an email relationship with him, chat back and forth. Maybe he'll realize how capable I am *before* we actually talk on the phone or meet in person."

"Charlie must have told him you're a woman."

"He didn't, because the conversation never got that far. Avenaco said he was looking for a ranch manager, and Charlie told him he knew a couple of good prospects and would send them his way. That was it."

"But surely…"

"This guy doesn't exactly own the King

Ranch, you know?" Riley argued. "Who's ever heard of Echo Springs? How demanding can it be?"

"Who'll watch the girls while you're out digging postholes and herding horses?"

"The twins are getting old enough that they should expect to help out. Didn't Mom and Dad have a whole slew of chores for us to do when we were their age? Time for them to stop playing with dolls and start making a real contribution."

As expected, Jillian's eyes went wide. Their parents had been pretty tough. Memories of the family ranch in Oklahoma weren't filled with parties and fairy tales.

Riley laughed and gave her sister's arm a shake. "I'm kidding," she said. "I'd never turn them into the slaves we were."

"Still, it seems like awfully hard work, Rile. A lot harder than crunching numbers as a bookkeeper."

Riley set her jaw and shook her head. "You know what *real* hard work is? Trying to find a reason to keep a marriage alive with a man who'd rather be with his mistress than at the hospital with his own sick child." The words came out angrier than she expected. She had thought she was all through with that. She forced out a deep, calming breath. "I can handle this, Jilly. I know I can."

Unexpectedly, Jillian reached down to give her a hug. "I don't want you and the girls to move away."

"Beaumont's only a five-hour drive from Cooper. Charlie thinks there's a decent-size apartment on the property. You could come and visit us."

"But—"

Riley held up one hand. "You can't talk me out of this. Besides, the email's sent. Please don't make me feel bad about it. When Charlie suggested I send my résumé, it just felt…right. And if Quintin Avenaco isn't interested, if he's too dumb to recognize what a catch I am, then someone else will. I'm not giving up on this idea."

Jillian reached out again, hugging her even tighter. "I hope you're right. You know I want you and the girls to be happy, after everything Brad put you through."

Riley couldn't have agreed more, but a lump had formed in her throat and she couldn't respond at the moment. She had wasted nine years trying to make her marriage work. *Nine years.* She shouldn't have to be reinventing herself at age thirty-one. It wasn't fair or right. But that was life. And if she didn't take a few chances, how would she ever get back on track?

Unexpectedly, the computer chime went off, notifying her that she had mail. She and Jillian both glanced down at the laptop in surprise.

"Who's after me now?" Riley complained with a laugh. Secretly, she was afraid it might be the automatic notification for her car payment popping into her in-box. She didn't want Jillian to see that she was late with it. Her soft-hearted sister would just try to give back the money Riley had shelled out for this month's share of the groceries.

She opened her email. After reading the subject line, she jerked back as if something had tried to reach out and grab her. "Oh, my God," she said softly. "What's he doing up at this time of night?"

"Who?" Jillian asked.

Riley gave her a stunned look. "Quintin Avenaco. He's already answering my email."

STANDING ON THE BACK PORCH of the Echo Springs ranch house, Quintin Avenaco stared out at the property he now owned lock, stock and barrel.

The dilapidated cattle chutes and a rusty-looking windmill that creaked in the early-summer breeze.

A sagging barn the color of tomato soup.

A line of perimeter fencing as jagged and crooked as a jack-o'-lantern's teeth.

This house, a three-bedroom Victorian with a century-old foundation and a family of raccoons playing in the attic.

He'd closed on the place last month and moved in two weeks ago. It was his now. All of it.

God help him.

He tried to remember that, on the surface, there might not seem much to recommend about Echo Springs. But a year ago, he hadn't been searching for a spread to call his own. He'd wanted only to lease good pastureland, and he'd found that here. But now his plans had changed. In spite of the deplorable condition of the horse and hay barn, the poorly-maintained equipment and loafing shed, the investment he'd made was sound.

The life he planned to carve out for himself could work.

At least, he'd been sure of that until about a week ago.

From the corner of his eye Quintin caught movement. He turned his head to see his best friend, Ethan Rafferty, coming around the corner of the wraparound porch. In one hand, he carried a bottle of Jack Daniels. In the other, two glasses.

"I rang the bell, but it doesn't seem to work," Ethan said with a grin.

"One more thing I need to fix."

"Long list, I'll bet."

"Getting longer every day." Quintin indicated the booze. "What are you up to?"

Ethan shrugged. "Just paying a visit to my best friend and ex-partner."

For years Quintin had been Ethan Rafferty's equal partner in Horse Sense. Three years ago they'd brought the business down here to Beaumont from Colorado Springs. Since then, Horse Sense had flourished, garnering a reputation in the horse world as *the* place to go if you had a problem horse or wanted mounts trained to interact with the public.

But last month, Quintin had sold his half of the company to Ethan. The amount they'd settled on had made it possible for Quintin to buy Echo Springs, and since then, they'd both been so busy there was little time for social calls.

"You look like hell, man," Ethan said with a sad shake of his head. "Like you haven't slept in a week."

"I'm not sure I have."

"Well, I can fix that." He wiggled the whiskey bottle. "Time we had a celebratory drink and a little guy talk."

They settled into a couple wooden patio chairs Quintin had picked up yesterday. Their newness looked out of place on a porch with missing balusters and rotted railings.

Ethan uncorked the bottle, poured a generous amount in each tumbler and passed one over. Then he raised his glass. "Congratulations, pal. You're now officially a Texas rancher." He glanced out at the land, chewed the inside of his cheek a moment, then turned back to Quintin. "Poor dumb bastard."

Quintin couldn't help laughing. Ethan could always lighten his mood, and they'd been friends too many years for him to mind being gigged.

"You still mad about me quitting Horse Sense?" he asked.

"Hell, yeah. I miss you, man."

That was nice to hear, even if it couldn't possibly be true. Ethan had a business going, a big ranch to oversee and a pregnant wife at home.

"I had a great run with Horse Sense," Quintin admitted. "But I was ready for a change."

When it came right down to it, Horse Sense had probably saved his life, giving it meaning and purpose for a long time. What had started out small and shaky had grown into a thriving business over the years. Quintin and Ethan, and Ethan's father, Hugh, knew how to coax ground manners and fearlessness into the most stubborn, skittish animal. Now they had contracts with mounted police associations around the country to train cops and their mounts. Those contracts kept Horse Sense's books in the black these days, and the six-week course for horse and rider was booked solid until winter.

Ethan turned his head, giving Quintin a serious look. "I mean it, Quint. You may have lousy people skills, but even Dad can't hypnotize a horse the way you can."

"I need more in my life than a good set of parlor tricks," he countered. "And all that wheeling and dealing you seem to enjoy these days... It isn't for me. I'm just a nag wrangler at heart, and you know it." He glanced toward the far pasture. "It's one of the reasons I bought this place."

Ethan blew out a resigned breath. "Okay. I get that. But now what? You still planning to run Dutch Warmbloods?"

"As much as I can. They've got the best temperament for police work."

For a couple years now, Quintin had grown more and more disgusted by the quality of the stock they saw coming through Horse Sense. At the start of every new session, cops showed up with sleek, expensive trailers marked with law enforcement decals and filled with equally sleek, expensive horseflesh. Some of the animals were top-notch and would serve their masters well. But others were completely unsuitable as mounted police horses and had to be washed out of the program by the end of the second week. It frustrated Quintin to see how many of those hay burners couldn't cut it. A year ago, he'd decided to do something about it.

"I don't know where most of these cities are buying their stock," he went on, "but they're getting ripped off."

Ethan nodded. They'd talked about this before, but there seemed to be little they could do except deal with the bad apples on a case-by-case basis. "You remember Bob Simmons with the Louisville bunch?"

"Yeah."

Ethan refilled his glass before answering. "He called me a week ago. He has two Thoroughbreds he wants to put through the program. They were donations. Couldn't cut it on the race track, I guess."

Maybe it was the whiskey helping him out, but Quintin felt the heat of his blood kick up a notch. "Donated." He swore softly in disgust. "It wouldn't matter if they were Secretariat and Man O' War. Prima donnas on toothpick legs. These guys are putting their own police officers at risk just to save a little money, and Horse Sense is supposed to fix the troublemakers."

"Well, it *is* what keeps Horse Sense in business," Ethan remarked with a light laugh. "You start supplying them with Warmbloods and I won't have anything to fix."

"I can give them good stock, but that doesn't

mean the horse can cut it. At best, it will only make your job a little easier."

Ethan pursed his lips, seeming to consider. "How many head are you going to run?"

"No more than fifty at first. I want to concentrate on quality, not quantity."

Ethan pointed north, past the pines and toward the far pastures of the ranch. "You still got your six-pack out there?"

Last year, when Quintin had decided to quit Horse Sense, he'd begun to put his plans for a new career in place, purchasing a gelding and five mares at an auction in Houston. He had needed someplace to put them, and that's what had led him to Echo Springs.

He nodded. "They're out there. Getting fat on sweetgrass."

"I still don't understand why it had to be here. You know you could have set up temporarily at my place. Granted, we mostly run cattle at the Flying M, but we could handle another small herd of horses. Hell, Cassie's Arabians would probably love the company."

"I'm not sure I'd want my herd mixing with those spoiled show ponies your wife insists on breeding."

Ethan laughed. "She'd cut out your heart if she heard you say that." He pressed the toe of his boot against one of the raised floorboards on the porch. The house might have a sound foundation, according to the county inspector, but the wrap-around porch was a goner. "Why didn't you get Meredith to show you something in better shape than this old relic? Surely she has enough turn-key operations available, given the economy."

Instead of answering, Quintin stood and went into the house. From the kitchen table he scooped up a file folder, withdrew a single sheet of paper and returned to the porch.

He handed the paper to his friend. "You know how mineral-poor the land is in this area. Take a look at the report from the Department of Agriculture."

When Ethan finished reading, he looked up at Quintin, surprise clearly stamped on his features. "Damn, Quint. The soil may be even better than what I've got going at the Flying M."

Quintin nodded. "Nutritional content. Potential carrying capacity for twice as many head as I've got planned. The guy who owned this place before me may not have known how to keep a ranch from going belly-up, but he started out right. He made enough improvements to the pastures that it's nearly perfect for raising stock. Some of the best I've ever seen."

They fell silent as Ethan seemed to be absorbing what he'd said. After a long moment, his former partner turned back to Quintin, eyeing him speculatively. "So what's keeping you up nights? Why don't you sound more excited? You get this place up and running, and you'll be on your way."

"I would be excited. I *am*. Except…I've run into a little hiccup." He shook his head. "I think I let my mouth get ahead of my brain."

"Cassie claims I do that all the time," Ethan said with a grin. He reached over to fill Quintin's glass again. "Tell me. I find it gratifying to know I'm not the only one who screws up sometimes."

Quintin swallowed a large gulp of whiskey. It licked his insides like wildfire. "I told James Goddard I'd be ready for him by October."

Ethan frowned. "Who's James Goddard?"

"Head of purchasing for the National Mounted Police Association. Every fall, he and a couple of buyers come down to Houston to negotiate stock contracts. I've been making a case with him for better horseflesh for months, and now he's actually agreed to consider my proposal."

"So? That's a good thing, isn't it?"

"He wants at least three-dozen horses ready for him to check out by then. More, if I can swing it."

Ethan frowned. "Ouch. That's a lot of stock to move and evaluate between now and fall."

"That's why I asked Charlie Bigelow to keep

an eye out for me. If what I'm looking for passes through East Texas stockyards, he'll know it."

Charlie ran one of the largest stock auction houses in Texas. Both Quintin and Ethan had become friends with the man over the years, Quintin slightly more so because Charlie had a fascination for all things Native American, and Quintin could lay claim to being part Arapaho.

"I'm going to do my best to make it happen," he said. "But if I bring Goddard here, this place has to look like I'm a viable player. The house doesn't have to be a showplace, but I should at least have decent barns and corrals where he can check out the stock. I want him to take me seriously."

Ethan looked a little incredulous. "Be reasonable, man. You can't really believe you can make all this appear respectable by fall."

"I don't have a choice. It has to look like a working ranch by then."

"It's been a long time since you ran a ranch."

"You don't forget how. And I like the idea of watching things take shape here, making the place productive again. I just wish I had more time."

His friend nodded slowly, considering. "You can't do it alone."

"Well, I've just signed a contract with a renovation outfit for the house, and I'll bet Cassie knows someone who would make a good house-keeper."

Ethan tipped his head toward the outbuildings. "And who's going to tackle the rest?"

"You're not making me feel better about all this."

"Sorry," Ethan said. "But how are you going to pull this together if you're out on the road buying stock? Suppose I loaned you a couple of my guys?"

"I appreciate the offer, but I need to do this myself. I can work some of it in between buying trips. I've got three hands starting in a few days. And I've hired a ranch manager. A guy named Riley Palmer from up near Cooper. Charlie referred him to me."

Ethan cocked his head. "Palmer," he mused out loud. "Palmer… Where do I know that name? What did he look like?"

"Hell if I know. We haven't met. I'm trusting Charlie's judgment, and a pretty good résumé that Palmer emailed me. I made a conditional offer. Told him if he gets here and we talk, and either one of us doesn't like the deal, no harm done. Otherwise, he can start immediately."

"You're moving pretty fast, aren't you?"

"I have to. I don't have a lot of time. The sooner I get someone here, the better."

"When does he start?"

"He says he can be here tomorrow or the day after." Quintin grimaced. "Which brings up another problem. I'm taking off later tonight. Charlie called just before you got here. There's an auction in Dallas that I need to make. Some really nice stock coming through. I've emailed and left a voice message on Palmer's phone, but haven't heard back. So when he gets here, he's going to be on his own for a little while. I just hope he doesn't take one look at the place and hightail it back to Cooper."

"You want me to come by tomorrow? Get him settled in?"

"Isn't Cassie planning to kidnap you for your anniversary?"

"Oh, crap, that's right," his friend said with a scowl. Then he smiled. "Sorry, pal. No way am I missing that. We're going to San Antonio, and she's promised to rock my world. You're on your own, I'm afraid."

"It'll be fine. I wanted us to get a slower start, see if we were going to hit it off and be able to work together, but with the deadline, he'll have to hit the ground running. I've told him where to find the keys, and left my cell phone number."

The two men talked a few minutes longer. There wasn't anyone Quintin trusted more than Ethan, anyone whose opinion he valued more, and it helped to walk through a few details and concerns that had kept him sleepless at night.

When they returned to Ethan's truck in the front drive, his friend looked him straight in the eye. "You know I've got your back, Quint. I'll help any way I can."

"Thanks. I know I can count on you," he replied. He ducked his head, then met his friend's gaze. "Actually, I'm sort of looking forward to putting down roots again. And this place can use someone to bring it back to life."

Ethan frowned. "I thought…"

Quintin waved a hand. "I know what I said back then. But that was a long time ago, and we were both drunk."

Years ago, he and Ethan had been snowed in during a Colorado winter. Four miserably cold nights. When they'd run out of tall tales and worked their way through enough beer, they'd both ended up confessing their biggest fears, their wildest dreams, their greatest regrets. Quintin had never told anyone else what he'd admitted to Ethan that night. And although it had felt pretty damn good at the time to unload, looking back, he wished he hadn't opened his mouth. That kind of past shame needed to stay buried and never see the light of day.

"Look how things have turned around for you," Quintin pointed out, hoping to focus attention away from himself. "Five years ago, could you have imagined that you'd be back with Cassie? That you'd have a nearly-grown son and a baby on the way?"

"Is that what you're really looking for?" Ethan asked. His voice was soft, like a leaf falling. "A wife and kids?"

"Hell, no," Quintin replied with a laugh. Why had he ever taken this detour? "I'm not crazy enough to bite off *that* much more than I can chew." When his friend remained silent, he added, "I'm just saying that I feel like I need a change. Like I'm ready for something different."

He shrugged, as if it was no big deal, but Ethan was no fool. From personal experience, they both knew that so much of grieving was just holding things at bay. No more. Quintin had spent a decade trying to forget the life he had lived and lost. Teresa, his pretty young wife. Tommy, his son, a cheerful little boy who could make the most ordinary day seem special.

Sometimes Quintin could see both their faces so clearly in his mind's eye. But these days their features were often like mists across a pond, formless and just out of reach.

As though he knew they needed to switch topics, Ethan pulled his truck keys from the back pocket of his jeans. He took one last look around.

"You've got one hell of a job ahead of you, but if anyone can do it, you can."

"Thanks."

He clapped Quintin on the shoulder. "Call me if you need anything. And look at it this way, if all your plans end up in the toilet, you know where you can get a job."

## CHAPTER TWO

FIVE MILES FROM BEAUMONT, the weak sunshine that had spilled through the SUV's windows all morning faded. It started to rain, hard. Definitely not a good sign from the gods, Riley thought.

She glanced in the rearview mirror. Both girls were napping in the backseat, curled against one another like puppies. Wendy flinched in her sleep as the first clap of thunder sounded in the distance. She'd always been afraid of storms, the exact opposite of Roxanna, who thought rain and wind made perfect dancing partners.

"Girls," Riley said softly. "Wake up. We're almost there."

They sat up with groggy interest, watching water streak down the side glass of the SUV. Neither one said a word, and Riley was glad for the silence so she could concentrate on negotiating the road.

She almost missed the turnoff to the ranch. The sky had darkened to a muddy gray and bruised purple. The trees beyond the wildly swishing windshield wipers looked as if they were doing a mad waltz with the wind. The dirt drive had potholes nearly large enough to swallow the car, and she came upon the house so suddenly that she had to brake hard to keep from taking out a couple bushes in the yard.

Because of the way she'd parked, the headlights sent a direct beam of harsh light onto the Echo Springs ranch house.

It wasn't what Riley expected.

In his few emails, Quintin Avenaco had told her that the original home was still standing—a three-bedroom Victorian. It needed work, he'd said, but it had potential, and a sound foundation.

Riley had pictured a quaint dollhouse of a place. Perhaps with the look of a tattered Southern lady, but charming. A house just waiting to be nurtured back into a real home.

But this…this place needed more than a woman's loving touch.

Shutters that must be hanging by a single screw bracketed some of the second-floor windows. There were cockeyed porch balusters, crumbling bricks along the entry stairs and whole sections of gingerbread trim missing along the eaves. The house probably hadn't been properly cared for since Roosevelt was in office. Teddy, not Franklin.

The disrepair gave it a sad, slightly creepy

appearance. The fact that a storm was raging, whipping rain and debris everywhere, didn't help.

Roxanna had unfastened her seat belt and hung over the seat back. "Cool!" she exclaimed, her eyes alight with excitement. "Do you think it's haunted?"

*I hope not,* Riley said to herself. *I certainly hope not.* In as steady and upbeat a voice as she could master, she replied, "It's not haunted. It just needs a little work." *And a bulldozer.*

Wendy was hanging over the front seat now, as well, but her face told quite a different story from her sister's. "Are we going to have to live there?" she asked in a whispery tone, her eyes full of grave concern.

"Of course not," Riley replied. "We have a cozy little place all to ourselves. Somewhere…" She squinted through the rain and eerie darkness until she spotted the watery image of a big barn a short distance away. "Over there, I think."

"I want to go back to Aunt Jillian's," Wendy said, unswayed.

Roxanna sniffed. "Big baby."

The rain beat a hard tattoo on the roof, making Riley's headache pound in unison. She released her seat belt and turned to face both girls. "Stop it, you two. We've come all this way and we're not going to turn back now without even getting out of the car."

"We can't get out of the car," Roxanna pointed out. "It's raining too hard."

"I *mean* we're not going anywhere until we've given this a fair chance. The man who owns this place wants me to help him turn it into a real ranch. I'm going to work very hard for him, but I can't give it everything I've got if you aren't on my side. I know you're nervous and a little afraid—"

"I'm not afraid," Roxanna stated.

Riley eyed her with the most intimidating look in her mom arsenal. "I know you'd probably rather be back with Aunt Jillian. But girls, we have to give this our best shot. I need your help. So keep an open mind, will you?" She smiled. "For my sake?"

The twins nodded solemnly.

"Wait here," Riley added, giving Roxanna a warning glance. "Do *not* get out of the car. I'll find the keys, and then we'll make a run for it. This is going to be great. I just know it."

Her daughters looked at each other doubtfully, but refrained from comment.

Riley gasped as the first hard, cold raindrops hit her. It did little good to cover her head with her arms. In moments she was soaked.

She took the steps two at a time, nearly twisting her ankle as the wood gave under her foot. Flipping over the flowerpot by the front door, she retrieved the keys and an envelope Avenaco had left for her, then dashed back to the car. The whole ordeal took less than a minute, but by the time she slid into the front seat again, she had to wipe rainwater out of her eyes just to see anything.

The twins remained silent as she carefully drove toward the barn, splashing through more potholes. *Those will have to be filled,* she thought, automatically starting a to-do list in her head.

The map Avenaco had left for her indicated that the apartment was attached to the right side of the barn, a pretty standard setup. Most ranchers liked their second-in-command to be close, with easy access to both the main house and primary barn.

Riley parked, wrenched open the car door and hustled the twins out. They squealed as the rain hit them. She jammed the key into the lock, and was never happier in her life than when she felt the dead bolt slide back. They practically fell through the opening as the wind and rain swirled around them.

Gasping and dripping in near darkness, the three of them stood a moment, trying to catch their breaths. Riley's hand found the light switch by the door. She flicked it on, and the room sprang into life.

*Oh, dear God.*

The place was smaller than Jillian's. A miniscule kitchen to one side led out to a dining-living room combination. A closed door on the far wall probably accessed the only bedroom. Through another door Riley glimpsed a slice of sink and tub in a very small bathroom. The walls were wood-paneled in knotty pine, giving the place a gloomy, closed-in feel.

But it was the decor that had them speechless.

In Texas it wasn't unusual to decorate a ranch house with a Western flavor. Nor was it uncommon to outfit the manager's apartment with castoffs from the main house. But whoever had created this nightmare seemed determined to turn the place into a Western theme park.

There was a dining room table made out of an old wagon wheel. A sagging plaid couch draped with Indian blankets that looked as scratchy as steel wool. Two barrel chairs made out of actual barrels. Battered ten-gallon hats lined one wall, held in place by horseshoes that had been turned into hooks. Branding irons crossed one another like swords over the ancient television, while one corner of the living room boasted a fake saguaro cactus festooned with Indian dream catchers.

It might have been laughable. In fact, Riley

could feel a giggle vibrating in her chest. But there was one *big* decor issue that would have to be dealt with immediately.

A white-tailed deer head adorned the space over the couch and seemed to be in a direct face-off with the mounted antelope head on the opposite wall. An angry-looking bobcat sat on the coffee table, posed to feast on a helpless rabbit with beady eyes.

Wendy's fingers were already tightening around Riley's.

"Mommy…" her daughter began, her voice a mere whisper, as if she'd suddenly found herself in church.

Riley bent down, bringing her face level with Wendy's. "I know, honey. I know. But we can fix it."

Seeing the fear on Wendy's face, Riley felt a flicker of annoyance. All right. Granted, this was Texas, a state with some of the best hunting in the country. By why would anyone think stuffing the poor creatures he shot and using them for decoration was a good idea?

Wendy glanced back over her shoulder. Her features were as pale as milk. "They're looking at us."

Riley had to agree it must seem that way.

"I think they're kind of cool," Roxanna said,

giving her sister a superior look, but Riley could tell most of it was pure bravado.

"Can we put them outside?" Wendy asked.

"Not right now," Riley said. "It's still pouring." The rain made a good excuse. Truthfully, she wasn't sure about her options. If they stayed, would Avenaco allow her to get rid of poor stuffed Bambi and his pals? He might be an avid hunter himself and see nothing wrong with it. And he'd expected a man to show up, someone who probably wouldn't care one way or another about a few hunting trophies.

She felt Wendy start to shiver, whether from the rain or the taxidermy, Riley didn't know. Probably both.

The downpour had slackened, so she made a couple of runs to the SUV to bring in suitcases, bags of groceries and a box of supplies. The girls didn't move an inch until she tossed them towels and began drying them off.

Wendy particularly didn't need to catch a cold. Last year, just before Riley had left Brad for good, a case of the sniffles had turned into pneumonia, putting their daughter in the hospital. They'd nearly lost her. Now, anytime Wendy even looked like she was going to sneeze, Riley's heart leaped up in her throat.

She gave her daughters a big smile and nudged them farther into the room. "Let's check out the place," she said, even though there didn't seem to be much else to investigate. "See what the bedroom's like. I'm going to unload the groceries. I brought the stuff to make spaghetti tonight. How does that sound?"

Since that was one of their favorites, they nodded absently. Riley headed for the small kitchen, while Roxanna and Wendy drifted slowly toward the bedroom.

The range and fridge were old, but functional; work space was on the skimpy side, but manageable. There was a decent supply of pots and pans. A maid service card was on the counter. Avenaco had emailed her that he'd had the place cleaned, which was a relief. She wondered what the cleaning crew had thought of all the taxidermy.

On top of a cupboard she spotted a stuffed flying squirrel in midflight peering down at her. "Don't even think about trying to tell me how to cook," she muttered up at the creature.

"Mom…" Roxanna called from the bedroom.

*Now what?* Riley wondered.

She stopped at the bedroom door. The girls stood on either side of a queen-size bed. The space was less cluttered with tacky Western decor than the living room, and at least the bed looked comfortable. She had planned to give the twins the bedroom, since the setup had worked so well at her sister's apartment.

Thankfully, there were no stuffed animals on the dresser or in the corner, looking ready to pounce. A pretty normal-looking bedroom, actually.

As long as you didn't mind the huge stuffed buffalo head glaring down at you from over the bed.

WITHIN AN HOUR, the rain had stopped and sunshine made a welcome reappearance. Covering the buffalo head with the biggest bath towel in the linen closet seemed to reassure Wendy. They unpacked, though Riley couldn't help wondering if it was a waste of time. When Quintin Avenaco returned, would she and the girls find themselves back on the road?

Riley decided they should spend the rest of the afternoon checking out their new surroundings. The girls refused to stay in the apartment alone, and trooped after her, with promises not to squabble or wander off.

The main house was off-limits, of course, much to Roxanna's disappointment, but there were plenty of other things to see. Since the girls had been raised on a ranch, they didn't find anything particularly interesting, but nothing scared them, either. Inspecting the barn, the equipment sheds and stock structures, Riley saw that Echo Springs had potential, just as Avenaco had said, but most of it seemed buried under years of neglect.

There were signs that he had begun to make progress already. Fifty-pound bags of grain were stacked in one corner of the horse barn, along with fresh, sweet-smelling hay and vitamin supplement pellets. Several unidentifiable delivery cartons were tilted up against one wall, plus boxes of cooling blankets, rubber wash mats, breeding hobbles and cross ties.

They found a late-model ATV parked in a dilapidated-looking loafing shed, probably for quick trips out to the pastures. Both girls wanted to take it for a spin, but Riley found an easy no in the fact that she didn't have the key.

From the moment they'd left the apartment, they'd been aware of a high-pitched squeal coming from somewhere on the property. The sound was like nails on a chalkboard, and it was a sure bet they would never sleep tonight if it continued. They discovered the source of the problem behind the big barn.

A sixty-foot windmill stood beside a large tank, probably used to pump water to the pastures. Every time a breeze caught its weather vane and the fan blades turned, the screeching began.

Riley pulled out her pad and pencil, adding one more item to the list of chores she'd been compiling—fix windmill. Even as she wrote, the wind sent the blades whirling, and the twins cupped their hands over their ears.

Making a sudden decision, Riley tossed her list aside. "Come on, you two," she said as she turned to head back to a toolshed they'd investigated earlier. "Help your mother with her first project."

As a teenager growing up on her parents' ranch in Oklahoma, Riley had gravitated toward helping her father with his chores, while Jillian seemed more interested in, and adept at, assisting their mother. Riley felt sure she could handle silencing the windmill. How many times had she been at her dad's side as he tackled problems with their old mill?

She found tools and a cupboard holding replacement parts. She and the girls carried everything back out to the water tank. Riley glanced up, checking out the loop steps that led up to the platform where she could access the gear assembly. The mill seemed taller from this angle, and it had been a long time since she'd climbed a ladder that high, but no way were they going to put up with that noise tonight.

"What if you fall?" Wendy asked, her head tipped back as far as it could go as she looked up.

"She'll get squished," Roxanna added, and to Riley's mind, she sounded a little too gleeful about the possibility.

"I won't fall. Watch. I'll make it up there faster than a monkey going up a coconut tree."

That didn't turn out to be entirely true. Riley wasn't as limber as she'd been at fifteen. The loop steps were made of tightly welded metal, and the anchor posts of the tower were solid, but halfway up, the height got to her and she had to pause a moment to recapture her courage. Below her, the twins seemed impossibly small.

At last, she swung onto the tower platform. She sat down immediately to catch her breath. Below, the Texas landscape looked green, so full of abundance and grace. The buildings made it seem like a Monopoly board come to life.

Placing one hand to her brow in her best impersonation of an Indian scout, Riley stared off into the distance. "Hey!" she called down to the girls. "I can see Aunt Jillian's apartment complex from up here."

"Really?" they replied in unison.

She laughed and set to work.

The structure had to stand up to tough weather, so it was well constructed from galvanized metal, and looked to be in pretty good shape. Neither the vane nor blades needed replacing. Riley pulled out the screwdriver she'd tucked into her back pocket and removed the face plate from the gear assembly. Using detergent-free cleaner, she wiped down all the moving parts, then discovered the culprit—a rusty pump rod. Fifteen minutes later, she had it back in working order.

When she jumped to the ground from the last loop step, Riley couldn't help grinning. Not bad for her first duty. Even Wendy and Roxanna seemed impressed. Now if only she could persuade Quintin Avenaco that she could handle any job.

She wanted to explore further, but the girls seemed to be running out of steam. Riley settled them in front of the television while she sat at the dining table, making lists, writing down questions she'd need to ask Avenaco and studying a detailed layout of the ranch that she'd found in a desk drawer. Probably a previous ranch manager's paperwork. Her new boss had said he might be back by midafternoon tomorrow, and she wanted to be prepared if she had to fight for the chance to stay here.

By bedtime, all three of them were yawning. It had been a full day, and a nerve-racking one in some ways. A good night's sleep would feel wonderful, Riley decided, even on the lumpy couch with Bambi staring down at her.

Tucking the twins in bed went more smoothly than she could have hoped.

"Do we get to go to that camp tomorrow?" Roxanna asked as Riley plugged in their night-light.

"Tomorrow's Sunday, so not until the day after."

She had made arrangements before they'd left Cooper for the girls to attend a summer day camp that would keep them busy while she worked—movies, arts and crafts, games. The woman she'd spoken to on the phone had agreed to take the twins even though it was last minute, but Riley wished she'd had more time to check out the camp more thoroughly. It was barely within their budget, and suppose the girls didn't like it? Well, she'd have to cross that bridge if she came to it.

The twins scooted into bed. Wendy glanced up only once at the towel-covered buffalo head, and Roxanna, in a show of unexpected sisterly love, promised to hold her hand all night. "If it falls down on us, don't worry," she said solemnly, snuggling under the covers until Riley could barely see her face. "I'll pull you out."

Wendy's eyes went huge. The possibility of being crushed hadn't occurred to her.

Riley bent forward to plant kisses along her daughter's brow and move aside stray bangs. "It's not going to fall down. It's probably been up there for a hundred years."

"What do buffalos eat?" Wendy asked.

"Not people," Roxanna answered. "Unless they're starving."

"Not people, period," Riley said firmly, and kissed the girls good-night, giving them an extra ration of snuggling hugs.

A rocking chair made out of cattle horns and cow hair sat next to the bed. After snapping on the night-light, Riley settled into it. Since this was a strange, new place—big emphasis on the strange—she wanted to make sure her daughters didn't have difficulty falling asleep.

They tossed and turned a few times, fussed with one another over bed space, then seemed to accept that nothing could harm them, especially with their mom in the room to stand guard.

Within ten minutes Riley heard their soft, slow breathing. The sound always made her feel oddly content. Really, they were her own little miracles, these two. They were the most important part of her life and the *only* part of her old life she had wanted to hold on to. After some initial stubbornness, Brad had been willing to turn them loose with embarrassing ease. She would never forgive him for that, even though she'd been shaking with relief to have full custody.

In return she'd had to hand over her share of their ranch and everything in it.

Exhausted, Riley cocked her head to rest her cheek against her fist. She ought to make up the couch. *Go to bed,* her weary brain ordered. But it felt so good to just sit and drift for a while, to put all her worries in the basement of her mind. It was so hard to plow your way through a life that offered no guarantees about anything.

She heard the air-conditioning kick on, and knew she should get up and boost the thermostat. The shorty pajamas she wore would offer little warmth if the unit ran all night. But under the veil-like prelude to sleep, she couldn't seem to manage it. Really, who would have guessed that a chair made out of cattle horns could be so comfortable?

A SCREAM WOKE HER. High-pitched, terrified and familiar.

Wendy.

Riley's eyes flashed open, then fought against the bright sunlight streaming through the bedroom window. She shot out of the chair, her breathing tight, her heart missing beats. Both her daughters were awake. Roxanna was struggling with the covers, while Wendy, her blond hair falling into her face, jumped off the bed and threw herself against her mother's legs. Her eyes were wide and panic-stricken.

Riley caught Wendy by the shoulders. "What is it, honey?" she asked softly. "Did you have a bad dream?"

Her daughter pointed toward the buffalo head. "It moved, Mom! It's coming down to get us!"

"It can't come get us, dummy," Roxanna said in a grumpy voice. "It doesn't have feet any-more."

"Sweetie," Riley crooned gently, rubbing her hands up and down her daughter's slim back. "It's not going to hurt you."

"No, Mom. Look!" Wendy said. "See what it did?"

The girl snatched up the bath towel they had used to hide the buffalo head. Sure enough, when Riley glanced up at the wall, the creature was no longer covered. And from this angle, he did look pretty mad.

"He threw it over my face," Wendy exclaimed, tears sparkling in her eyes.

"Wendy. The towel must have slipped loose when the air-conditioning kicked on."

"No, really! He tried to smother me in my sleep!"

"Oh, brother," Roxanna muttered, sitting up in bed to scratch her head.

"Rox, be quiet," Riley said with a twinge of frustration.

Since she'd spent those days in the hospital last year, Wendy had become clingy and fearful. She also tended to be a bit paranoid. Everything from the tiniest ant on the sidewalk to Bigfoot was personally out to get her. Riley didn't have a clue how to fix it.

She sat on the bed hugging Wendy tightly, and stared up at the buffalo. Enough was enough. The damned thing was coming down.

Trying to lighten the mood, Riley yanked up her pajama bottoms and stood on the mattress. "All right, varmint," she told the head. "This apartment isn't big enough for the both of us."

With a giggle, Rox bounced to her feet, nearly sending Riley off the side of the bed. Wendy had planted herself in one corner, waiting to see how her mother would save the day.

Now that she was standing, Riley was nearly eye-to-eye with the thing, and she could almost feel sorry for it. Its dark hair was matted and dusty. A huge chunk had been taken out of its left ear. She couldn't help wondering if that had happened before or after it had met its tragic end. But it still had to go.

She reached up and grabbed a horn in each hand, wiggling the head to see if there was any give. There wasn't. Whoever had mounted it up there had intended it to stay secure through a tornado.

Riley tugged some more, every which way she could think of. "Come on," she groaned between clenched teeth. "Give it up. Come down from there."

"Don't touch it!" Wendy squealed from behind her, but there was a giggle in her voice.

"Go, Mom!" Roxanna encouraged. "You're like the Incredible Hulk."

The mounting plaque didn't budge. The buffalo looked bored. All Riley succeeded in doing was breaking a fingernail. She blew hair out of her eyes and redoubled her efforts.

"No one scares my kids, you hear me?" she threatened. "Don't make me get my chainsaw."

Roxanna, bouncing on the bed, laughed at that.

Poor Wendy gasped, but at least she seemed caught up in this crazy new adventure. "You're making it mad. What if it tries to eat us?"

Riley might have refuted that possibility, but she didn't get the chance. From the doorway of the bedroom, a male voice said, "I'm pretty sure the buffalo is a vegetarian."

This time, all three of them screamed.

# CHAPTER THREE

WHATEVER QUINTIN HAD thought he would run up against when he'd heard that scream, it hadn't been three pajama-clad females in a face-off with a stuffed buffalo head.

Returning from the trip to Dallas with five Dutch Warmbloods in his thirteen-horse trailer, he'd seen the muddy blue SUV parked close to the horse barn. He'd assumed it belonged to Riley Palmer.

But now, having let himself into the manager's apartment with his spare key, he didn't know what the hell was going on.

He'd found a woman, standing with her back to him, tussling with the buffalo head mounted above the bed. Two children—little girls—were cheering her on, and all three females were so intent on their mission that they were unaware of his presence. He blinked in surprise. It wasn't every day you ran into a woman trying to go three rounds with a buffalo head, accompanied by her own small cheering section.

But he'd expected a man. One man only. Riley Palmer. This was definitely not that man.

He watched, filled with curiosity, as the blonde continued to rail against the buffalo. He couldn't help staring—those thin, shorty pajamas defined her rear end nicely and complemented a pair of strong, slender legs that went on forever.

She seemed to be trying to amuse the children, or maybe lessen some unknown fear. That scream had been real enough. But now, with every one of her tugs, the kids urged her on, laughing in that little girl way that would make anyone want to be part of the fun.

The woman paused for a moment, and one of the kids gasped out her suspicion that the buffalo might eat them. Quintin had decided it was time to reveal himself, but answering the child's question only seemed to scare the crap out of them.

Almost as though it was planned, they yelped and squealed in unison. The woman reached to gather the children close, a sweet, protective gesture. He'd bet money these were her kids.

The problem was, they were probably Riley Palmer's, as well, and wherever the guy was right now, he and Quintin were going to have to talk. No mention had been made about bringing a family. Or even having one, for that matter. Lots of ranchers hired married couples to run both the house and the ranch, but that hadn't been Quintin's plan. He hadn't wanted to bring an entire family on board.

Kids at Echo Springs, for God's sake. Underfoot and in need of constant attention.

He felt a weary kind of irritation. Palmer should have told him. Now Quintin would have to send them packing. Valuable time lost, as well as an upheaval for this mom and her children.

They stared at him, mouths open, eyes full of uncertainty. Twins, he realized, with a lot of their mom in them. Same silky blond hair. Same eyes, the color of a tropical sea.

Their mother, obviously realizing how scantily clad she was, snatched up a portion of the sheet and pressed it against her breasts. In spite of his annoyance, Quintin almost laughed at that.

*Relax, honey,* he wanted to tell her. *Believe me, I've pretty much seen everything you've got.*

She might be another man's wife, but Quintin could still appreciate a good-looking female, and this one had prettiness to spare. He'd been out of circulation for a while, but he couldn't deny the effect a pair of big blue eyes and honey-blond hair could have on his system.

When she lifted that strong chin as if to brazen out the awkwardness of the situation, Quintin felt his lips twist. Palmer had chosen well. This woman was no shrinking violet.

"I'm sorry to have frightened you ladies," he said. "I knocked, but I think you were too busy fighting with the buffalo to hear me."

The woman came off the bed quickly, but with surprising grace in spite of the fact that she pulled the sheet with her. She marched over to him, straight as a drum major. In her bare feet, she was much shorter than he was in boots, even with those long legs.

She held out her hand. "You must be Quintin Avenaco. It's a pleasure to meet you."

He took her slim fingers in his. Her handshake was firm, and he felt an odd twinge of regret that very soon he'd have to send this family on their way. And where was Riley Palmer while his wife and kids were taking on stuffed monsters?

"I'm Quintin," he confirmed. "And I assume you're Riley Palmer's wife?"

He saw her swallow hard before answering. Whatever she intended to say, she didn't like it. "Actually…I'm Riley Palmer."

Quintin felt a kind of lurch inside him, then a wild rush of anger as he realized what those four simple words meant. What they meant to his plans for the future. He had thought having this family show up was unacceptable. But this… The reality that he'd been deceived pretty much sent him over the edge.

Behind Palmer, her children were watching,

listening to every word. For their sake he fought to keep his face neutral. "You're not what I was expecting."

"I know, and I can explain that," she said quickly. "Just give me a minute to put on some clothes and get the girls in front of the television."

He still had her hand in his, and he used it to pull her forward so that he could reach her ear. "I don't think that will be necessary," he said in a low, crisp voice. "You have an hour to pack your things and go. Take the buffalo head with you as a souvenir if you like."

She inhaled sharply, but Quintin had already turned and left the room. "Wait a minute—" He heard her call after him, but he kept going, out of the apartment, out of her sight.

He took long strides back to the horse trailer. Halfway there, Riley Palmer pulled him up short by catching his arm. He noticed that she'd thrown on a robe, and her feet were tucked into a pair of unlaced sneakers.

"Mr. Avenaco..." She spoke his name with a raw undertone of clear desperation. "If you'll just listen for a moment. Let me explain—"

"There's no need," Quintin replied. "We agreed to hold off making this job offer final until we had a chance to meet. We've met. You're not what I'm looking for."

"You mean because I'm a woman asking to be considered for a man's job?" Her voice was flat, reproachful.

In his entire life, no one had ever accused Quintin of discrimination. Of any kind. Part Native American, he'd grown up with too much of it in Wyoming to ever indulge in the same himself. Her claim nearly tore the breath out of him.

Deliberately, his eyes riveted to hers, with an intensity he hoped would send her back to the apartment to pack. "No, not because you're a woman," he said plainly. "Because you're a liar."

She had the grace to flush. That flawless, creamy-white complexion went beet-red, even if the look in her eyes remained determined and defiant. "I never lied to you, really. I can't help it if you assumed I was a man."

He sighed and shook his head. "Lady, I don't like being played for a fool. You made every effort to keep your sex a secret. Now I understand why you weren't answering my phone calls. Whose voice was that on your voice mail?"

"My sister's boyfriend. But I didn't have him record the greeting to fool you. He did it months ago, because I was getting some crank calls."

"Convenient. I don't know how you thought you were going to pull this off once you arrived, but it doesn't matter. There's no job for you here."

"I didn't intend… I hoped we could talk this out, that you'd be fair—"

"*Fair* seems like an odd word coming from you. But I think you've wasted enough of my time. Have a safe trip back."

He shook her hand off his arm and unlatched the back door of the trailer. He didn't trust himself to speak, and hoped that being on the receiving end of the cold shoulder would do the trick and send her off. But while he ignored her and went through the process of removing safety gates and dividers that would allow him to back the first horse out of the trailer, he was aware of Riley Palmer standing there.

She was in an old-fashioned fury, he could tell, but she could hardly act on it. Not if she thought she could still sway him. Which she couldn't. She could stand there until hell froze over if she wanted to.

"So you won't even consider me for the job?" she asked, unable to keep a touch of belligerence out of her voice.

"Afraid not," he replied mildly, in spite of the anger churning inside him.

He guided the first gelding backward, forcing the woman to move aside. Some horses didn't trailer well, and he was pleased to see this one step down to the ground without the slightest sign of nervousness. Alert and curious, but definitely not afraid.

He began to lead the animal to the pasture gate, but Riley Palmer blocked his way. It seemed ridiculous that she was still here, standing with a stranglehold on the neck of her robe, trying to persuade him to change his mind. She looked like a woman controlling herself at some cost. He recognized it because that was pretty much the same way he felt.

He suddenly didn't know whether to be annoyed or amused by such determination.

"You read my résumé," she said. "My experience—"

"Was any of that résumé even true?"

Oddly, the color didn't come up in her cheeks again. They went a little pinker maybe, but mostly she seemed…hurt. In the bright sunshine, her features suddenly looked very young. He almost felt sorry for her.

*Don't,* he cautioned himself.

She said in a voice that was slightly less antagonistic, "In spite of what I did, what you might think, I'm qualified for this position. I ran a three-hundred-acre spread for nine years while I was married."

"If you ran the place, where was your husband?"

"Managing the Bar Seven, outside of Cooper."

She lifted her hand to stroke the gelding's neck. "We raised cattle mostly, but I know horses, too."

"These aren't hack ponies I plan to rent out to Sunday riders. They're going to need specialized attention and a nutritional regimen as stringent as any racehorse in Kentucky."

"I understand that. I'm not afraid of hard work. And what I don't know, I can learn. Very quickly, too."

He took her hand from the gelding's neck, clearly surprising her. Turning it upward, he inspected the fingers, the soft palm, then lifted his eyes to hers. "This isn't the hand of a woman familiar with manual labor."

"I said I did it for nine years. Before that I was a bookkeeper. Since my divorce, I've been looking for work in that field, but the job market's flooded."

"So you decided to be a little more creative in your search."

Her nostrils flared as though she'd caught an unpleasant scent. He noticed that she had a small nose, snubbed at the end, as though it had been drawn by an illustrator of children's books. "You spoke to Charlie Bigelow. Would he have referred me to you if he didn't think I could handle this work?"

Quintin realized he was still holding her hand, and dropped it immediately. "I'm not sure *what*

Charlie was thinking," he growled. "Someday I'll ask him."

The woman held his gaze and wouldn't turn loose. "I can do any job you give me. I swear it."

"Mrs. Palmer—"

"Just listen for a moment," she said, cutting him off. "What do you hear?"

He didn't understand what she meant, but he fell silent. The air between them felt charged with tension, the stillness electric. At last he said, "I don't hear anything."

"That's right. Nothing but peace and quiet. Want to know why?"

He thought about it for a moment. Then, in mild surprise, he swung his head in the direction of the water tank. "The windmill."

"Exactly. I fixed it yesterday. No big deal. I just thought a good night's sleep might be nice for everyone."

He turned back to her. She looked pleased. His eyes narrowed. "You climbed up there and fixed it."

"I did. It was a rusted pump rod, and it cleaned up fine. That's only one of dozens of things I have on the list I've started. I can get this place in shape. All I need is the chance."

He had to admit he was impressed and intrigued. He didn't like that. Admiration. Sympathy. Any of those feelings for this woman could be fatal for what he wanted to accomplish here. With a rush of discipline as sharp as a steel trap, he drew back from any willingness to see her side.

"Thank you for fixing it," he told her. "I appreciate your efforts. Send me a bill when you get home." It occurred to him that she might not have enough money to *get* home. "Or tell me what I owe you right now," he added.

Quintin tugged on the lead rope and the gelding followed. He opened the paddock gate, unhooked the halter and sent the animal off with a light slap. Resting his arms on the top of the gate, he stood there, pretending to admire the wild gallop of a creature delighting in its freedom.

"Courageous. Friendly. Intelligent. Dependable. Eager to work."

The Palmer woman stood looking at him, and though her eyes were full of challenge, he thought he saw little tremors in the muscles around her mouth.

He frowned at her. "What?"

She came closer, facing him, jaw set. "Those are the five attributes you need in a mounted police horse. The ones you're probably looking for in a Dutch Warmblood."

"How do you know that?"

"As I said, I learn quickly. You told me in one

of your emails what you wanted to do with this place. I made it my business to find out the kind of horse you would look for, and what kind of care they'd need. I assumed it would all be part of the ranch manager's job."

Scowling, he stared at her, and this time he studied her from head to toe. She didn't flinch or look away. She didn't say a word. Maybe she'd run out of them. Or out of arguments, at least.

He told himself that anyone could parrot back a few lines from the internet or a book. And even if she'd burned the midnight oil learning everything she could, that didn't take the place of real experience. So she was a woman who'd been forced to run the ranch while her husband did his thing on a bigger spread. Did that mean she knew anything, really? Did that mean she'd be an asset to him?

In order for Echo Springs to make the October deadline, the ranch manager would need to work his ass off. Hard, demanding, hands-on work, not simply overseeing a bunch of hired help. The toughest guy in the business would have found it a challenge. But this woman? With two kids in tow?

"Look…" he began with what he considered an air of great reasonableness.

"I know how to properly fertilize, test pH levels, correct for mineral deficiencies and maintain disease control." She rattled off the list. "I managed for herbicides and parasites. I've treated horses for colic and thrush, and I've even floated teeth. If yours need something special, I can learn to do it. I'll do anything I can to help you succeed." She stopped, and he watched as her lips turned inward, making her mouth disappear as she bit on them. "Isn't that what's important here?" Her voice sank lower, as if it had begun to tire.

He remained silent for a long time, unsure he could speak. He'd never met any woman more willing to fight for what she wanted. Sure, she was probably desperate, but there was something else, too. There was some quicksilver quality about Riley Palmer, something nimble in her spirit. He had the random, unexpected thought that she'd probably make one heck of a partner in bed. Full of passion and life. He could imagine what being married to her must have been like. Her husband probably thought he'd hooked up with dynamite.

Quintin knew it would be a major miscalculation in judgment if he let her stay, but he had to admit he was curious about her.

His silence must have smacked of rejection. Her shoulders moved impatiently, and she said with more anger than she'd likely intended, "I guess hiring me is a chance you're not willing to take. Too bad, really. You'd have gotten more than your money's worth." She raked a hand through her already mussed hair. "We'll be off your property in fifteen minutes."

She marched away, looking as dignified as a person could in a bathrobe and unlaced sneakers.

"What about the kids?" he called after her.

She swung around. "What about them?"

"This isn't the place for them."

She walked back. Those blue eyes were watchful, but tinted with hope. "Why not? They've been raised on a ranch. That's all they know. If you're worried that they'll get in the way, they won't." A little more quickly, she added, "I've already lined up a summer day camp that starts tomorrow. When they're on the ranch, I won't allow them near anything, and I'll have a baby monitor with me to keep tabs on them. You'll hardly know they're here."

He crossed his arms over his chest. "You're their mother. Is that what you want to do? Work like a dog and hardly see them?"

"I'm a *divorced* mother," she replied, her neck arching back. "I've learned that there are things a single parent has to accept. I need the money. Besides, your email said half days off on Saturday, and all of Sunday. I'll have nights and weekends with them."

She radiated confidence, and as far as bluffs went, she was damn good. Given the challenges ahead, Quintin thought he could use someone that positive. But again, was she the *right* someone? He couldn't afford to make too many mistakes between now and October.

"No, I'm sorry…." He shook his head and watched her blink in disappointment. "But I'll tell you what I'll do," he continued. "You and your children can stay here for a while—"

"I'm not asking for charity—"

He lifted his hand to stop her. "Hold on. I'm not offering any." When she pressed her lips tightly together, and he seemed to have her full attention once more, he said. "Stay and work for me until the end of the month."

"That's barely three weeks away!"

"That will give me time to do what I should have done in the first place—run an ad, interview, do a background check. Once I get someone hired, you're done here. But you'll have enough time to regroup."

"And *you'll* have enough time to see what I can do."

He shook his head again. "That's not the way this is going to play out."

She pinned him with a shrewd glance. "If I prove to you that I can do this job better than anyone else, would you be honest enough to admit it and hire me?"

His brow lifted as he feigned surprise. "Do you really think it's *my* honesty we have to worry about here?"

Her mouth quirked. "Touché."

"So three weeks," he said. "Take it or leave it."

"I'll take it," she replied quickly.

He felt suddenly weary and yet oddly invigorated at the same time. He wouldn't allow himself to wonder if, by this time in his life, he shouldn't have had a little more sense than to make such a foolish offer. But it was too late for rational acts and plain logic.

They shook hands, and she began walking toward the apartment. Her stride was confident, her back straight.

"It's not your day off yet, Mrs. Palmer," he called out to her. "Meet me at the house in thirty minutes, and we'll get started. Bring your list."

"I'll be there in twenty," she said without looking back.

## CHAPTER FOUR

RILEY SAT THE TWINS DOWN in front of the Cartoon Network with bowls of cereal and some toast.

Quickly, she slipped into a pair of jeans and comfortable boots. She bypassed her most worn work shirts for a fairly new one the color of Texas bluebonnets. Makeup had never been her thing, so she kept it pretty simple. A little mascara and lipstick, and she was done. She didn't want to look like she wasn't willing to get down and dirty for this job. First impressions were important.

Although it was probably too late for that.

She picked up her pad and pen, then went back out to join the girls.

Seated on the rug behind the coffee table, they were absorbed in their program. Riley twisted her hair into a ponytail and tried to catch their attention. "I'm going to the house to talk to Mr. Avenaco. You know the drill. Put your dishes in the sink, brush your teeth, comb your hair. Your clothes are on the bed."

She glanced at the television. Three cartoon kids in space suits were cautiously walking through alien territory. They looked nervous.

*I know just how you feel,* she thought.

"Can we go outside?" Roxanna asked without taking her eyes off the TV.

"Later. When I get back."

Wendy glanced up at her. Her forehead creased. "Is that man your new boss?"

"Yes." *For nearly three weeks, anyway.*

"I don't think he likes us very much."

"Once he gets to know you, he'll love you just like I do." She caught Wendy's head in her hands and planted a noisy kiss on her daughter's blond hair. Then she did the same to Roxanna. "You two behave. And don't make a mess."

The twins nodded absently. On the television, the space adventure was heating up—bubble-headed aliens were shooting ray guns at the kids.

Riley took calming breaths as she walked the short distance to the house. Somewhere nearby she could hear two squirrels having an argument, and overhead the sky looked as if it had been painted in oils. After yesterday's cleansing rain, today would be a hot one.

She knocked so determinedly on the front door that little chips of white paint flew off. The entire house needed a fresh coat. After a significant amount of rotted and missing wood got replaced.

The door swung wide and Riley straightened. As expected, Quintin Avenaco stood there. He wasn't scowling, exactly, but his expression looked as though it had been permanently set on skeptical.

"Morning!" she declared, putting more confidence in her tone than she felt. "I'm ready to get started."

He expelled a deep sigh. Then, as though he had no choice, he stepped aside. "Let's go to my study."

She followed his broad back as he led her past the foyer and a nondescript staircase, through a sparsely-furnished living room and down a gloomy hallway. Idly, she took in the sight of linoleum floors rippling like tide pools, dark paneling from the sixties and flocked wallpaper stamped with faded square ghosts where photographs had once hung.

It would be generous to say the house spoke of gracious neglect. More like dilapidation. It was pretty depressing, actually, and desperately in need of a makeover. Did Avenaco live here alone, amid the wreckage of former tenants? In their emails back and forth, he hadn't mentioned having a wife or family.

The study was a different matter. A big desk

with the requisite computer setup. Comfortable looking chairs and a leather couch in front of a fireplace. Surprisingly little clutter. Stylish and tasteful, but definitely a man's room.

"This is a great house," Riley said, feeling the need to start making a connection somewhere.

He looked at her and did an eyebrow hike. Checking for sarcasm, maybe.

"I mean, it has great potential. Obviously it needs work."

"I have a renovation crew starting tomorrow."

"Will I need to be involved with that in any way?"

"No."

Well. A very definite negative to that question. She stood in the middle of the room, waiting as he moved behind the desk and shuffled through papers.

During their earlier conversation she'd barely had time to notice, but it struck her as she watched him now—the guy was good-looking. Not *GQ* material, but the kind of handsome a woman should feel comfortable with, not intimidated by. His hair was silky and black, worn at a length that wouldn't please a boardroom, but looked right on him. A calligraphy of lines around his eyes suggested he might have a killer smile, though she'd yet to see it.

Maybe they were just squint marks from too

much Texas sun. Regardless, he had a great body, like a man who'd been an athlete once and kept his shape.

He motioned absently toward a sideboard holding a carafe and mugs. "Do you want coffee?"

"I'm fine, thanks."

"Give me a minute."

She nodded, though he didn't see it. Unwilling to just stand there with her pad and pen hugged against her breast like a census taker, she tried to find something to take her mind off how nervous she was.

She found it on the sideboard. A photograph. A woman tucked close to a man who held a child in his arms. All three were smiling for the camera, dressed in denim and cowboy hats. Even the little boy. There were trappings of a rodeo in the background, but it couldn't have been Texas. Enormous snow-capped mountains loomed in the distance.

Riley guessed that the man was Quintin Avenaco, though he looked at least ten years younger. The woman next to him, probably his wife, wasn't beautiful, but she had appealing features that spoke of deep experience and rural wisdom. Definitely Native American with those prominent cheekbones and all that dark, flowing hair.

It was the little boy's face that made Riley smile. He was a miniature version of his father, and his slightly lopsided grin seemed to say he knew magical secrets. He couldn't have been more than four. She remembered the girls at that age. Complete charmers.

She wondered if his family was living some-place else right now, waiting for Avenaco to get Echo Springs on its feet. Funny he hadn't men-tioned them, but maybe that explained why he was in such an all-fired hurry to make headway here. Missing his wife and kid, no doubt.

She picked up the frame and held it toward him. "Nice looking family. Yours, I assume?"

He glanced up, then straightened. After too long a silence he said, "My wife, Teresa, and our son, Tommy."

"Do they live here, as well?"

Avenaco's mouth pulled flat as his eyes met hers, black as night and unyielding. "No."

She returned the photo to its place on the sideboard. Okay. He wasn't willing to go fur-ther down that road. He looked calm, almost as though he had no interest in the picture, but the muscles in his jaw betrayed him.

Probably a messy divorce. *Join the club, buddy.*

Clearly, the door had been slammed on any

more discussion of his family. Silence fell, and she couldn't think of anything to say.

"Let's get started, shall we?" he said at last.

She approached the desk and waited until he took a seat, before she slipped into the chair in front of him.

"I didn't see a strange horse in the barn," he told her. "So I assume you didn't bring your own mount."

Memories rushed in. The image of Ladybug, the sweet-faced mare she'd ridden for so long, still stung. With no way to take care of her, and Brad determined to hurt Riley in any way he could, she'd been forced to leave the animal behind, another victim of the divorce.

"No," she said. "My ex-husband got the ranch and everything on it."

"Sounds like you could have used a better divorce lawyer."

Had she sounded bitter? Better work harder on that. "I came out of the marriage with what I wanted," she said, as though unfazed by one of the most traumatic events of her entire life. "Do I need my own horse?"

"Not necessarily. I have ranch stock stabled at a friend's right now. As soon as the main barn's ready, I'll move them over, and you can use one of them. I assume you can ride?"

Wow. After finding out she'd been less than

honest just to get here, he really had no trust in her. She gave him a mild look, determined to be pleasant and professional. "Very well, actually."

"Can you drive a stick shift?"

"Yes."

"Even with a trailer attached?"

"We had a six-horse. I think I can manage."

"What about an ATV?"

"No problem."

"Do you know how to take care of horses?"

The way he looked at her was starting to bug her. As if he was trying to match her face to one he'd seen during his last visit to the post office. "In my résumé I told you we had horses," she said briskly.

He cocked his head to one side. "Yes, well… I think we've already established that your résumé wasn't…completely accurate. I'm simply trying to get a feel for what duties you're capable of handling."

She suppressed her annoyance. When it came to her employment for the next three weeks, this man held all the aces. "Yes. I know how to take care of them. My family had a small herd, and we always kept horses at the ranch my husband and I owned."

"Can you groom?"

"Of course."

"Pitch hay and carry bags of feed? You're not very muscular."

She opened her mouth to say something she shouldn't, thought better of it, and instead said, "I'm stronger than I look. I'll manage fine."

"What about hoof care?"

"What about it?"

"Do you know how to clean and check for problems?"

"One of the first things my father ever taught me. No hooves, no horse."

"Can you muck out a stall, Mrs. Palmer?"

His eyes were so watchful now. Did he expect her to balk at that lowly task?

Deliberately, she gave him her most winning smile. "With the best of them," she said. "And really, Mr. Avenaco, if we're going to get down to the nitty-gritty and talk horse manure, I think we should be on a first name basis. Please call me Riley."

He gave a little snort and raised his eyebrow infinitesimally. She couldn't tell if that was a bad sign or not. Then he turned his attention back to the desk, searching for something. Riley sat there, her insides feeling as though they'd just spent time against the rough side of a cheese grater.

Finally, he handed her a page torn from a legal pad. "This is the schedule for hauling hay to the pastures. You'll need the truck for that. The ATV can be used to make smaller runs. Extra keys for both are on a hook in the tack room."

She scanned the page of instructions. Nothing much out of the norm.

"I'd like to keep to this schedule as closely as possible," he said. "If you can't make a run, then I'll do it."

"I don't see a problem." She frowned as something caught her eye. "Pretty heavy on the protein supplements, considering it's summer. They'll sweat like crazy."

"These animals are going to need a good set of chest muscles for police work."

Darn. She should have realized that. She nodded, placed the paper inside her pad and smiled up at him. "All right. What else?"

He frowned. "What do you mean, what else? That's it."

"Surely there are other things you'll need me to do."

"If I think of any, I'll let you know."

The small blister of annoyance inside her got a little bigger. She sat straighter in her chair, fixing her eyes on him with intense determination. "Mr. Avenaco, let's be clear with one another. You weren't looking for a stable hand. You wanted a ranch manager. And while I'm perfectly willing to do the work you've just given me, I'm capable of handling a lot more than this."

He tilted his head back slightly. "Mrs. Palmer—"

"Riley."

"Riley. Since you'll only be here until the end of the month, I don't see the point of involving you in anything long-term."

"Perhaps not. But it doesn't have to be all or nothing, does it? Surely there are things you need help with besides grunt work. I'm good. I'm willing. You've already told me you don't have the luxury of time to waste, so why not make the best use of it?"

Silence descended again as he seemed to consider her words. She saw the indecision in him, the way his shoulders shifted uncomfortably. His lips pursed to form a rejection but he never voiced it.

Instead he said in a polite, businesslike and slightly chilly tone, "Have you ever managed men?"

Her heart bounced upward with hope. "I assume you mean ranch hands. Yes. We often hired seasonal help when we needed them."

"But did *you* manage them?" His mouth quirked. "Please don't give me the stink eye. I'm the one who has everything at stake here. Just answer the question."

The stink eye? It seemed she had something else to work on besides a bitter tone. "Yes. I was the one who managed their work. My husband was…" She almost said that Brad was busy boinking his mistress, but decided against that. "…Brad was needed at the Bar Seven, where he worked."

"I have three men starting tomorrow at 10:00 a.m. The Ramseys. Cousins Jim, Steven and Virgil. I don't know them well, but they seem reliable. They can do most of the manual labor. One of them used to be a carpenter. Jim, I think. If I decide to bulldoze the main barn, I'll want his input on rebuilding, but right now they should be able to handle the schedule I've given you."

"I walked the barn yesterday. It needs work, but…" She stopped there, wishing she hadn't voiced an opinion where it probably wouldn't be welcomed. "I'm sorry," she amended quickly. "You were saying?"

"Tomorrow I'll get these fellows started. Then you can take over. If they don't want to take orders from you—"

"Because I'm a woman?"

"For whatever reason, then I'll handle them, and we'll have to find something else for you. Agreed?"

"Agreed." Irritating to think Avenaco had such

little faith in her ability, but she'd show him. The relieved smile she gave him was sincere. "What else?"

For a half second, before he remembered that none of this was to his liking, the man's mouth tilted upward, just a little, and Riley saw those creases at the corners of his eyes deepen. Oh, yeah, she'd been right. There *was* a killer smile hiding in there somewhere.

"You're a very stubborn woman," he said.

"I am. I like to think that's a good thing."

As though resigned, he shook his head slightly, then turned to pull a rolled tube of paper from his credenza. He swung back and opened it across his desk. It was a blueprint of Echo Springs, both the house and the surrounding land.

"This is a layout of the property," he said. "Pretty straightforward, really."

Riley scooted forward in her chair. She tried to focus on the task at hand. Inside, though, her heart was doing somersaults. He seemed ready to take her seriously.

"You've seen the pasture closest to the house," her new boss continued. "With the stock I brought in this morning, it'll be maxed out for grazing soon." He circled his finger around the area behind the barn. "Two small corrals here, plus a sacrifice paddock in between." He glanced up at her. "You know what a sacrifice paddock is, right?"

She resisted the temptation to scowl at him. "Back in Oklahoma, we called them all-weather paddocks. We used to joke that Texans like to make everything sound more dramatic."

He barely nodded. "It needs to be torn down, as well. Too much rotted wood." His finger slid across the drawing to the upper right corner. "This piece will eventually carry most of the herd. It needs work. Right now, those are my priorities."

"Is the pasture already under fence?"

"Barbed wire."

She grimaced. Horses were farsighted and needed to have very visible fencing so they didn't go crashing into it when they chased each other around. "Great for cattle, but not a good idea for the kind of horses you're buying."

"Exactly. I've seen the damage a horse can do to itself when it's tangled up in barbed wire. All of it needs to go. A truckload of lumber is being delivered tomorrow. The Ramseys should be able to handle the tear downs."

Quintin stared at her thoughtfully, for a long enough time that she began to feel uncomfortable. He had the darkest, most intense way of looking at a person. Sort of unnerving.

After an agonizing wait, he seemed to come to

some decision. He pointed toward a meandering circle notated at one end of the pasture. "Have you ever put in irrigation?"

With that, things got easier. He walked her through every nook and cranny on the drawing, until she thought she could have traveled the property blindfolded. In an easy, confident voice, he told her what he hoped to accomplish and how he planned to do it. He remained somewhat aloof, but at least he stopped patronizing her, and actually seemed interested in her responses.

From their earlier emails back and forth, Riley knew basically what he wanted to create here. But when he spoke again of his eagerness to provide the best horseflesh to police departments around the nation, perhaps internationally, as well, she saw the real passion in him and couldn't help finding it infectious. She tried to keep her features professional, interested, but inside she realized that her heart had slipped into a faster rhythm. The guy sure knew how to sell an idea.

One thing took her by surprise even more. As they sat hunched over the property layout, heads nearly touching, she became intensely aware of him as a man. She inhaled his scent, something citrus and musky and completely male. Again and again her eyes were drawn to the short hairs that feathered around his temples like black silk, with just a few threads of gray woven in. To the dark shadow that lay along his jawline, and the strong flex of his arm muscles when his hand reached out to stab a spot on the map.

And those hands. Long fingered. Tapered at the end. Roughened slightly, but still managing to look gentle and kind. Riley had always been a sucker for a man with great hands.

Not that she was looking to be a sucker for any man these days.

She yanked her mind back, forcing it to concentrate on what her new boss said, not on how he looked. The conversation was winding down. With all the bases covered and her pad full of instructions and notations, they were nearly done. Avenaco was rolling up the map, clearly ready to see the last of her, no doubt.

Straightening, Riley gave him a positive, reassuring smile. *Forget those hands and all the rest,* she told herself. *You've got a job to do.* "So you want to make all this happen by October."

"Yes."

"Beginning or end?"

"October 3."

"Then there's no time to waste, is there? I'll get started right away."

He shook his head. "You can start tomorrow. Today's Sunday. I assume you'd like to finish getting settled in, and spend some time with your kids."

The offer surprised her, but she wasn't going to look a gift horse in the mouth. "Thank you. I will." She produced another self-confident smile and offered her hand. "I'm not going to disappoint you, Mr. Avenaco."

He shook her hand, but didn't indicate one way or the other whether he honestly believed that or not. There wasn't anything else for her to do but leave. She swung around and headed for the door.

"Riley…"

She turned back. He just looked at her, another one of those unnerving stares that made her feel as though he was sizing her up. Maybe he was.

Finally he said, "I think you're right. We should be on a first name basis. Call me Quintin."

She was smiling by the time she hit the front door. Three weeks, she thought. A lot could happen in three weeks.

## CHAPTER FIVE

By EIGHT O'CLOCK THE NEXT MORNING he had finished going over the plans with the renovation crew foreman. Quintin stood in his study, trying to prepare himself for the workers who were about to take over the house like an invading army.

He'd lived alone too long to like the idea of being closely surrounded by other people, but if Echo Springs was going to be presentable by October, it was necessary. First the downstairs area, then the upstairs. And in between all that, the exterior would be spruced up so it no longer looked like the set of a horror movie.

After draining his coffee from his cup, he picked up the photograph he'd set on the sideboard. His son grinned out at him, and beside him, Teresa, the smile on her lips so gentle it made Quintin's heart stutter even after all these years.

She would have loved this renovation. When they'd bought their run-down ranch in Colorado Springs, newly married and hoping to turn it into something grander, they hadn't had the money to hire outside help. Not that it mattered. Working on the place together had only brought them closer.

He carried the photo to his desk. At times, when the past lay heavy on him and guilt was like a yoke, he felt depressed just looking at their faces. This shot had always been one of his favorites—that last golden summer afternoon spent at the Cheyenne Frontier Days Rodeo. They'd had so much fun, and he'd won enough money in the events that they'd been able to repair the ranch-house roof.

Even in the still photo, it wasn't difficult to see the delight his family had found in one another. Quintin stared at his own face—younger, flush with excitement and love. Not a worry in the world. So...oblivious.

How could he have been so carefree? It felt wrong somehow. Shouldn't his features have revealed *something,* some hint of the grief that would come only a few months later? Stillborn dreams for his marriage. A future for Tommy that would never happen.

He yanked open a desk drawer and placed the photograph inside, forcing himself to concentrate on the present. He had charted a different course now, set ambitious goals and found new purpose. Alone. And as hard as that was to think about, he would not turn back. The sensation of feeling something, after years of numbness, was a novelty, and he wouldn't give it up.

Somewhere in the house he heard a skill saw start up. Men called to one another. He could tell they were already ripping out the outdated paneling in the dining room next door.

The new hands would be here soon, needing instructions. He punched the toggle switch on his computer. Time to search the employment sites, post ads and go through the steps necessary to find a replacement for Riley Palmer. Things he should have done in the first place.

He had to grudgingly admit that during their meeting yesterday, the woman had held up her end of the conversation pretty well.

She'd come up with good suggestions and shown a talent for innovative thinking. Even when he'd annoyed her, she'd hung on to her temper. He could tell she'd wanted to push back, but she had enough sense to know when it was appropriate and when it wasn't. He admired her determination, that straightforward way she had about her. Who would have guessed there was that kind of grit inside such an attractive package?

One tough cookie, that Mrs. Palmer.

Riley.

Still, she wouldn't work out for what he had in

mind. Not for the long haul. He'd have to keep an eye on her. Make sure she didn't get in over her head or create any new problems. The time she was here would go fast.

He'd just completed an online classified ad when he heard a knock on the study door. He looked up to see Cassie Rafferty stick her head around the corner.

"The front door was open," she said, loudly enough to be heard over the sound of hammering.

He motioned for her to join him. She entered, and he winced inwardly. He'd forgotten that he'd agreed to let her bring over a prospective housekeeper for an interview. The day was starting to get away from him.

Quintin thought Cassie was one of the prettiest women he'd ever met. His best friend's wife was now well into her sixth month of pregnancy. She and Ethan had been married for a couple years, and though the way back to one another had been long, and deep with emotional quicksand, the two had never looked happier.

"How are you doing?" he asked.

Ethan and Cassie planned to host a big wedding reception next weekend. Since the announcement, Cassie had been like a field general marshalling troops. Ethan fretted over her constantly, but today she looked well rested.

"I'll be glad when this is all behind me," she said with a sigh. "The reception *and* the baby. I'm not sure which is more work to get ready for."

"So where's this woman you want me to hire as a housekeeper? Mercedes's sister."

"Lilianna should be here any minute. I promise, you're going to like her. Although I'm not sure I'm doing her any favors. This place looks like a war zone."

Cassie wandered around the room, straightening a picture on the wall, repositioning one of the couch cushions. "Ethan says that if you can pull all this together by October, the payoff could be huge."

"It's a big if, but I'm trying."

"All this…" She swept her hand out to encompass the room. "I think it's exactly what you need."

He frowned at her. "What do you mean?"

"I just think having a real home will help establish you in the community. And it won't hurt you to be around more people."

"I'm around people every day."

"You know that's not what I mean. Time to come out of that cave, Avenaco. Time to start participating in real life."

"Cassie…"

He stopped, uncertain what to say. Both the

Raffertys knew that he'd lost his family, but only Ethan was aware of the details, and Quintin wanted to keep it that way. He wasn't looking for anyone's pity or help, but Cassie seemed determined to play matchmaker. That was the curse of the hopelessly in love. They'd do anything to make everyone else as happy as they were.

Cassie swung around to face him. "What's wrong with meeting new people? Building new relationships?"

"I don't need—" He jerked upright. "Wait a minute. How old is this Lilianna?"

Cassie laughed. "She's at least fifty, with two grown children and a husband she adores. Don't be so suspicious. I'd never try to set you up. At least, not without talking it over with you first."

"Really? Because I distinctly remember getting blindsided by you and a couple of single women last Christmas."

"I can't help it that I know a lot of lonely women who would like to have something to do on a Saturday night."

"So start a sewing circle. Just leave my love life alone."

"What love life?" She smiled. "And what's so wrong with trying to help a friend?" Glancing down, she ran her fingers across her extended belly. "You've agreed to be this baby's godfather, but we're still in the market for a godmother."

"Check the internet. I hear there's a website for everything these days."

She laughed again, and he watched her move to the window. He knew she meant well, but he could find women on his own to deal with…the basics. He wasn't a monk, for God's sake.

He wondered how the conversation had drifted so far off course. He made a point of looking at his watch. "I have hired hands coming anytime now. Where *is* this woman?"

"Any minute." She nudged aside the curtains to watch the activity in the side yard, where construction trucks were now parked. Men hurried back and forth from the house. "So you hired the Ramsey cousins?"

"Yes."

"What about the ranch manager Ethan told me about? Did he show up?"

*"She."* Quintin couldn't help frowning, remembering that shock. "Yes, she got here."

Cassie looked back over her shoulder. "She? Ethan didn't tell me you'd hired a woman."

"That's because he didn't know, and neither did I. But she's only here until the end of the month. Until I hire a replacement." He indicated the computer. "I just finished running an ad, in fact."

"The end of the month. Is that her choice or yours?"

"Mine. She's not what I'm looking for."

Cassie made a face. "Why? Because she's a woman?"

"No. Of course not."

"Then what's wrong with her?"

"She's nice enough. But before she ditched her husband she was a housewife stuck doing chores on their ranch. That gives her some experience, I suppose, but I want someone more…seasoned. Someone who's lived and breathed ranch management." He considered leaving it at that, but Cassie's eyes were sharp, and he felt impelled to add, "Someone unencumbered. She brought two kids along. Little girls. So it's out of the question."

"I didn't realize you didn't like children." Cassie let her eyebrows lift in polite disbelief.

He thought of the picture in his desk drawer, Tommy grinning as only a kid could. He thought about the impenetrable veil between life and death. To Quintin, watching children, being around them—especially little ones—was a painful reminder of what he'd lost. He didn't need that in his life right now.

Cassie continued to look at him closely.

"Children don't have any place here," he explained. "We're in chaos, and it's going to stay this way for the next few months."

She didn't seem to find that a reasonable explanation, but before she could say anything, they both became aware of movement at the study door.

*"Señora?"* A dark-haired Hispanic woman stood there, waiting to be acknowledged. This had to be Lilianna, and Quintin was relieved to see that she was indeed middle-aged, with the same motherly look as her sister Mercedes, the longtime housekeeper at the Flying M.

"Here you are!" Cassie said, extending both hands and pulling the woman into the room. "This is Quintin Avenaco." She ushered Lilianna into the chair in front of the desk. "Sit. You two get acquainted, and I'll make myself scarce." She gave Quintin a warning look. "Don't scare her off."

What was that supposed to mean? He wasn't in the habit of scaring people off. And even if he tried, he must not be very adept at it. It certainly hadn't done a bit of good with Riley Palmer.

He turned on a hundred-watt smile for Lilianna's benefit and extended his hand. If she was as fine a cook as Cassie said, and could mind her own business, he'd hire her. This, at least, seemed like a quick decision that couldn't possibly come back to bite him in the ass.

As soon as Riley pulled into Echo Springs's front drive, she saw that everything was in full swing.

The house and barn were surrounded by parked cars and trucks, some displaying the logo of a local renovation company and bearing all kinds of equipment and supplies. Busy, boisterous construction workers were everywhere.

She wedged her SUV in between a Jeep and an old truck slowly dying of cancerous rust. Time to pull it together. She had a job to do. She just hoped she didn't look as if she'd been crying.

Earlier, she had taken the twins to their summer camp in Beaumont, where they would spend the weekdays while she worked. Since she'd made the reservation over the internet, she'd been relieved to see that the place looked clean, bright and full of fun things to do. The woman in charge made them feel very welcome. Riley's stomach had begun to relax just listening to her, and the girls seemed excited about having other kids to play with.

However, on the drive back to Echo Springs, Riley's mood had deteriorated. For so long it had been just the three of them. The girls were her world. Last night, as she'd watched them sleep, life had seemed so complete. Now it felt as though an essential piece was missing, and five o'clock was very far away.

As soon as she opened the door of the SUV, three men who'd been sitting in the ancient truck got out and approached her. Noting the vague similarity among them, Riley suspected they were the Ramsey cousins. They were all tall, tanned, typical cowboys, the kind of men employed on hundreds of ranches in Texas. Over the years, Riley had hired plenty of their kind.

"Hello," she said, turning on a welcome. "You must be the Ramseys."

The one who had a face beaten by time, probably the oldest, seemed to take the lead. "We are. You the boss man's lady?" he asked, ramming his hands into his back pockets.

"No, definitely not." *The boss man's lady.* She had to hide a smile, just thinking about the absurdity of that notion. "I'm Riley Palmer."

Introductions went quickly. When Riley told them she was the ranch manager, it took a moment for the information to sink in. There was a little surprise, perhaps, but no rebellion that she could see.

That didn't keep her stomach from swooping in nervous anticipation. In spite of his promise, Avenaco would probably find a way for her time here to come to a screeching halt if these men balked at taking orders from her.

She spent a few minutes laying out the plan for today, watching them size her up, as she did with them. She used her most commanding tone, the one that worked best on the twins. The one her sister called her General Patton voice. After a while, their heads began to nod in unison, like top-heavy flowers caught in a breeze.

Relieved, Riley headed for the barn, and the cousins followed. In another five minutes, they'd picked up tools and were already headed for the paddock.

Tearing down fences was a boring, simple assignment, but it would allow her to see what these guys could handle. After loading the back of the ATV with supplies and retrieving work gloves from the apartment, Riley would join them, but first she began filling a beaten watercooler from the spigot behind the barn. One look at the cloudless porcelain sky told her it would be another hot day, and they would all need to stay hydrated.

So far, so good, she thought. The work would be dirty and hard, no picnic—but no worse than some of the things she'd had to do on her own ranch.

She was bent over, trying to maneuver the full watercooler onto her knee, when she glanced up and saw a woman approaching from the side yard. A pretty redhead who was obviously several months pregnant.

As she came closer, the stranger smiled. "Hello. Need some help with that?"

"No, thanks. I've got it." Riley managed to get a solid grip and wrestle the cooler into the bed of the ATV. Then she turned back to the newcomer.

The woman held out her hand. "You must be the new ranch manager. I'm Cassie Rafferty. My husband, Ethan, is Quintin's best friend."

"Nice to meet you. I'm Riley Palmer."

"Riley," the woman said, as though trying out the name. A touch of humor lit her eyes. "*That* explains why Quintin thought you were a man." She stared so intensely at her that Riley frowned, and Cassie laughed lightly. "I'm sorry. I don't mean to be rude. It's just… I know Quintin wanted some grizzled old crowbait for a manager, and you are so…not that. He must have flipped when you showed up."

"He wasn't exactly thrilled."

"Was it awful?"

"Brutal," Riley admitted. "But I'm determined to win him over."

"Hmm. Good luck with that," Cassie Rafferty said with a touch of amused skepticism. She squinted toward the back of the paddock. "I see you've got the cousins hard at work."

The Ramseys were at the far end, out of earshot, knocking boards and tossing them on the ground.

Riley took the opportunity to study the woman. Her husband was Avenaco's best friend, but what was she? Best friend to Avenaco's wife? Riley could imagine the four of them going out to dinner together, playing cards, maybe sharing a rental house on family vacations. All the fun things couples did with other married couples. Just the kind of life Riley had hoped for with Brad, but never got.

Cassie turned to look at her again. "We built an arena at the Flying M last fall, and the Ramseys did a great job."

"They seem capable."

"You might want to watch Virgil. He tends to let his blood sugar get too low when he's focused on work. He's diabetic, but thinks he can tough it out and just ignore it."

"Virgil. The young one with the prominent Adam's apple?"

"Right. Jim's the oldest. Then Steve, with the big mustache."

"Looks like it was cut out of a carpet sample?"

"That's the one. He's a Tom Selleck wannabe."

Riley noticed the other woman's fingers absently begin to smooth over her extended belly. Remembering how uncomfortable and unattractive she'd felt carrying the twins, Riley thought

Cassie looked darned good. "When are you due?" she asked.

"Three more months, and then I can stop looking like I'm smuggling a basketball. I can't wait."

"First one?"

"Might as well be. I have a boy who's just turning sixteen, so I'm a little out of practice. Ethan treats me like I'm made of glass, and to tell the truth, it's starting to make me nervous." As though embarrassed to have admitted such a thing, she made a face and pulled her hair back, refastening the clip that held it. "I hear you have twins."

"Wendy and Roxanna. They're eight." It was Riley's turn to make a face. "Double the trouble, that's for sure. But double the love, too."

"I assume you're a single mom. That can't be easy. What do you plan to do with them while you work?"

"They started a summer day camp today. I miss them already."

She wondered what the girls were doing this very minute. Did they hate the place? Did they wish their mom would come and take them home? Her cell phone was in her back pocket, and for the hundredth time she had to fight the urge to check it for messages she might have missed.

"What program?" Cassie asked. "Camp Buddies, by any chance?"

"Yes. Near the park by the river."

"They'll have a ball! Amelia Watkins runs it. She loves kids and has *loads* of experience. I sent my son there when he was little, and he still talks about it. And it's very safe. Trust me. Your girls will be in good hands."

Riley had been shoving toolboxes next to the cooler. She looked up and smiled. "That's good to hear. Makes me feel less like I've deserted them."

"We moms have to stick together."

Cassie watched her as she continued loading the ATV. Riley tried to think of anything else the men might need. No sense wasting time coming back for stuff.

She wished she could spend more time with Cassie, and suddenly realized how few conversations she had with her own sex. Her sister, sure, but that was different. A friend would be lovely to have, and Cassie seemed like a nice person. Then Riley remembered that she might not be here all that long, and the idea seemed silly.

She pulled the ATV keys out of her jeans pocket, and Cassie took the hint.

"I'd better let you get to work." Cocking her head, she gave Riley a kind smile. "If there's anything I can do for you while you're here, just let me know. Maybe I'm way off base, but I think…"

She stopped as they both sensed movement at one end of the barn. Quintin Avenaco was rounding the corner, his long, easy stride eating up the distance.

They waited for him to join them.

Cassie crossed her arms and gave him an inquiring look when he came up beside her. "Hello, boss man. So. Did you hire Lilianna?"

"Yes. You knew I would when she told me she makes *tres leches* even better than Mercedes."

Cassie laughed. "I thought that would do the trick." She tossed a glance toward Riley. "Here's a secret for you about Quintin. He can't say no to a great dessert."

Avenaco's lips curved. "I can't tell you anything, can I?"

"You didn't have to. I see it every time you come for dinner."

It was obvious he liked this woman, and Riley suddenly wished he would speak to her that way. But she and Quintin had a completely different kind of relationship, and not a particularly good one at that. Heck, not a relationship at all, really. He was her boss, not a friend.

She moved restively, and Avenaco seemed to remember that she was standing there. The change in his expression was immediate. Nothing nasty or unkind. Just a cool disinterest. "Good morning."

"Morning."

He glanced past her, spotting the newly-hired help along the paddock fencing. His eyes captured hers again, and he looked so surprised, Riley almost laughed. "You've already put the Ramseys to work?"

"They showed up early, so I thought I might as well," she said, feeling in command of the moment. Then she wondered if she'd overstepped. Maybe he had wanted to meet with them first, lay out his plan. "Would you prefer they do something else? I can call them back…."

"No. No, that's fine. I just thought I'd need to get them started, but it looks like you've already handled it. "

Did he really have such a low opinion of her ability? "They seem to be doing fine," she said. What had he expected? All of them just sitting around waiting for the big boss to show up?

"No…attitude?" he asked. "No grumbling?"

Riley caught Cassie rolling her eyes. She wanted to do the same, but the small, steady voice inside her said to let it go as much as possible. It was going to take a while for Quintin to realize what she could do.

"You mean, did I have to convince them to take orders from me?" She shrugged. "Not really. I'm sure they'd *prefer* to get directions from a guy, but I told them they could sit out here and wait for you to finish up at the house...or grab a hammer and start earning a paycheck."

"I'm sure they were grateful to get on the clock," Cassie remarked.

Riley nodded. "Nothing cowboys hate worse than sitting around with nothing to do. Especially if they aren't getting paid for it."

"Great," Quintin said, and though his features didn't change, Riley could sense him backing off just a little. He tipped his head toward the ATV. "I think I'll just run that stuff out to them and say hello."

She held out the key ring with two fingers, as though it were a dead seagull. "You're the boss."

She dropped the key into his open palm. While the two women watched, Quintin jumped on the vehicle, backed it up carefully, then headed across the paddock. When the cousins saw him coming, they stopped and came toward him as though they'd just reconnected with a long-lost brother.

"Men," Cassie muttered. "Can't live with them..."

"Can't send 'em to the moon?" Riley finished for her, and they both laughed.

Cassie looked thoughtful. "He's not usually a control freak. It's just that this...this thing he wants to accomplish here is very important to him."

"I get that. I really do. I just wish…" Swallowing a frustrated sigh, Riley walked over to the spigot to make sure the water stopped dripping. No point in complaining.

"Don't get discouraged. You're going to be a wonderful addition to this place."

Riley smiled over at her. Nice to hear, even if it wasn't her new boss saying it. "Thanks. I hope you aren't the only one who feels that way."

"Oh, I think you're just what Quintin needs, whether he knows it or not."

"I'm sorry?"

Cassie let a half smile slip out. "Just a feeling I have. Some silly, pregnant-woman thing, probably."

Riley had no idea what she meant, but the redhead seemed to know Quintin pretty well, so it wouldn't hurt to pump her a little for more information. She straightened, wiping her wet hands on the back of her jeans.

"How long have you known him?"

"Long enough to know he can be a hard sell. He and Ethan formed a partnership in Colorado, working with problem horses. They moved the business down here three years ago, and that's when I met him." She cast a glance toward the far paddock, where the men still stood talking.

"Although…I'm not sure anyone really 'knows' Quintin. Except maybe Ethan. He's a pretty private guy. I'd trust him with my life, but he's got that stoic-Indian thing going on most of the time. He doesn't let anyone…in. Very guarded." She turned back to Riley. "Too guarded, if you ask me."

"What about his family? Surely he's close to them. I saw a picture of his wife and child in his study. They looked so happy."

Cassie's brow furrowed. "He didn't tell you?" Before Riley could answer, she muttered, "No, of course he wouldn't."

"Tell me what?"

The woman shook her head sadly and said in tones of pure heartbreak, "Quintin's wife and son died ten years ago."

# CHAPTER SIX

CASSIE'S WORDS MADE A shiver run up Riley's spine. "How?"

"I'm still not entirely sure. My husband's the one who told me, and even he doesn't know all the details. A fire, I think. It happened before he and Quintin met. Ethan says Quintin's always blamed himself."

"But why?"

A tight smile stretched across Cassie's mouth, but there was no joy in it. "I wish I knew. He never, *ever* talks about that time in his life. That's why I'm so pleased to see him determined to make a go of things here." She shifted her attention to the far paddock. "There's something terrible and lonely in him, something no one can reach. Having people around, getting involved in life again…" She swung back to Riley. "It's just got to be better for him, don't you think?"

Riley barely heard her. She couldn't help it. She was remembering last year, reliving the absolute terror that had coiled around her heart every time she'd watched Wendy struggle for a breath. She completely understood the boundless scope of parental love, and how fragile a hold you could have on a young life.

But to lose a child…*and* his wife. Anyone looking at that photograph in Quintin's study could see the depth of their love for one another. How had he survived that kind of total devastation? The kind that made tears seem quaint and impotent, and promised a future of sterile emptiness.

"How awful," she said, almost to herself. "That sweet-looking little boy…" She couldn't seem to take her gaze from Quintin, who was engaged in conversation with Jim Ramsey, gesturing toward the pasture behind the paddock.

"I know," Cassie said in a soft, contemplative tone. "Children make life seem more precious, don't they?"

"One of my daughters was very sick last year, and if the worst had happened—" Riley broke off, feeling chilled in spite of the day's heat.

It hit her suddenly. Why Avenaco might have been so adamant about not wanting a ranch manager with children. She looked at the woman she was already starting to think of as a friend. "No wonder he wasn't happy I'd brought my kids along. It must be difficult for him, being around little ones again."

"Well… It probably wouldn't hurt if they kept

a low profile for a while. Just until he adjusts to the idea."

"He may not need to adjust. Did he tell you I'm officially on the payroll only for three weeks?"

"He told me. But nothing's written in stone, is it? He could change his mind."

"I thought you said he's a hard sell."

"He is," Cassie agreed. Then she grinned. "But he also likes a challenge. Having you around may be just the stimulation he needs."

Riley frowned, wishing it was going to be that easy. She shook her head. "Where I'm concerned, I think the only challenge he's interested in is how fast he can send me packing."

Cassie briefly commiserated with her over that possibility before giving Riley her phone number and making her promise to call if there was anything she could do. Riley would have liked to give the loss of Quintin Avenaco's family more thought, but right now she had a job to do.

When she joined the Ramseys, they stopped talking and ambled away to resume work. She turned toward her boss, ready to use the I'll-take-over-from-here approach. She was surprised to see him pull a pair of work gloves from the back pocket of his jeans.

"I think I'll keep you company for a little while," he told her. He stated it without apology or explanation.

She gave him a bold look and wondered if he saw the leap of suspicion in her eyes. Didn't he trust her to manage such a simple job without his help? "They won't need you at the house?"

"Not right now. I'll just be in their way."

She wanted to stare him down, but didn't see how she could in the face of such a polite performance. Undoubtedly, he derived some satisfaction when she said nothing more and simply turned away.

So she was stuck with him. What could she do but make the best of it?

She moved along the fence line to the right of the Ramseys while he went left, helping Virgil.

She dug into the work, finding that the idea of physical labor held a lot of appeal. Anything to keep her mind off missing the girls, the depressing thought of how briefly she might be employed here and, surprisingly, her awareness of Quintin Avenaco.

The Ramseys gave her little cause for concern. They were hard workers. They went at it almost nonstop, and they weren't talkers or complainers, thank goodness.

As for Quintin, she tried to ignore him. Very seldom did she let her gaze move even one degree in his direction, and they exchanged less than a dozen words the whole morning. To his credit, he worked just as hard as the rest of them.

She was relieved that he never took charge, never countermanded her instructions. He might have been just another member of the hired help.

But his presence still annoyed her.

The hours passed, and the sun continued to beat down on their heads like a mallet. Quintin stopped to wipe sweat from his brow with his sleeve and called out to the cousins, "No one expects you to roast out here, guys. Mrs. Palmer has seen bare-chested men before." He glanced at Riley. "Okay with you if they take off their shirts?"

Riley, who was nearly dying in the heat herself, felt foolish not to have thought of that before. "Yes, of course."

The cousins expelled relieved sighs, as though they'd been hoping someone would say something, which only made Riley feel worse. In the blink of an eye, the three stripped to the waist, tossing their shirts over fence posts.

Jim, the oldest, had a bit of a pot belly. Virgil seemed slightly embarrassed, probably because he had an obvious farmer's tan, his white chest set off by the deep bronze of his neck and forearms.

Steve, however, wasn't shy. He peeled off his shirt like a Chippendale dancer, revealing a smooth, muscular torso. If he was trying to be Tom Selleck, as Cassie Rafferty had claimed, he certainly succeeded. A very young, buff Tom Selleck.

*You're just one of them,* she told herself. *Just one of the guys.*

It had been a long time since she'd been around so many shirtless men. She glanced over at Quintin. "Sorry to have been so oblivious—"

She stopped as she lost her train of thought.

While she'd been focused on the Ramseys, Quintin had shrugged out of his shirt, as well. He wasn't bare-chested; he'd stripped to a T-shirt. A white one that clung to his sweaty body in all the great ways that kind of garment could. He probably had ten years on Steve, but it didn't seem to matter one bit.

A dark, soft-looking mat of hair peeked out the top of Quintin's shirt. The material was thin enough that she could see the strength in him, the bulge of muscles across his chest. He looked almost offensively healthy and powerful.

Something warm and unfamiliar unfurled in the pit of her stomach. *Nerves,* she told herself.

Quickly, she lifted her head to the sky, as though she had to gauge the time by the position of the sun rather than her own watch. "Another hour before we'll break for lunch. All right?"

The Ramseys murmured their assent and went back to work. So did Riley. From the corner of her eye she saw Quintin scoop up his hammer again.

For the rest of the morning she set herself a killing pace. If she had pretty much ignored him before, she now refused to even glance his way, trying to pretend he was invisible.

By lunchtime, a little less than half the paddock fencing remained, and frankly, Riley was whipped. Her back and shoulders ached. Since she didn't have the luxury of taking off her clothes, every inch of her body felt covered with grimy sweat. Even her hair hurt. It had been a long time since she'd worked like this.

The Ramseys went off to retrieve packed sandwiches from the cooler in their truck. Riley intended to grab something from the apartment and make a call to Amelia Watkins, just to check on the girls. She was relieved when Quintin told her he wouldn't be back after lunch, that he had work he needed to do if the renovators didn't chase him out with their racket.

She watched him go, glad he wouldn't be with them again the rest of the day. Having him nearby made her feel edgy, off balance, and she was smart enough to know that her feelings weren't completely the result of having the boss hanging around. Smart enough to know, too, that she had no business feeling anything about this man.

Idly, she wondered if the time in his study would be spent trying to find her replacement. At the moment, feeling the ache of so much hard, physical work, she wasn't sure she cared.

After lunch, they redoubled their efforts. The brutal sunshine demanded their surrender, but they kept at it.

Late in the afternoon, she pulled Jim off the job to help her load and run feed out to the horses in the far pasture. She watched them eat, made notes in her pad—mostly to help her remember which animal was which—and spent a few minutes familiarizing herself with the irrigation system that brought water from the main well. Then she and Jim rejoined Steve and Virgil.

Finally, by the time the sun had just begun to sag, they called it a day. The horses had been tended. The paddock had been cleared. Rotted fencing lay in a huge pile, ready to be hauled off to the dump. Shading her eyes against the lowering sun, Riley surveyed the area.

Not bad. Not bad at all. With new fencing and a little ground maintenance, it would look like the real deal in no time.

"Great job today, guys," she told the men as they trudged wearily toward their truck, using their shirts to mop their faces. "Are you willing to come back tomorrow? The barbed wire in the big pasture needs to go."

"Oh, boy," Steve said sarcastically. "More fence to pull down."

Virgil groaned.

Jim nodded slowly. "Guess so, Mrs. Palmer."

Not the most enthusiastic responses she might have hoped for, but she could hardly blame them. She wasn't really looking forward to it, either. Still, the fact that they were willing to come back at all was a plus in her book.

"Tell you what," she said. "I'll look at the weather report. If tomorrow is supposed to be as hot as it was today, we can work in the main barn. It's on the boss's to-do list, too."

The three men looked relieved and marched off.

She collected the last of the tools they'd used, checked the area to make sure nothing was left behind, then drove the ATV back to the loafing shed. She considered putting the vehicle in the barn instead, since the shed looked to be on its last legs. Quintin had said it needed tearing down, but it wasn't very high on the priority list.

Tomorrow or the next day, she thought wearily. Or the next. She was too tired to think about it right now.

Her fingers hurt. Really hurt. As she pulled off her left glove, it stuck for a moment. Something gave way, and her hand stung badly enough that she gasped. In the shady light, she saw that a blister on the palm of her hand, one of many, had been torn open and was weeping.

She cursed as she lifted her fingers to the fading light. What a mess. "This never happened when you worked in accounting," she muttered.

"How bad is it?" a male voice behind her asked.

Riley turned quickly and found Quintin standing at the open-air entrance of the shed. She dropped her hands, not hiding them, exactly, but she didn't want to make a big deal of a few blisters. "It's nothing," she said with a shrug. "No more than you'd expect."

He came to stand in front of her, and the first thing she noticed was that he'd changed into fresh jeans and a pale blue polo shirt. His hair looked black as midnight from a shower, and he smelled nice. Manly. It only made her feel more grubby.

Unexpectedly, he caught her wrist and lifted it for his inspection. "Ouch," he said with a frown. When he brought her other hand up so that he could compare the two, he added, "Ah. A matched set."

"They'll get tougher."

He barely had hold of her hands, so she didn't understand why his touch should make her nerve endings sizzle, leaving her with a vague feeling of vulnerability.

She just knew she was inordinately glad when he let her go.

"I have something in the house that will help," he told her.

Self-consciously, she curled her hands into loose fists and wedged them into her pockets, where they throbbed like crazy. "That's all right. I brought first aid stuff with me." She gave him a quizzical look, eager to find some other topic of conversation besides herself. "Did you need something?"

"I saw the Ramseys head out. Just thought you might want help getting things settled for the night."

She'd get blisters on top of blisters before she'd let him think her too weak to finish up. "I can manage, thanks."

To prove that, she began pulling things out of the bed of the ATV. She'd turned her back on him, and she wished he'd just go. She felt awkward and uncomfortable, when all she wanted to feel was strong and capable. Like an insect trapped on the end of a pin, she sensed him watching her.

"What about the afternoon feeding?" he asked eventually.

"Did it around four o'clock."

"Everything look all right?"

"Fine," she told him as she wiped down a couple hammers with one of the old towels. "Pretty good-looking horseflesh you've got there."

"That's what I'm going for."

"If you have no objection, I thought I'd start the men working on the barn tomorrow. Didn't you say you wanted those stalls ready to hold stock as soon as possible?"

He nodded. "Do you want to come up to the house for a cup of coffee? We can discuss a few changes I'd like to make."

She looked at her watch and grimaced. "Can't. I'm a mess, and I…" She hesitated, not wanting to mention having to pick up the girls at the day camp.

"Oh, that's right. You have to get the kids, don't you?"

"I don't want to be charged an overtime fee."

"Yes, of course." His tone was curt, but polite, and there was something else buried in it she couldn't name. "I'm sure you missed having them around today."

"When we stopped for lunch I called to check on them. Evidently, they managed fine and didn't miss me at all."

"I'm sure that's not true," he told her, the corners of his mouth lifting in a not very convincing smile. Suddenly he was moving away, and though only minutes ago she'd been wishing he'd leave, she discovered that she didn't feel that way right now. He inclined his head. "I'll see you tomorrow, then."

## CHAPTER SEVEN

RILEY BARELY MANAGED TO wash her face and hands—gingerly—and run a comb through her hair before she had to hurry into Beaumont to get the girls. In the future, she'd have to watch her time more closely if she was going to keep from being late. The money she'd budgeted for the camp wouldn't survive too many overtime fees.

She was relieved to see that the twins weren't the last kids to be collected. Children surged out the door of Camp Buddies as she came up the walkway, cute little whirlwinds intent on greeting their parents.

As soon as Riley entered the playroom, Wendy and Roxanna came charging in her direction.

"Mommy!" they cried in unison.

She knelt down, spreading her hands wide to receive welcoming kisses and hugs. "Did you miss me? You'd better say yes because I sure missed *you.*"

They smelled like modeling clay and apple juice and their own unique scent that Riley could have identified them by even if she'd been blindfolded. Their soft breaths fanned each side of her neck like a warm caress, and she couldn't help it; for a moment her throat closed, and she thought she might cry from the sheer joy of holding these two precious little beings.

Roxanna was the first to pull away, her nose wrinkling. "You smell like horses."

"I do? Well, you smell like...dirty socks. But I love you, anyway."

"Don't listen to her," Wendy said, glancing sternly at her sister. "I think you smell nice. I missed you. I wanted Miss Amelia to call you to come and get us, but Rox said I was being a baby and to just make you something. So I did." She held a piece of construction paper three inches from Riley's nose. "Do you like it?"

Riley examined the drawing. "It's beautiful. That's the prettiest horse I've ever seen."

"It's a dog," Roxanna said as Wendy frowned.

"Oh. Well, it's still very pretty. What else did you two do today?"

The twins began to talk at the same time, excited, happy snippets about the day's adventures. They'd obviously had a great time, and one thing that came through loud and clear was how much they'd enjoyed playing with the other children.

It made Riley feel better about having enrolled them in the camp. Even if this job didn't work out, the twins would have benefited from their time here.

"Mom, your hands!" Roxanna said with a horrified gasp. "They look so gross!"

Riley wiggled her fingers at them, trying to make light of the situation. "They do, don't they? And they hurt, so don't make me spank you tonight."

"You never spank us."

"I will if you squeeze my hands."

Both girls giggled. Then Wendy, with another dark frown on her sweet features, said, "Did you get those 'cause that man made you work so hard?"

"I did. I had to work all day in the hot sun until I thought my brain would melt." Riley lowered her head and said dramatically, "But then I escaped, and I came racing down here to get you. Do you know why?"

"'Cause you only paid for us to be here during the day?" Roxanna guessed.

"No! Because I knew just seeing you two would make me feel all better." She rose, and tucked them close against her. "And it does. It really…" She planted a noisy kiss on the top of Roxanna's tangled blond hair. "Really…" She did the same to Wendy. "…does. Now let's go home."

Her daughters raced off to get their backpacks,

and Riley spent a brief time talking with Amelia Watkins, who swore she found the twins delightful. The words made Riley feel almost walking-on-air relieved.

She wasn't a horrible mother. She hadn't made the wrong decision. At least, not about this.

BECAUSE HER BODY—and her hands—hurt so much, Riley fed the twins a simple dinner of macaroni and cheese while she took a bath. She would have liked to stay in the tub indefinitely, but that was just wishful thinking. Long soaks in hot, steamy, bubbling water had been pretty much impossible since motherhood came along.

Roxanna and Wendy were bathed, fed and in their pajamas by the time their favorite television program came on. While they watched it, Riley sat slumped on the couch, wishing her body would stop hurting, and wondering how she'd let it get so out of shape.

She was so focused on her various aches and pains that she almost didn't hear the knock on the apartment door. She belted her terry-cloth robe tighter, and discovered Quintin Avenaco on the doorstep.

"Hello," he said.

She blinked in surprise. This was his place. He could come over anytime he wanted. But she hadn't expected he would want to be within ten feet of her when he didn't have to.

"I hope I'm not catching you at a bad time," he went on, when she just continued to stare.

"No, not at all," she assured him, finally remembering her manners. "Would you like to come in?"

"No, thanks." He held out what looked to be an old mayonnaise jar filled with a dark liquid that sloshed against the sides. "I just thought you might be able to use this." He motioned toward the deep pockets of her robe, where her fingers rested. "For your hands."

"Oh."

"I know it looks pretty disgusting, but it's an old home remedy that really works."

"Thanks." She took the container from him, unscrewed the lid and gave the contents a sniff. She grimaced. It smelled like mouthwash…and something nasty. "How much of it do I have to drink?"

He laughed.

Nice to hear, that sound. Rich and genuine and sexy. It was also the first time he'd ever laughed around her. She was aware that her blood surged giddily in response.

"What's so funny?" she asked.

"You drink it, and you'll have more than blisters to worry about. I'd have to take you to the hospital to have your stomach pumped. Chill it a little, then soak your hands in it. I don't suppose you have a pair of silk gloves?"

She suddenly felt silly and careless, and would have snapped her fingers if it wouldn't hurt so much. "Darn. I packed them away with my ball gowns."

"I was afraid of that. How about petroleum jelly?"

"I have some."

"Good. After you soak your hands, don't rinse them off. Cover them with petroleum jelly and then wrap them with gauze. I guarantee they'll be nearly back to normal in no time."

"What's in this stuff?"

"You don't want to know. Let's just say I've never had a horse suffer with a saddle sore."

"Great. I was looking for a new perfume. Eau de Mr. Ed."

She saw his mouth twitch, and felt a jolt of pleasure. They stood silently for a long moment. Undoubtedly, this was where she should thank him one more time, wish him good-night and close the door.

But…maybe not. He didn't seem all that eager to go.

"Can I smell?" she heard Roxanna ask, and became aware that her daughter had joined them.

Riley removed the lid again. Roxanna brought

her nose down cautiously, then made the antici-
pated face. Wendy had come over, too, but shook
her head quickly when Riley offered her a whiff
of the concoction.

Roxanna looked up at Quintin. "Why do you
want our mom to stink?"

Riley laughed. "He doesn't, honey...."

Wendy grabbed a handful of Riley's robe. "He
wants to cook Mommy's brain!" she told her sister.

"I beg your pardon?" Quintin was clearly uncertain he'd heard right.

"Mommy said you tried to melt her brain
today."

"Wendy!" Riley said quickly, touching her
child's shoulder. Her eyes flew to Quintin's as
she shook her head. "I didn't say that."

"Yes, you did," Roxanna confirmed.

Riley stared down at the twins, giving them
both a wide-eyed look that should have silenced
them. "Well, I didn't mean it that way."

Roxanna could be like a terrier with a bone
sometimes. "Why don't you like her?" she asked
Quintin, her jaw thrust forward.

"I like your mother just fine," he said, his tone
an unexpected mix of bewilderment and amusement.

Embarrassed and uncomfortable, Riley turned
to her daughters. "Girls, go brush your teeth.

Right now. And use the toothbrush, not your finger." She turned back to Quintin, flustered. If he was annoyed, he wasn't showing it. "Sorry about that," she said, giving him a pained look. "They get things mixed up sometimes. I didn't say you were trying to melt my brain."

His sudden grin made something inside her go off like a grenade detonating. "Good, because I know people think I'm a hard-ass, but I've never, *ever* tried to Hannibal Lechter anyone's gray matter."

"I was trying to explain to them how hot it was out there today."

"Yeah. That's what it sounded like."

All of a sudden, the strain of the past couple of days seemed to have vanished. Maybe she was just too tired to keep her defenses at the ready. Maybe he was starting to see her as a person, instead of such a disappointment.

Whatever it was, her senses didn't seem to be exhausted at all. When she nervously touched her tongue to her bottom lip, Quintin's gaze followed the movement, and her pulse reacted in a way it hadn't in a very long time. Racing. On fire.

A totally inappropriate response, and not good. Not good at all.

Another long moment stretched between them, and Riley developed a sudden interest in the jar she held. She felt heat start to crawl up her neck. This was getting embarrassing.

"Today in the paddock…" Quintin said at last, then stopped. He cleared his throat. "You and the Ramseys did good work."

Her head came up. The compliment pleased her, but she wouldn't make a big deal out of it. "I think so. They seem like decent guys. You didn't need to…"

"Babysit you?"

She'd been tempted to say that very thing, then thought better of it. She shook her head. "I was going to say you didn't need to worry."

"Uh-huh," he replied, as though he didn't believe her. But what he said next took her by surprise. "I'm sorry if I made you feel as though I was hovering."

She barely knew what to make of that. He didn't strike her as the kind of man to apologize often. She shrugged. "You worked as hard as the rest of us, and as you've said, you have a lot at stake here."

"Still… I'll try to resist micromanaging from now on."

Okay. Now he was really starting to confuse and worry her.

Even in the short time she'd known him, she'd come to expect certain things. When he wasn't being gruff and a real hard case about her lack of management experience, he had often unnerved her with his scrutinizing stare, and she could only imagine the sarcastic remarks being framed and discarded as just too cruel.

But now, this evening, he was suddenly being…almost nice to her. Human. For once there was no mockery in his eyes. No mistrust or skepticism. And an apology, for Pete's sake. What was up with that? She made a cursory stab at sorting out his motives for such affable behavior, and came up empty.

She gave him a genuine look of gratitude. "Thank you," she said simply.

He nodded a few times, quickly, as though what he'd come here to do was finally over. After a few moments, he said good-night and drifted back into the darkness, heading for the house.

Riley shut the door, then leaned against it.

"Wow," she said out loud. "What the heck was *that* all about?"

She realized suddenly that Quintin's apology tonight wasn't the only thing that had her stunned and searching for an answer. There was that…that reaction she'd had to him. Where had it come from?

*Lust,* she told herself firmly. Had to be. Too long without a man and too long since one had actually said anything nice about her to her face. She must really be desperate to prove herself.

Yes, that's what it was. That's all it was. Meaningless, forgettable lust.

But why now? And why him? Why, with all the men on the planet, did she have to be attracted to the one person who would probably wreck her world in three weeks' time?

## CHAPTER EIGHT

RILEY DECIDED SHE WOULD refuse to think about her new boss. Not in *that* way, at least.

The next day started out great. When the Ramsey cousins showed up and joined her in the horse barn, Quintin was with them, but he didn't stay long. They discussed his plans for the building, then he left them and disappeared back inside the house. Riley breathed a sigh of relief and they all got to work.

A structural engineer had certified that the barn was sound, but needed a great deal of repair if they intended to move horses in before the end of the week. She and the men began replacing missing shingles on the roof and broken ventilation louvers. They cleaned gutters and downspouts, then regraded the foundation for better drainage so that water would no longer collect to rot the wood.

The four of them established a rhythm that seemed to work well, and Riley was pleased with their progress. As for Quintin, by the time they broke for lunch, she had almost convinced herself she'd imagined that little moment between them last night.

Then, disaster.

She returned from the noon break to find Quintin in the barn, chatting with the Ramseys. He claimed that he couldn't get any work done in his study with all the noise made by the renovation crew. Before she knew it, he had scooped up a hammer and crowbar and begun prying off damaged siding as if he intended to be with them the rest of the day.

So much for not hovering, Riley thought, but just as quickly she realized that her irritation had less to do with the possibility of him usurping her authority than the fact that he was now sharing the same space with them.

With *her*.

Vowing not to be difficult about his presence, and more importantly, determined to shrug off the disconcerting effect Quintin had on her senses, Riley picked up where she'd left off before lunch, lubricating hardware that could be saved, and replacing what could not. For the most part, she would ignore him.

But throughout the rest of that day, and all the next, she found it one heck of a struggle. He was just so…*there*.

She tried to stay focused on the job, and didn't allow herself to relax an inch. She spoke to him, but only about business matters. They seldom worked side by side, sometimes not even within sight of each other. One or more of the Ramsey cousins was usually nearby, so it wasn't as if she and Quintin could exchange extended, personal conversation, anyway.

But none of that seemed to matter. She was constantly aware of him.

Constantly.

She listened to the soft roll of his voice when he talked to the men, and once, his quick, laughing response to one of Steve's remarks made a swift tingle of pleasure shoot up her spine. She liked the whiff she got of his aftershave when he passed in front of her the next morning. She watched him stretch after an extended period bent over some recaltricant wood, drawing her unwilling attention to his broad shoulders and the well-defined muscles in his arms. Something about the way he moved was worse than that first day in the pasture, when he'd stripped to his T-shirt.

There was just no way not to notice Quintin Avenaco, and it was maddening.

And her boss? Was he aware of her as a woman?

The jury was still out on that.

Most of the time he seemed oblivious to her. Their interactions were polite and professional.

He seemed accepting of her presence, but every so often she felt as though he watched her surreptitiously. She might have thought he was waiting for her to make some grievous mistake that could send her packing, but on one occasion his dark gaze was so intense it felt like a touch against her flesh. When she glanced suddenly his way, there was nothing remotely suggestive about the look on his face, but he didn't turn away, either.

She did her best to ignore his scrutiny. Common sense warned her not to do anything else. But she hated the way her blood quickened and her skin heated.

By the time they had called it a day on Wednesday, and she went to pick up the girls, Riley wasn't sure she would make it to the end of the month.

"SOMETHING WRONG with the eggs, *señor?*"

Seated at the kitchen table, Quintin glanced up at Lilianna in confusion.

In the background, the crew was already hard at work, the sound of half a dozen hammers pounding away in the living room, not two of them in unison. The renovators' day had barely started, and already he had a headache fierce enough to be nationally ranked.

Lilianna gestured toward his plate with her

spatula. "The omelet? It's not to your liking? You were frowning."

"No, it's great." To prove it, Quintin took a big bite, then jerked his head toward the outer wall. "It's all the noise. Hard to concentrate."

Lilianna nodded and turned back to the stove.

He watched her, admiring the efficient way she handled the pots and pans of her new domain. Multitasking to the max. After hiring her on Monday, he had allowed her to rearrange the kitchen to her liking. Today she'd shown up on time, jumped right into fixing breakfast and seemed to realize that he wasn't looking for conversation while he ate.

He had a feeling she was going to work out fine.

Unlike the *other* female currently on his payroll.

This morning his mind felt about as nimble as an aircraft carrier. Definitely not enough sleep.

For once, it hadn't been bad dreams that kept him awake. Sometimes, against his will, they walked him through memories of the past, those precious few years he'd had with Teresa and Tommy. The dreams started out lovely, but always ended in heart-stopping flashes of fear and crippling grief that jerked him awake, covered in sweat.

Nothing like that had kept him sleepless last night, thank God.

Instead, he'd just tossed and turned until his sheets looked as if they'd been whirled by a tornado.

All because of the Palmer woman.

Half the night had slipped away before he'd been able to drift into blissful oblivion, finally able to shake off the foolish, erotic images that seemed to occupy great segments of his brain. It was ridiculous that someone he'd known such a short time, someone he wasn't even sure he *liked,* should be able to invade his thoughts so thoroughly.

But there she'd been, damn her. Peppering his mind with reminders of the way she'd looked in the pasture that first day, and the two days they'd been working together on the barn. That startling sweet smile toward the Ramsey cousins when she gave them directions. The way she tilted her head to the sun, or curved her neck as she swept her hair back into its ponytail. That lift to her breasts when she arched her back to stretch out the kinks. A man would have to be dead not to notice.

And that night on her doorstep… Ah, hell. He'd been reduced to acting like some moony teenaged boy.

It had started out simple enough, that visit.

Good intentions. A professional interest. An effort on his part to show her that he wasn't completely oblivious to her welfare. Her hands *had* been a disaster.

But the moment she'd opened the door, all that concern for her blisters threatened to go right out the window. How could he think about them when she stood there, pink and dewy from her bath, fine tendrils of damp blond hair escaping down her neck? Without a doubt, she had the most kissable mouth of any woman he'd ever met.

All right, so she was attractive and had a great body. Plenty of other faces out there, and eventually, someday, he'd want one again. But not right now.

*Move past it, Quint. Stay focused.*

But that lecture didn't seem to work yesterday. Or the day before. Or last night, as he'd tried to get some sleep.

Why couldn't she have been the kind of ranch manager he'd been looking for? A guy, preferably one with about forty years' experience. Arms like thick cables, a face dented and marked by life, and the personality of a wire coat hanger.

Instead, he'd hog-tied himself to Cowgirl Barbie.

Annoyed, Quintin balled up his napkin. He

stood and scraped his chair back so quickly that Lilianna glanced over her shoulder in alarm.

"Lots of work today," he said by way of explanation for his abrupt behavior. "Better get to it."

He thanked her for breakfast, grabbed his Stetson from the peg near the front door and headed for the barn.

He wondered what kind of reaction he'd get from Riley when he showed up. He'd promised not to micromanage, and he thought he'd been pretty much hands off while they got the barn back in shape. Well, too bad if she was peeved with him. This was his baby, and he had too much invested here to leave it completely in the hands of an amateur. He should never have made that stupid promise not to interfere.

If he'd been thinking with his head instead of… Well, if he'd just been *thinking*.

Weaving past the vehicles in the yard, he hit the barn entrance. The doors at both ends had been thrown wide. Dust motes danced in the rays of light streaming through the low windows.

It was early, but he expected to find the Ramseys and Riley already making headway with today's work. On Sunday he'd told her about the eight boxed, prefab stalls that had been delivered a week ago. Now that they'd repaired the barn and stripped out all the damaged wood, they would replace the older, outdated stalls.

But there was no buzz of activity here. Not yet, anyway. Instead, he saw the men standing around their manager. Riley stared down at a large sheet of paper she held, spread out like a giant road map. Several shipping boxes lay open at their feet—tongue-and-groove lumber, grill doors, hardware and kick plates, all sorted and stacked.

He couldn't see Riley's face, but the way she stood was a clear sign she was annoyed. And maybe confused?

Quintin watched her tilt the paper—probably instructions on how to assemble the stalls—toward a shaft of sunlight. She pointed out something on the page. "This doesn't make sense."

Jim, who probably had enough carpentry experience to build a house from the ground up, shrugged. "It will, Ms. Palmer," he said patiently. "You just can't see it yet."

Riley grimaced and folded the paper with a frustrated snap. "Great. Since you seem to have a better understanding of all this, I'm officially making it your baby."

Virgil bent to pick up one of the pieces from the stack—a delicately-veined oak ball that had been carved to a point on one side. He bounced it in his hand. "What's this?"

"It's called a finial," she told him.

"What's a finial?"

"A fancy word for a useless decoration no one cares two beans about. It goes on top of the posts on either side of the stall doors."

Quintin almost laughed at Riley's description. He stepped farther into the corridor, figuring it was time to make his presence known.

Jim Ramsey spotted him and nodded a greeting. "Morning."

Riley's head snapped up. Even across the distance that separated them, Quintin could read her mind. She was flustered by the thought that he might have overheard her.

He smiled and inclined his head as he joined them. "Problems?"

"None that we can't handle," Riley quickly replied.

Crap. She might be feeling momentarily stymied by this project, but she still looked as perky as a parakeet. If she'd lost as much sleep as he had last night, she sure didn't show it. Her hair was loose, floating around her shoulders like a golden cloud. No makeup that he could see, but her fresh-faced good looks didn't need any.

She was wearing denim overalls, with a white tank top underneath so that her arms were bare. Overalls, he thought disgustedly. How could that be sexy? Kids wore overalls. But as far as he was concerned, with Riley Palmer inside them, they beat silk and satin hands down.

He glanced at the array of oak lumber and assorted parts. He'd decided to splurge on the stalls, wanting something more than a standard ten-by-ten box and Dutch door. He liked the European look, with their iron-grate half doors, low, curving side walls and brass kick plates.

Virgil scratched his cheek carefully with the claw end of his hammer. "We could probably throw up some stalls a lot faster than trying to make heads or tails of these directions."

Quintin shook his head. "I know these are a lot fancier than what Texans are used to. But I want to showcase the stock as much as possible for the buyer."

"As soon as we get the first one in place, the rest will be a piece of cake," Riley said confidently. He knew she was determined to give him the impression that everything was under control.

The men went to work, and Riley joined them in trying to make slot A fit into flap B. She wasn't very good at it. If her twins had gotten tricycles one Christmas, Quintin would have bet the ranch her ex-husband had put them together. Definitely not her area of expertise.

In spite of that, he began to feel like an interloper. They didn't need him, but there were a lot of projects that did. Besides, he kept catching himself taking more interest in the same thing that had intrigued him yesterday. The sight of Riley Palmer.

*Not today,* he thought. *Use your head, man.*

Clenching his jaw, he headed down the barn corridor.

"Quintin, hold up," Riley called. "I just need a minute."

He turned and waited.

He met her polite smile with an expression of amusement. "Let me guess. You have another confession to make. You have lousy spatial skills?"

She wrinkled her nose and frowned. He tried very hard not to find it cute. He hated cute.

"Was it that obvious?"

"Blatantly."

"Darn. But you know…the greatest coaches in the world don't have to play the game like superstars to be effective leaders."

"That thought occurred to me. Otherwise I wouldn't be willing to leave you and the Ramseys alone to figure things out."

She looked cautiously pleased. "Thanks for the vote of confidence."

Something was different about her this morning. He couldn't put his finger on what, exactly. She still wanted him to believe she was just as good as any seasoned ranch manager, so she probably thought a different approach with him would turn three weeks into a full-time job. Regardless, he liked it that they could almost speak, instead of fencing clumsily with one another.

Too bad for her it wouldn't work to her advantage. He'd placed the ad only yesterday morning, but already there was a printer tray full of résumés waiting. A quick glance had told him there were a bunch of heavy hitters in the pile.

"You're welcome," he said. "I'll let you get back to work."

"Wait!" She grasped his sleeve as he started to turn away. "I wanted to show you." She lifted her hands, palms outward. "Did you notice my blisters? You were right. They're practically gone."

She smiled up at him. All friendly, blue-eyed innocence. God, she was practically radiating sunshine and rainbows.

*Back away,* his brain ordered. But he was afraid this was one of those times when his mind simply wouldn't take instruction.

"They look good," he said, trying to sound as interested as a mechanic checking out a carburetor.

She didn't seem to notice. "That gunk really did the trick. And take a whiff." She brought one hand under his nose. "You can't even tell that nasty stuff was there, can you?"

If he'd had a little more sleep and a lot more
sense, he might have made some comment and
headed for the barn door. Whatever her game
was—if she was playing a game—he was too
old for it, too rusty. He'd sure as hell never been
the kind of guy to surrender to the moment.

But he suddenly realized that he didn't give a
damn about anything except finding out if her
skin was as soft as it looked. He supposed his
curiosity got the better of him. Never a good
thing.

"No, I don't smell it," he agreed, and then
slowly, deliberately brought her hand up to his
nose and inhaled. The only scent he caught was
*her,* sweet and intoxicating. As if he'd stuck his
face in a bunch of flowers. "You smell like…
warm roses."

She didn't stiffen or clench her hand. She
blinked a couple of times. Surprised, maybe?
*Join the club,* he thought.

He touched his lips to her knuckles, then
turned her fingers over and brought his free hand
up to cradle her palm. He laid his mouth gently
against the slight rise of an almost-healed blister. It felt so warm, and smelled ridiculously like
some heady perfume. When he kissed the spot,
he heard Riley drag in a deep breath of her own.

"Quintin…"

"I know," he said in a slow, husky voice. He

lifted his head to catch her eyes. Her mouth was parted, and she was frowning. "Insane, isn't it?"

"I…" The word was a trembling sigh, barely more than a whisper. She wet her lips. When she tugged her hand away, he released it immediately. "I think I should get back to the men."

He watched her walk away from the shadows and back into the soft peachy light where the men were. Watched her, and thought how much he had liked what just happened. How he had enjoyed it more than he had enjoyed anything in a long, long time.

But what he'd done had just made a difficult situation even worse, and he couldn't help but realize just how foolish he'd been.

By THE END OF THE DAY, as Riley drove back to Echo Springs from picking up the girls, she decided to assume that there must be days when a person's common sense went on vacation. In her case, it had gone to a whole other planet.

What else could explain the mistake she'd made with Quintin after the lectures she'd been giving herself lately?

For a while, his actions this morning had had a babbling-idiot effect on her brain, but that had more or less worn off by now. Those few minutes alone with him in the barn had been dissected a dozen times, and still she couldn't come up with any logical explanation.

She knew she had rather limited experience with men. Brad had been the only serious relationship she'd ever had. She'd never played around behind his back, even though she'd known their marriage was over long before she left him. In spite of her impulsive nature, she wasn't a flirt or tease.

So the idea that she had been foolish enough to behave that way with Quintin Avenaco...well, it just had to be a momentary, but monumental, lapse of good judgment.

He wasn't like Brad the Cad. In spite of those stray glances she'd caught from him the past couple of days, Quintin hadn't struck her as the kind of man a woman should play games with. A red-blooded male he might be, but he was focused on the single goal of making a success of Echo Springs.

And her *boss,* for God's sake. The idea that she had waved her hand under his nose like a medieval princess offering a token to a favored knight...

It was embarrassing. Stupid.

Some seriously messed-up stuff was going on in her head where he was concerned.

Her mind first jumped at the idea, then backed away, like a kitten tricked into pouncing on a shadow. But the truth couldn't be ignored. After that night at her apartment door, after that little glimpse of…of *something* that had arced between them, and two days spent in close, intense proximity in the barn, she couldn't help her curiosity getting the better of her.

So when the opportunity had presented itself, before she knew it…

*Let's test drive this baby and see what she can do.*

And boy, the response had been terrific. Definitely scary. But terrific.

Yes, she had her answer. Now, what was she going to do about it? What *should* she do about it?

*Nothing,* a weak but sensible voice inside her warned.

She had the tiniest toehold on this job. Maybe not even that. If she had a hope in hell of keeping it, making a decent living so she could support her girls, then she mustn't sabotage herself.

This attraction between them couldn't go anywhere. Time to reorder priorities. No more indulging in wayward, reckless thoughts about Quintin. No hoping for sexy banter or erotically charged moments. Their future conversations should be brisk and impersonal.

No socializing.

No dawdling.

All business.

Besides, now that he'd had time to think over what had happened, that was probably the way Quintin wanted things to go, too. A man with a mission, that guy. And in that mission, she didn't have a place. Not really. Three weeks, and then adios.

"Mommy?"

Riley glanced in the rearview mirror at Wendy. "What, sweetie?"

"You look sad. Are you mad at us?"

"No. Just a little tired," she lied. "Tell me more about your field trip to the zoo today."

Wendy started recapping the excursion again, and Riley tried to find a new way to look fascinated. It wasn't easy. Wendy didn't have Roxanna's dramatic flair for storytelling. Riley found it difficult to wrap her mind around images of monkeys and tigers when she couldn't stop thinking about Quintin's sloe-gin smile, the softness of his breath sending leaping awareness to every nerve in her body and, most of all, the tingling warmth of his lips on her skin. Even now, the memory made her lungs feel like an accordion being crushed under a giant's foot.

*No, no, no. No more of that nonsense.*

She was determined to keep that silent vow. All the same, she felt her stomach contract with a little spasm of regret at the thought.

She ignored it.

Wendy twisted in her seat to catch Riley's attention. "I drew you a picture. It's in my backpack. It's a horse this time. It's better than the dog."

"They still all look the same," Roxanna muttered from her spot in the back, and Riley shot her a warning glance in the rearview mirror.

She smiled at Wendy. "I can't wait to see it."

The renovation crew was gone by the time she swung the SUV into the front drive, and Quintin's truck stood alone in the yard. After this morning's foolishness, Riley hadn't seen him the rest of the day. The ATV sat at the bottom of the front steps. She frowned. After returning from the afternoon feeding, she'd parked the vehicle in the loafing shed.

As she pulled up next to the barn apartment, Quintin came out of the house. By the time she'd collected the girls' things from the backseat, he was beside her, perched on the ATV, a caddy of supplies next to him. She spotted bandages nestled among hoof picks and currycombs.

"Something wrong?" she asked. Everything had looked fine earlier, and she hated the thought she might have missed something.

"Nothing serious. I was just out in the pasture, and one of the mares got in a tussle over personal space. Ended up with a good-size bite on her neck. Just making sure it doesn't get infected."

Catching sight of an unlabeled container in the caddy, one that looked very similar to the concoction he had given her to treat her blisters, Riley motioned toward it. "Another homegrown remedy?"

"Your hands are living proof that stuff like this works," he said pleasantly enough, but then his gaze drifted off to some point beyond the barn. She wondered if he was sorry he'd brought up any reminder of what had happened between them this morning.

For a wild second or two, her mind detoured into dangerous territory about just how therapeutically wonderful his mouth had felt, but she quickly shut those thoughts down. "Would you like me to take care of it?" she said instead.

"I've got it, thanks."

He smiled a little, but those lines around his eyes, the ones she'd come to think of as devastatingly sexy, didn't show up. Maybe he'd decided to go back to polite indifference in his dealings with her. For both their sakes.

The twins had come around the car to join her. "Can I take a ride on that?" Roxanna asked Quintin, indicating the ATV. "Just in the yard."

Quintin parted his lips as if to respond, then closed them again. For the first time since she'd come here, Riley thought he seemed at a loss for words.

She caught Roxanna's eye and shook her head. "This isn't a toy, honey. It's for work."

"I bet I can drive it, and I'll be real careful."

"I'm sorry," Quintin finally said, looking more uncomfortable by the moment. "Maybe some other time your mom can take you and your sister out."

"I won't go fast."

Riley handed her daughter her backpack. "Roxanna, you and Wendy go inside and wash up for dinner."

With one sullen glare at both adults, Roxanna stormed off toward the apartment.

Riley gave Quintin an apologetic look, but it was Wendy, still standing next to her mother, who spoke up.

"I have a present for you," she said to Quintin.

"For me?" he echoed.

"Uh-huh."

Riley still held Wendy's backpack, and the child reached out and unzipped the top compartment. From it she withdrew a piece of slightly crumpled drawing paper. Very solemnly, she handed it to Quintin, who stared down at it, obviously confused.

After a long moment, his eyes came back to Wendy's. "You drew this for me?"

Riley had to hide a smile. Wendy's artistic talent was almost nonexistent. The drawing looked as abstract as a Picasso. She felt compelled to say, "It's a horse."

Wendy groaned. "He knows that, Mommy."

"It's, uh, it's very pretty," Quintin said with a tentative smile. Riley could almost feel his uncertainty. "Thank you."

"You're welcome, mister."

"You can call me Mr. Ave… You can call me Quintin, if you like."

"Okay."

Riley watched this exchange with more than a little bewilderment. Wendy hadn't said anything in the car about having drawn a picture for Quintin, and when he'd brought over the blister medication, she'd seemed almost afraid of her mother's new boss. Kids. Go figure.

Quintin set the picture on the seat beside him, catching one corner with the caddy so that it wouldn't be blown away as he drove. He gave Wendy a tight smile, and Riley a look she couldn't interpret. She stepped away from the vehicle, pulling her daughter against her.

"I'll leave you to your doctoring," she said. "See you tomorrow."

He nodded. In another moment, he was bumping slowly down the rutted road that led out to the back pasture.

Riley locked the SUV, then she and Wendy headed for the apartment. "It was very nice of you to draw a picture for Mr. Avenaco."

"He said I could call him Quintin."

"How many pictures did you draw today?"

"Only one."

Riley stopped, frowning down at Wendy, whose soft blue eyes looked up at her in sweet innocence. "You gave him the picture you drew for me?"

"Uh-huh."

"Why did you do that?"

The little girl shrugged. "I can draw pictures for you anytime. I think he needed it more than you."

## CHAPTER NINE

THE NEXT DAY, when Riley returned from dropping the girls off at day camp, she noticed two things right away—Quintin's truck was missing from the yard, and the Ramseys' beat-up Chevy was already parked next to the house.

She had no idea where her boss might be. As for the hired help, she hoped the three cousins were busy on their next project.

Cutting through the barn, she admired yesterday's accomplishments. Quintin should be pleased. The final touches had been put on the new stalls, and she had to admit they looked pretty spectacular, even if they had been a pain to put together. Thank goodness Jim was such a wiz at construction.

She found the Ramseys behind the barn, working on another item from Quintin's to-do list—rehabbing the wash station where sweaty horses who had rolled in the dirt could be cross-tied and then hosed down, made to look like show ponies for prospective buyers.

"You just missed the boss," Jim told her. He

plucked an envelope from his back pocket and handed it to her. "He left this for you."

The note said Quintin would be away for the weekend. No explanation as to why, but then, he didn't owe her one. Someone from Horse Sense would be bringing over his personal stock today, and he wanted her to have two stalls ready. Other than that, she was to keep to the work schedule they'd laid out. If she ran into any problems— he'd underlined *any*—she should call him immediately on his cell.

She frowned down at his crisp, clear handwriting. She appreciated the fact that he felt confident enough to leave her in charge. She even told herself that she was relieved she wouldn't have to be around him for another uncomfortable day. But she had to admit she was a little disappointed, too.

Was he deliberately avoiding her?

Almost immediately she rejected the idea. He'd already said he would be away frequently from the ranch on buying trips. That was one reason he'd wanted an experienced manager. This was probably one of those times. Although... neither of the horse trailers was missing from beside the barn.

Then out of the blue, the thought came that maybe Quintin had a girlfriend nearby. Riley would bet money he could have his pick of women, though, come to think of it, Cassie Rafferty had said he was pretty much a loner.

Of course, being married to Brad had shown Riley that the ability to socialize or share sparkling conversation with a woman wasn't a big priority for most men. Mitzy Freeman, the daughter of Brad's boss at the Bar Seven and now Brad's fiancée, had barely been able to put two words together to make a sentence. But boy, could she fill a pair of jeans.

So maybe it was as simple as that.

*And why should you care if it is?* Riley chided herself. *He's your boss, not your boyfriend.*

Except…she did *care.* Sort of.

In spite of the fact that she'd sworn not to entertain romantic fantasies about Quintin, she had to admit to being…fascinated by him. During the past few days, working in close proximity, they'd had very little personal interaction, but that didn't mean his every movement hadn't played on her senses with sharp awareness. No doubt about it, the man had sex appeal.

But besides just a physical response, Riley thought she was starting to understand him a little, to get a better feel for the kind of person he was. He might be unreasonable about not wanting her as his ranch manager, but in everything else he seemed sensible, thoughtful. Likable, even.

Cassie had said he was too guarded, but why

wouldn't he be? There were some mistakes you never got to erase, and if he honestly thought he was to blame for what had happened to his family, it wasn't surprising he seemed so uncomfortable around the twins. But he—

"Mrs. Palmer?"

Riley looked up quickly, startled to discover Jim at her elbow.

"Everything all right, ma'am?" the oldest Ramsey cousin asked.

Definitely time to stop thinking about Quintin and get busy. She smiled at the man. "Fine," she told him. "After we finish this, we have to start tearing down fence in the back pasture."

By 10:00 a.m. they were all toiling in the hot sun, pulling up posts and using cutters and their thickest gloves to carefully remove the barbed wire that was so dangerous to horses. For every section they stripped out, they replaced it with solid lumber boards.

The horses, curious and probably hoping for a handout, hung around to keep them company. They were such beautiful animals, every one of them, and Riley could easily imagine them decked out in police equipage. She noticed that the bite mark on the black mare Quintin had doctored had already dried up, though it would take a couple weeks before hair regrew to cover the spot.

By the time lunchtime rolled around, Riley's shoulders were aching again, but not quite as badly as they had her first day. Her hands seemed tougher, too, with no fresh blisters. She went back to the apartment, made herself a sandwich, then toed her boots off just to give her feet a rest.

She must have dozed off, because a knock on the door brought her sitting straight up, her heart hammering. A quick look at her watch showed that it was nearly time to get back to work.

When she opened the door, she was half hoping it would be Quintin. Not a sane way to be thinking, but there it was. Instead, she found Virgil standing on the stoop, his hat in one hand and a toolbox in the other.

"What's up?" she asked quickly. The last thing she wanted was a problem she would have to call Quintin to resolve.

"Sorry to interrupt your lunch, Mrs. Palmer, but Mr. Avenaco told me this morning to get with you first free chance I got."

"Get with me? About what?"

"He said I was to haul out some animals you got in here." His eyes traveled past her into the apartment, like a cop expecting to see marijuana growing in the living room. "Some stuffed deer and such. And a…a buffalo head that was scaring your kids?"

"Oh," Riley replied with some surprise. She stepped back, allowing Virgil to enter.

He made quick work of the assignment, releasing stuffed Bambi and his friends from their positions of honor on the walls, and carting them outside. Even the flying squirrel above the kitchen cabinet went, though Riley had to admit she'd sort of grown used to him staring down at her. Virgil struggled a little getting the buffalo head down, but eventually it gave up the fight, too.

"What are you going to do with them?" Riley asked as he muscled it out the door.

"Take them up to the house," he replied, tossing his screwdriver into the toolbox. "Mr. Avenaco said they weren't to show up anyplace your kids might go. Anything else I can do for you, ma'am, before I head back to the pasture?"

"No, thanks. I'll be out to join you shortly."

After Virgil tipped his hat and hurried away, she surveyed the newly excavated apartment. The twins would be thrilled. Especially Wendy, who had continued to give the animals a wide berth, and constantly asked Riley to recheck the towel she'd tied over the buffalo's head.

It had been thoughtful of Quintin to send Virgil. Unexpected, too. It pleased her. She'd never mentioned how unnerved the girls had been, but maybe he remembered when they'd first met—

her struggling on the bed to pull down the buffalo head and the twins squealing nervously behind her.

Her heart stumbled a little. Really, no matter how much Quintin liked to come across as gruff and no-nonsense, he had it in him to be kind.

THE FISH WEREN'T BITING at Little Sabine Creek, but the mosquitoes were. And it was hot. Damned hot. Quintin knew that Ethan thought he was nuts for suggesting they go camping in the middle of a brutal Texas summer. With only an hour's notice.

So far his friend hadn't complained, but it was coming. Quintin had felt the man's questioning glances on him all day yesterday. Now it was Saturday night, and those glances had turned into frowning, open curiosity.

And how could Quintin explain anything when he wasn't sure himself just why he was out here in the wilderness? Why was he sweating through his shirt and trying to keep two steaks from turning into shoe leather on the grill, when there were about a million things he should be doing at the ranch?

He saw Ethan pull a couple of beers out of the ice chest, then pop the tops. He sauntered over to check the progress of their dinner, and handed Quintin a can.

His friend looked down at his steak as though it had turned into roadkill. "That's a damn fine cut of meat," he said. "I'd prefer it if you didn't burn mine to a crisp."

"I'm not going to burn it."

"As distracted as you've been, I wouldn't be too sure. Care to tell me what this is all about?"

*Here it comes,* Quintin thought. He tried to look confused. "What are you talking about?"

"This impromptu fishing trip."

"You're the one who's been bugging me to go fishing."

"Yeah, except I've been saying that since last fall, and the answer has always been no. Too busy. No time. Now suddenly you call me and say be ready to go in one hour. What gives?"

Quintin shrugged. "A window of opportunity opened up, and I took it. Figured you could use some downtime, too."

"You're lucky my wife didn't slam that window on your fingers," Ethan replied with a short laugh. "Josh and Meredith's wedding reception is next weekend, and Cassie has a mile-long list of things I need to do. You owe me big-time for this little getaway. Especially since we haven't caught any fish."

Quintin motioned toward the can in Ethan's hand. "Quit bitchin' and drink your beer."

"Quit dodging my question and give me a

straight answer." He tilted his head. In the primitive light put out by the two Coleman lanterns, his features were suddenly serious. "What's up, Quint? Are you in some kind of trouble?"

"No. Don't be an idiot."

"I don't mean it like that. I mean with Echo Springs. Are you going to miss the October deadline?"

Quintin's gut tightened at the mere suggestion of that happening. "No. Not if I can help it." He took a swig of beer and shook his head. "I just needed to get away. The damned house is like Grand Central Station with all the renovations going on. Hammering and sawing the entire day. I needed some peace and quiet. Time to think."

"So think at night, when everyone goes home."

"That's a joke. At night all I can think about—" He handed off the empty beer can to Ethan. "Give me another one."

His friend's brows rose, probably because he knew Quintin wasn't much of a drinker. Still, he fished out another cold brew and handed it over. "Buddy," he said, shaking his head, "I don't know what burr is under your saddle, but you need to get it out. I've never seen you this edgy."

Quintin stabbed one of the steaks with his fork. "I tried to remove it," he said sourly to the meat. "I gave it three weeks to find someplace else to go. But right now, I'm stuck with it." He looked up at Ethan. "And by *it,* I mean *her.* I'm stuck with *her.*"

"Her who? Why do I feel like I've either dropped about a hundred IQ points, or you're not making any sense?"

"*Her.* My ranch manager. Riley Palmer."

"The woman you hired sight unseen? The one Cassie told me she met?"

"That's the one."

"Is she incompetent? Hell, Quint. If she can't do the job, why are you putting up with it? Fire her ass and find a replacement."

"She's not incompetent. She's…" He grimaced. How could he explain, when his thoughts were growing so tangled they didn't seem to make sense anymore? "She's not incompetent."

The light must have dawned, because Ethan suddenly grinned. "Ohhh…I get it now. Cassie said she was a looker."

"She is. And in spite of all the ways I've tried not to notice, it's damned hard to ignore."

"Is she coming on to you?"

"No. If anything, I'm— No. But I can't seem to stop thinking about her. And I need to, because all that's important right now is getting Echo Springs ready."

"Then good-looking or not, cut her loose. Out of sight, out of mind."

"I can't. I agreed to keep her on until the end of the month."

"So pay her for that amount of time and send her off with no hard feelings. She'll probably thank you for it."

"She won't. She's determined to prove she can do the job, and I'm beginning to think she can. She's a lot tougher than I thought." He slapped a mosquito from his neck and shook his head again. "She's not just an attractive woman. She's interesting and smart, and I like the way she—" He flipped one of the steaks so viciously that it almost sailed off the grill. "Aw, hell, I sound like your son when he tells me about his latest girl-friend. I'm too old for this kind of crap."

Ethan snorted in disbelief while Quintin remained silent, his gaze fixed on his beer. "You're not exactly ready for the nursing home. Maybe it's time you pulled out the old playbook and took a run at a beautiful woman again." He tossed back a swallow from the can, then eyed Quintin closely. "There's more to life than just work, you know?"

"In spite of what you and Cassie might think, I don't need a woman in my life. I'm fine being a bachelor. I don't understand what's going on. For God's sake, I barely know the woman."

"So what's wrong with getting to know her a little better? Or even ending up in bed together?"

"I can't."

"Can't? Or won't?"

Quintin scowled. "I'm not completely opposed to passion. In theory and in small, manageable doses. But I don't believe in starting something I have no intention of finishing."

Ethan stared at him for a moment, open-mouthed. Then he grinned again. "Wow. That was one hell of an impressive speech. How long have you been rehearsing it? And when do you plan to lay it on her?"

"I don't know why I've bothered to tell you any of this. You're not helping."

A minute or two passed while Quintin fussed with the steaks, and his friend just watched him do it.

Finally, Ethan said in a softer tone, "You can't hide from real life forever. And finding a woman attractive, wanting her, isn't being unfaithful to your wife, Quint."

He gave his friend a hard stare. They'd known each other too long, been through too much for him to take serious offense, but sometimes Ethan could really piss him off. "Shut up and get me a couple of plates."

"Quint—"

"Leave it alone, Ethan."

"Teresa and Tommy have been gone a long time—"

"You think I don't know that?" he said tightly as he swung toward his friend. "I can tell you to the day, to the minute how long…." The words sounded harsh, and a little wild. Deliberately, he clamped his teeth together. "I don't need this kind of complication right now," he said at last. "Neither does she."

"How do you know what she needs or wants? Maybe you should ask her."

"She's in no better position than I am. For one thing, she's my employee—"

"Not for long."

"All right. But when she finishes up at Echo Springs, she'll be jobless and maybe even homeless. Not a great time to be worrying about your love life. She's barely come down from a divorce, and it was a bitter one from the sounds of it. And…she has two little girls."

"What's so bad about that? Are they brats?"

"I don't know. I haven't been around them much. One of them gave me a picture of a horse she'd drawn."

Ethan made a scandalized sound that he probably thought was pretty amusing. "The little monster! You can't put up with behavior like that."

Quintin jabbed his fork toward his friend to make a point. "Don't act like you don't know what I'm talking about. I remember how long it took you to get comfortable around Donny, and he was your own son. I haven't been around kids—little ones, anyway—for a long time. Frankly," he muttered, avoiding Ethan's gaze, "they scare the crap out of me."

"You'll get used to them."

"I don't want to get used to them. They don't have any business being on a working ranch that's in chaos."

"So what do you plan to do?"

"I wish I knew. At the very least, I owe her an apology. I acted like an ass the other day. The last thing she needs is me trying to get her into bed."

Ethan sent him a dry glance. "Have you considered the possibility that if you two were… willing to *explore* things a little, shall we say… that maybe you could get her out of your system?"

"Like that got you over wanting Cassie?"

"That was different. Cassie and I had a history together. We still had a lot to resolve."

"The timing is just all wrong," Quintin said doggedly.

"When will the timing be right?" Ethan asked quietly. "Ever?"

Quintin muttered a curse. "If you can't come up with decent advice, then quit talking."

"Might as well, since you're not listening."

"Right now, I'm just happy to be away from the ranch for a while and have a little time to think."

"Fine. Be a stubborn ass. I only have one more thing to say."

"What?"

Ethan pointed toward the grill. "Stop burning my steak."

AFTER DROPPING ETHAN OFF at the Flying M, Quintin arrived back at the ranch late Sunday night. He took a hot shower, scrubbing away sweat, dirt and mosquito repellent, then sorted through a stack of mail and checked on the progress the renovation crew had made while he was gone.

Exhausted, he fell into bed. The camping trip hadn't rejuvenated him as he'd hoped, and his brain felt as sluggish as his body. The conversation he'd had with Ethan had brought no new perspectives or ideas on how to handle this ridiculous fixation he seemed to have for Riley Palmer. If anything, it had left him with more questions.

When he finally fell asleep, he dreamed about the fire.

*The air was so cold that it burned his nostrils. The packed snow beneath Windwalker's hooves crunched as the smooth surface gave way, and* the animal struggled awkwardly to find its footing. Rounding up strays in the middle of a bitter Colorado winter was one of the worst parts of owning your own spread. Teresa had wanted him to wait until tomorrow, but money being tight, Quintin couldn't afford to lose even one steer to the weather.

Just thinking about Teresa made him smile. When he returned, he'd have to kiss her into a better mood. She'd been angry with him this morning because the house was too chilly, and the damned furnace—which he'd promised to fix—was on the blink again. The old relic had to be babied into working most of the time, and he'd refused to replace it until they could pay cash for a new one.

But when he got home, he'd see to it. By then, Teresa would have probably forgiven him, and if she hadn't, well...he knew ways to bring her around.

God, he thought, as he pulled his collar up so that the wind didn't send frigid air down his back. He was a lucky man to have a wife who loved him in spite of all his faults, who had given him a terrific son like Tommy. Just thinking about them made his smile deepen, and almost unconsciously he turned in his saddle to look back toward the house, hidden now behind a barren ridge of snow.

He saw it then. Streaks of red light on the

horizon. Bloodred, like the most magnificent Colorado sunsets in summer. But this was the wrong time of year for that kind of show. Quintin frowned, not understanding at first just what he was looking at.

And then he did know. He knew it in his head and in his gut and in his heart.

The house was fully engulfed in flames by the time he reached it. He slid off his horse, panting, running, heading for a front door that was no longer there. He dived into thick, black smoke and searing heat, shouting Teresa's and Tommy's names over and over, with no response. The house that he had practically built with his own hands seemed so foreign to him now. No recognizable touchstones. Everything gone in a wall of flames and falling timber.

Something cracked and roared and then hit him across the back, hit him hard, and when he came to, he realized that the roof had caved in, that a single support truss had pinned him to what remained of the floor. He struggled, gasping for breath, pain swelling in his chest. He had to find his family! His brain was screaming at him to do so, but he couldn't make his body respond.

Staring up at the hole where the roof had been, he sensed that he was going to die. But it didn't matter, didn't matter at all, because he *knew that with the house had gone the woman he loved and the son he adored. There was nothing he wanted more in that moment than to let the flames take him, too....*

Jerking awake, Quintin sat upright. He stayed like that a few long moments, gasping for breath. Then he swung out of bed. No more sleep. There was nothing new in those memories—there never was—but tonight they seemed especially unbearable.

He prowled the bedroom, then headed for his study.

At his desk, he resisted the temptation to flip on his computer. In the black mood he was in, accomplishing anything worthwhile seemed unlikely. Instead, he remained sitting in the dark, rubbing his temples and waiting for his heart to return to its normal rhythm.

Tonight, that took a long time, but it gave him plenty of opportunity to think.

He was so tired of this. The life he had established after the death of his wife and son had been all right for a while. It had become so easy, so much less painful to withdraw and isolate himself, to be wary of anyone who tried to pull him out of the protective shell he'd built over the years.

But something wasn't working anymore, and he suspected that Ethan was right, damn him.

It was time to stop battening down the hatches somewhere deep inside. Time to stop ignoring the world. Especially now that he had launched all these plans to bring the world to his doorstep come October.

Whether he liked it or not, if he was really going to make any of this work, could he afford to hold everyone at arm's length anymore?

Pensively, he stared down at his desk. In the moonlight, he could barely make out the stark-white piece of paper that lay on his blotter. He picked it up, realizing it was the picture Riley's daughter had given him the other day. Was her name Willa? No. Something from literature, but damned if he could remember it.

He smiled a little, tracing the lines of the horse she'd drawn. Cute little girl. Pretty like her mom, but no budding artist. Still, it was the thought that counted, right? This sudden gift had shocked the heck out of him. God, had he even remembered to thank the kid?

He got up and walked to the window that looked out over the side yard and the barn. The manager's apartment was dark, the curtains drawn tightly.

It occurred to him that Riley Palmer was part of that world he'd been trying to shove away for too many years. He didn't know why he found her so appealing, why it had to happen now, when he could least afford the distraction. But he knew he was doing a really poor job of controlling his interest. She might be wrong for him in every way he could conceive of, and probably a few he couldn't.

But that didn't mean he had the willpower to stop imagining her in any number of creative and daring scenarios. How could it be a stretch for any man to link thoughts of Riley Palmer and a warm bed?

And what was so unusual about that?

He was a single guy who'd made a pass at a very attractive single woman. He'd regretted his behavior the other day because he'd seen it as a failing, a weakness on his part. Not because the impulse had been wrong.

But now he could see it for what it was, and suddenly, he knew what he had to do. He spent the rest of the night slouched in his desk chair, thinking about tomorrow and the woman sleeping just across the yard.

## CHAPTER TEN

IN SPITE OF THE DECISIONS he'd come to in the middle of the night, it took Quintin until midday Monday to find an opportunity to act on them.

The camping trip had cost him valuable time. There were a dozen phone calls he had to return, emails to answer. The crew chief of the renovation team had concerns that needed to be addressed. Even Lilianna wanted his input on matters in the kitchen that he couldn't have cared less about, though for her sake he tried to seem interested.

Before he knew it, lunchtime had arrived, and Lilianna showed up at his study door, announcing that her special chicken enchiladas were waiting on the table for him.

He got up, ready to follow, but the housekeeper hung in the doorway, looking sheepish. "What is it?" he asked, hoping he was misreading her obvious concern.

"*Señor*, I am so sorry," the woman said nervously. She reached into the pocket of her apron and pulled out a folded piece of paper. "I forgot to give you this earlier. It was lying on the doorstep when I got here this morning."

He took it from her, and she trotted away as though making an escape. Was he really such a formidable employer that she was frightened of how he would react to something so minor? Was that how everyone saw him? Maybe some of the decisions he'd come to last night were a lot more overdue than he'd thought.

His name was scrawled across the face of the page. When he opened and read the note, he frowned, a little surprised and uncertain just what he was looking at. Finally figuring it out, he couldn't help smiling. Then he refolded the paper and stuffed it into his back pocket.

His eyes were drawn to the window. The usual army of vehicles sat in the yard, but beyond them he glimpsed Riley seated at a picnic table the previous owner had placed under the oak trees. She was eating her lunch, her laptop computer open in front of her. She was alone.

Although she must have seen his truck in the drive and known he was back, she hadn't come to the house this morning. She was probably determined to show him that his presence didn't matter to her one way or the other. She had things under control. She could manage. That would be so like Miss Invincible, he thought as he left the room.

He found lunch waiting for him like an elegant display, far too grand for his tastes. Catching a glance of himself in the mirror over the buffet, he realized how scruffy he looked. Menacing, even, with a weekend's worth of stubble on his jaw and dark circles under his eyes from lack of sleep. Now didn't seem like the ideal time to try out any of his new resolutions, but he figured he'd better do it before he changed his mind and retreated back to his old, comfortable ways of thinking.

Hurriedly scooping up what he needed from the table, he went outside.

As he approached Riley, she looked up. He saw no welcome on her face, but no rejection, either.

She straightened on the bench as he stopped across from her, setting a plate of enchiladas on the table, then another that he'd been balancing on his arm, then a glass of iced tea. From his shirt pocket he removed two napkins cradling silverware. He scooted one plate across the table until it sat next to Riley's plastic bowl of…something that didn't look like anything a sensible person should eat.

"What's this?" she asked, staring down at the plate.

"Chicken enchiladas. Lilianna set out lunch for me, but it felt too much like teatime with the queen, so I figured I'd come out and share." He pointed at Riley's bowl with a rolled napkin. "Unless you'd really rather stick with that," he added, then scowled. "Whatever *that* is."

She glanced at the contents. "It's what's left of the salad I made last night for dinner."

"Aren't you supposed to ditch lettuce when it turns that brown?"

"Old wives' tale. Besides, I'm trying to eat lighter."

"Well, then…if you'd rather…"

He started to slide the enchiladas back to his side of the table. Quickly, she used her fork to stop him, catching the edge of the dish.

When he looked up, she grinned. "Then again, what's another pound or two?" She speared a cheesy bit of chicken and slipped it between her lips. Her eyes closed in delight as she moaned. "Oh, my gosh. Whatever you're paying that woman, it isn't enough."

He swung his leg over the side of the bench and sat down. While he watched, she took another bite.

The light behind her created a halo of sunshine around her head, a hundred different shades of gold. When she moistened her lips with a slow, utterly distracting movement of her tongue, Quintin felt his throat go so dry it was hard to swallow the sip of tea he'd taken.

"Thanks," she said after another couple of bites. "And welcome back. How was your trip? Since you didn't take one of the trailers, I assume it wasn't to buy more stock."

"It wasn't."

They spent a couple long seconds studying one another in silence, then Quintin dug into his own lunch.

He motioned toward the laptop with his fork. "What's with the computer on your lunch break?" He realized suddenly that maybe he had no business asking, and added quickly, "Or is it private?"

"Not at all. And unfortunately, I'm not accomplishing much. You know how it says 'User' when you first log in? Mine should say 'Idiot.' I made a mistake and let the girls play on it, so now it locks up on me all the time. I've been looking for a new wheel for the muck bucket. So far, no one locally carries them. I thought maybe I could order one, but..." She grabbed the edge of the computer screen with both hands and made an annoyed sound as she shook it.

"Come up to the house," he told her. "You can use mine."

She leaned back, obviously surprised by that suggestion. "I wouldn't want to be in your way."

"You won't be. As a matter of fact, I've got a list on my desk that keeps growing. Things I need to order from Sheplers' supply website, but just haven't had the time. I'll let you take care of it. If you don't mind."

"I'd be happy to," she said with a small smile, and Quintin felt heat pool in his stomach. He needed to keep his wits about him, but that might be more difficult than he expected. He supposed it was because he was so out of practice with women, but surely inspiration would come to him.

When it didn't, he took another swallow of iced tea, aware of her eyes on him.

He placed the glass on the picnic table again, then cleared his throat and asked, "So. How did it go while I was gone?"

She laughed, and the sound sank into his senses. "I expected that question as soon as you sat down."

"I wanted to use the enchiladas to lull you into a false sense of security first."

"Nothing exploded, fell apart or got sick," she told him. "None of the Ramseys quit. Your two stock horses—very impressive animals, by the way—arrived and got settled into the new stalls without a problem. Pretty routine stuff, mostly."

"Good. I'll be gone again this afternoon. There's a Warmblood I want to take a look at on the other side of Houston, and I'm going to pick up an industrial-size water cooler for the back pasture."

A frown puckered her forehead. "A water-cooler. For the horses?"

He nodded. "I think summer's going to continue to be brutal, and I've noticed that the trough water is nearly boiling by the end of the day. Not good for a horse's delicate digestive system. So I want it cooled down."

"That makes sense," she said, then pushed aside her empty plate and leaned forward a little. "As long as we're talking about the back pasture, there's something I have to tell you."

He saw that she was suddenly hesitant. She clutched her hands together tightly, and chewed on her bottom lip. He couldn't help it; the sweetly vulnerable sight made him stare at her mouth. It was all he could do to look away, because something stirred in him that, until the day she'd come into his life, he'd thought safely mothballed.

She drew a deep breath. "While you were gone, I made what I guess you'd call an...executive decision. Not much of one, really, but still…"

She had his attention. Cautiously, he asked, "What kind of decision?"

He tried not to look overly concerned. Even if she was going to be the ranch manager for such a short time, shouldn't she be allowed to make decisions and act like one? On the other hand, he'd yet to hear just what kind of "executive decision" she'd made.

"Well…let me start at the beginning. You know the big water trough in the far back quadrant of the pasture?"

One thing he'd discovered about her: she was lousy with directions. "The west corner. Yeah."

"It's got about ten feet of space behind it. You mentioned you might reconfigure the irrigation back there. If so, I think the trough should be moved."

"Why?"

"It's just a suggestion," she stated. "But horses like to congregate around the water."

"Yes. Go on."

She cleared her throat. "Well, when I was a kid, we had a gelding that used to bully the other horses by getting them trapped in a tight pocket. Until we moved the water out, I spent a lot of time cleaning up kick and bite marks. I thought maybe that black mare you had to doctor got her battle scar that way. So I'd like to suggest that you bring the trough out a ways."

"How far?"

"Another twenty feet ought to put an end to any reign of terror. But since you weren't here, I had the men do the next best thing. When we tore out that section of barbed wire, I directed them to pull the fencing back a bit. We rounded off the corner, too, so there'd be more of an escape hatch. Oh, and it will make that little patch much easier to mow."

She sat back on the bench, waiting for his reaction.

He didn't say anything at first. What she'd done was of no consequence, really. Any good ranch manager might have made a similar call. His silence wasn't the result of annoyance.

It was the realization that Riley Palmer was giving this job everything she had, and for him to continue being unfair to this woman about her capabilities was small and petty and unworthy of him. Yeah, he'd still rather have an old pro as his ranch manager, and eventually he intended to get one. But that didn't mean he could withhold his approval when it was warranted.

His eyes met hers. "That idea didn't occur to me, but I think you made a good call. I appreciate your ingenuity."

She actually blushed. It had been years since he'd seen a woman have that kind of reaction to a compliment. He found it incredibly charming, and a craving for things he couldn't put a name to built inside him.

She looked away as though finding sudden interest in the renovation crew returning from lunch, then turned back to him. "Thank you," she said softly. "I think that's the nicest thing you've said to me since I've been here."

Time seemed suspended. Quintin couldn't explain the spell she cast over him, any more than he could deny it, but in those moments not a single cell in his body was responding to any of the coping mechanisms he'd fashioned for himself since Teresa's and Tommy's deaths. Which was one reason why what he had to say to her was going to be so difficult.

But he was determined to get his life under control again. Starting now.

"Riley," he said gently.

She must have heard something in his voice, seen something in his face, because a tiny frown creased her brow. Her eyes became wary, and her shoulders went back.

"You did fine while I was away," he told her. "But I don't want you to read too much into what I just said. I'm sorry, but it doesn't mean you have this job permanently."

She drew a deep breath, and he caught a glimpse of the woman he'd collided with that first day. "I don't understand. What more do I have to do to persuade you that I can be a great ranch manager for Echo Springs? For you?"

He shook his head. "I don't think that's really the issue anymore. I've seen the one-hundred-percent effort you give, even when you're not completely sure you know what you're doing. I've seen you manage the Ramseys with no problems. I know you're trying very hard."

Reaching across the table, he put his hand on her arm, which was a terrible mistake. A warrior's gleam came into her eyes, and her jaw went rigid.

"Why do I think I hear a 'but' coming?" she asked.

"*But,* if you stay, there would be the potential for an even bigger problem than whether or not you're capable of the job."

"What problem?"

"It's one of the reasons I came out here. So we could discuss it. The elephant on the table."

He waited for the words to sink in. She looked momentarily confused, then her eyes widened. There was no artifice about her. She stared at him, which was what he wanted. "You mean what happened between us the other day."

"Yes."

He saw her swallow. Then she said, "I've been thinking about that. I have to apologize. In the past, I've been known to be a little too…impulsive. I've done a few things without really thinking them through."

"You mean like applying for this job?" He hoped the humor in his voice would wipe away some of the tightness he saw in her face.

Her mouth twitched. "You really shouldn't stop someone when they're trying to say they're sorry." She swiped away a lock of blond hair that the breeze had tossed against her cheek. "Anyway, I might occasionally do foolish things, but I swear to you, I don't usually act the way I did that day in the barn. I don't know what was wrong with me. I just…" She frowned. "What's so funny?"

He realized that her words had brought a smile to his lips. "You," he said quickly. "Offering up an apology when I've just spent the entire weekend trying to figure how to do the same thing without turning it into a big deal."

"So *you* want to apologize?"

"I shouldn't have done what I did. I'm sorry." She shifted on the bench and her expression darkened. "Don't look so annoyed," he said. "I'm not saying I didn't enjoy it. I did. That's the problem."

"This conversation is getting a little awkward," she muttered in a desert-dry voice. "I have a feeling I'm going to wish I hadn't said yes to the enchiladas."

Well, at least she was still listening. He took it as a positive sign and decided to plunge ahead. "Look, Riley, let's be honest here. In spite of the way things started out between us, I think it's a given that we're attracted to one another. I'm not sure why or how that happened so fast. Even if you were my type—"

One eyebrow arched. "Your type?"

*No. Definitely not the right way to get through this.*

He grimaced. "I'm not good at this sort of thing. What I'm trying to say is that I haven't been in a relationship in a very long time, and I haven't been looking for one."

"Well, neither have I."

He gave her a tentative smile. "This whole… *thing* between us… It caught me by surprise, and I'm not a man who likes surprises."

"Yes, I know. I figured that out the day we met."

"My point is, I thought we could ignore it. Keep it polite and professional. But that's not really working, wouldn't you agree?"

"I… You—" Sighing, she left the sentence hanging. He watched her tip her chin and lift her hand to knead the back of her neck as though it hurt. Her face had paled to the color of new milk. Finally, she said, "No. It's not really working."

He realized that a drop of sweat had started to trickle down his backbone, and hoped it was just the heat. But at least he knew now that he hadn't imagined Riley's interest.

He shook his head. "If this was another time or place, or maybe different circumstances, it might be simple enough to resolve. But right now, it leaves us in a pretty tough spot."

"Because you're my employer."

"God, yes. That's a huge issue. I don't even want to think about how inappropriate my behavior was. But there's also the fact that I'm at a critical point with what I'm trying to build here. I have to stay focused. Having you here, having your kids here—"

"Are you saying they've been a problem in some way?" she asked in a mother's defensive tone.

"No. I'm sure they're great. But I'd be lying if I didn't admit that having them around makes me…uncomfortable. Knowing Cassie, I'd be willing to bet she told you that I lost my wife and son several years ago."

"She did. Only because she wanted to warn me that the girls shouldn't get in your way."

He doubted that was the full extent of the conversation, but he let it go. Cassie's big-hearted interference in his love life drove him crazy, but she meant well.

He took a deeper breath, trying not to think about the past, when he was working so hard to change the future. The memory of what he'd lost was still there, of course, still powerful. And just as dangerous to his peace of mind.

"Tommy was only four when he died," he said,

determined to stay focused. "Seeing you with your daughters brings back a lot of memories. Things I'd rather not think about." He dragged a hand through his hair impatiently. "What I'm trying to say is that I don't need—I can't afford—distractions that could in any way screw up what I'm trying to accomplish here."

"So are you asking me to pack up and leave today?"

"No. I gave you until the end of the month. I don't go back on my word."

"Great. A man with a conscience. What a refreshing change from my ex-husband." He heard the slightly unsteady tone in her voice. She must have, too, because she frowned and lifted her chin so that her eyes were in line with his. "What exactly do you want from me, Quintin?"

He'd begun to feel very foolish. He'd taken a risk telling her all this, admitting how he felt. But so far so good. Well…not *good,* exactly. But not a complete disaster, either.

He allowed a smile to play over his lips. "Honestly, I don't know, and I don't think I've got the right to tell you what you should do." He cleared his throat. "But I know what I want for myself. In spite of everything I should or shouldn't do, I want to stop pretending. I've never been good at playing those kinds of games. To me they're a waste of time and energy. I think you're an attractive and talented woman. I want to admit that and move on from there."

"Which means…what, exactly?"

"Which means I'm leaving myself open to whatever happens between us. Maybe nothing will. Maybe this thing is just a flash in the pan, and we'll both get past it soon enough as we continue to work together."

She moved restlessly on the picnic bench. "That's possible, I suppose." She didn't sound convinced.

"Regardless, I won't be able to get anything accomplished if we spend every moment trying to avoid one another or walking on eggshells. If we do that we'll only end up driving one another crazy."

"I agree. That isn't the way I want the rest of my time here to go."

"Then you're with me so far?"

"No. I'm afraid I'm still confused about just what it is you're getting at."

He blew out a breath, unable to think of a way to make this conversation any easier, but resolved to push through somehow. "Let me see if I can clarify my position."

She laughed a little. "Clarify your position? You sound like a lawyer."

"Sorry. I haven't lived the life of a monk for ten years, but I'm a little rusty when it comes to male-female interactions. I'm just trying to make sure we're honest about this. That we're clear with one another."

She leaned forward. Her eyes were very direct. "What do you want to say to me, Quintin?"

He let his gaze linger for a moment on her face. A week ago he would have been surprised by what he was about to suggest. Now it seemed almost like common sense.

"I told you I'm not interested in a serious relationship," he said plainly. "But I like you, and I think you like me. I don't have a problem with flirting. What's wrong with feeling good? With giving each other something to smile about? I think it's more sensible than trying to constantly second-guess ourselves over every word or action."

She was staring at him now. A look that could have been anything from irritation to astonishment.

"I'm trying not to be crude here, but..." He blew out a breath, disgusted with himself for his inability to be straightforward about this. "But if this...this thing we've got going gets away from us, just how averse are you to sharing something...short-term?"

She didn't reply for a long moment. A very long moment. "You mean...a one-night stand?"

she asked at last. "How averse would I be to having sex with you?"

"Yes, if that's where it led."

She blinked. More than once. "I guess being married all those years makes me pretty rusty, too, because I can't ever recall having a conversation like this with a man. Certainly not my ex, who was an expert at subterfuge and playing games."

She seemed suddenly tense, probably debating whether or not she was dealing with someone certifiable. But Quintin decided there was no point in trying to back down now. "I'm sorry you spent so many years married to someone who didn't treat you like an adult," he told her. "You're a smart lady who deserves respect."

She remained still and quiet for so long that he felt foolish again. Finally, her eyes narrowed slightly and she tilted her head. "Are you flirting with me right now?"

"No. Just telling the truth." That won him a smile, giving him the courage to go on. "I'm not trying to make you uncomfortable. It's just that you don't strike me as the kind of woman who would agree to something like that lightly."

"I'm not."

Disappointment began to curl through him.

"But I'm also a woman," she went on. "And

I can't help being flattered when a guy like you says he's interested."

"So you'd consider it?"

"No, I'm afraid not."

God, this was embarrassing. He hadn't made such a muddle of things since he was a teenager, asking Darla Harris to the prom and being told politely that he must be out of his mind. When he gave an absent nod, Riley reached across the table to grasp his hand.

He looked up at her and her lips lifted slightly. "It isn't what you think, Quintin. I'll admit it. I am seriously attracted to you. But I can't. A little fling with no strings attached might be lovely and fun for both of us—"

He chuffed out a short laugh. "At last we're in agreement."

She shook her head. "But things can get out of hand if you're not careful, and I can't take a chance on that right now. My daughters are the most important part of my life. The divorce put them through the wringer, and I'm determined to make things better for them now that it's behind us. That means I don't want them to be confused or uncomfortable in any way."

"I would never want to hurt them, either."

"They aren't babies. They're old enough to be aware of everything I do. I'm supposed to be the person they look up to. So I can't just go tripping over to your place for a little fun and games whenever I want, no matter how much... I just can't do it."

He scraped his hand along his jaw. "I do see your point."

She settled back, seeming relieved. "Good. So there have to be some limits. Some boundaries. And I'm afraid that means no sex." Her mouth twitched. "But we can still be friends, can't we? We're not children, and I'm not going to be here all that much longer. Can't we keep it light and pleasant?"

"I suppose that's best for everyone."

"It is."

"So then..." Quintin was eager to change the subject and move on, now that he had struck out in the casual sex department and managed to create an incredibly awkward situation. He pulled the folded piece of paper out of his back pocket and laid it in front of her. "What would you like to do about this?"

## CHAPTER ELEVEN

TWO HOURS AFTER THAT unusual lunch, Riley found herself back at the picnic table, on the cell phone with her sister. She hadn't talked to Jillian for nearly a week, but if ever she needed a woman's opinion, now was the time.

The Ramseys were tearing down fence in the pasture. Quintin had left the ranch. Riley was waiting for the irrigation company to show up, and she'd just told Jillian about the extraordinary conversation she'd had today with her boss.

"Oh, good grief," her sister said for about the tenth time. "I'd never have gotten through it. How in the world did you manage?"

"Part of me wanted the earth to open up and swallow me, mostly because it was just so awkward. But I have to admit, part of me appreciated his candor. And *all* of me liked the compliments."

"So then what happened?"

"Then I said, 'Oh, the heck with it!' and we knocked the rest of our lunch off the table and had sex right out here in the open." When Jillian gasped, Riley laughed. "I'm kidding."

Inwardly, however, the impulsive side of her nature could freely admit she wouldn't have minded. Maybe not out in the open, but the idea of having sex with Quintin definitely held a lot of appeal.

"That isn't funny," her sister said.

"Believe me, none of it was funny. I've never had such a serious discussion about sex with a man. Not even Brad. And then, when I thought we had gotten it all behind us, he put this piece of paper in front of me and shocked me even more."

"He wanted you to sign some sort of agreement?"

"No, silly! It was an invite to dinner. Wendy made this pretty invitation for him to come over for pizza."

"Your Tuesday pizza and game night?"

"Yep. She even drew a picture of me twirling a pizza over my head. Only with Wendy's talent, it looked like I was being beamed aboard a flying saucer."

"But that's family fun night. I thought the rule was no outsiders."

"Not this time, evidently. She didn't ask me if it was all right. She didn't tell me she was going to give it to him. She just did it. She must have snuck over and put it on the doorstep this morning while I was in the apartment looking for my car keys."

"Wendy did this? Not Roxanna?"

"She's getting more like her sister every day, and I'm not sure that's a good thing. Anyway, it all looked very sweet and cute and colorful, and I wanted to strangle her."

"What did you say?"

"What could I say? After I got over my surprise, I said he was welcome to come. He was actually very nice about it and said that, considering the conversation we'd just had, he didn't want me to be uncomfortable—a word I'm beginning to loathe, by the way—and if I'd rather, he'd make up something to let Wendy down easy."

"That was kind of him."

"I know. So, of course, I laughed that off and pretended it was no big deal. Come on over. The more the merrier. Then I changed the subject, and we started talking about work again."

"And that was that?"

"More or less. He came out a few minutes ago and asked me to handle the irrigation company when they get here, walk them through the changes he wants to make. Then he left. They haven't shown up yet, so I figured I'd call you while I'm waiting."

"I'm glad you did. I've been worried about you and the girls. The way things started out, I was sure I'd see you back here by now."

"Don't give up my spot on the couch yet," Riley said lightly, but it sounded so cheerfully fake that she grimaced. She hated the thought of having to go back to her sister's place at the end of the month, one more failure to her credit.

Jillian must have heard the disappointment in her voice, because she went into sisterly pep talk mode. "Don't give up. Your three weeks aren't over yet."

"They might as well be. Honestly, I realize that a lot of people are having to reinvent themselves in this economy, but why on earth didn't I just sign up for some classes or something? That's what sensible people do."

"Hmm. The sensible part. That's the problem."

"I suppose the girls are just lucky I didn't join the circus and pretend to be a bareback rider. Or drag them out to Silicon Valley so I could try to become a computer programmer."

Jillian laughed. She was well aware of how limited Riley's skill set was when it came to computers. "In that case, you'd definitely be back on my couch by now. *And* you wouldn't have met Quintin Avenaco."

"Maybe that wouldn't have been such a bad thing," Riley muttered.

In spite of all her best intentions, in spite of what she'd told Quintin the rules had to be, there was something irresistible about knowing he wanted her.

The silence on the line had gone on too long, and Jillian must have felt compelled to fill it. "No one judges you more harshly than you do, Rile," she said gently. "No matter what happens, I admire you for trying to make this job work. You're so fearless."

The words brought a thickness to Riley's windpipe. All her life she'd accepted her sister's sweetness as a given, but sometimes Jillian really got to her.

"I love you, Jilly," she said. When the words sounded a little shaky, she cleared her throat. "I miss you, and I'm sorry I haven't called more."

"It's all right. I know you must be busy."

"I am." Eager to get back on even ground, she added, "I'm so tired every night, I just fall into bed. And during the day, there's never enough time for a real chat." She sighed. "But I don't want to talk about that. That's what I signed on for. Tell me what you think. What would you have said to Quintin?"

"What difference does it make what I'd have done? You have your agreement."

Frustrated, Riley dragged a hand through her hair. "I know. But I need you to say I'm right about shutting him down on the we-can-have-sex-and-it's-no-big-deal thing."

"Well… This guy sounds like he'd be quite a…um… I think it would be hard to say no. But any offer that could possibly hurt the twins has to be a no-go."

"That's how I saw it," Riley said, unable to keep from wishing, even now, that it didn't have to be that way. "But wow. It was just so tempting to say yes, let's go for it. He seemed absolutely sincere. And it's so refreshing to meet a man who's not afraid to admit what he wants. Someone who's honest."

"That's only because you're used to dealing with Brad the Cad. Compared to him, Quintin sounds like Honest Abe."

"Believe me, he doesn't look anything like Abraham Lincoln." She frowned as they heard the call waiting beep come through the phone. "Hang on, Jilly. This might be the irrigation company."

She clicked over to the second call. It was Amelia Watkins from the day camp, and as soon as she explained why she was calling, Riley switched back to her sister.

"I have to go," she said quickly. "I'll call you when I can."

"What's wrong?"

"I have to pick up the girls. Wendy's sick."

She hung up. Then she jumped off the picnic table and ran to get the keys to the SUV.

LESS THAN AN HOUR LATER, Riley ushered the twins into the apartment.

They headed toward the bedroom. She dropped the SUV keys on the kitchen counter and the girls' backpacks on the couch, then plopped down beside them. The adrenaline she'd experienced as she'd driven into Beaumont had dribbled away. Now all she felt was exhausted. No. Make that exhausted and discouraged.

The twins were whispering in the bedroom. "You two, get into your pajamas," she called to them.

As expected, Roxanna popped back into the living room to give her an annoyed look. "It's not even dark outside!"

"Just do it," Riley told her wearily, wishing that, just once, her daughter would be meek and malleable.

"But it's not fair. Miss Watkins said she's not running a fever, and I didn't see her puke. Not even once."

"That doesn't mean she doesn't feel well."

"I can hear you!" Wendy yelled from the bedroom. "Don't talk about me like I don't have ears."

Roxanna ignored that. "I wanted to stay," she

told her mother. "*She* wanted to come home. So she just faked being sick until Miss Watkins called you. If I did that, you'd be mad."

Sighing, Riley rose and went into the bedroom, Roxanna close behind. Wendy was sitting on the side of the bed, kicking her heels against the mattress. She threw a sullen glance toward her sister, but other than that, she seemed calm. And very healthy.

Riley knelt down, gently taking both Wendy's arms to get her attention. She pressed her hand under her daughter's bangs to feel her forehead. Cool as spring water.

"What's the deal, Wendy?" she asked softly. "Where do you feel sick?"

"I don't know exactly. My stomach. I guess my head. I'm probably sick everywhere inside."

After all Wendy had been through last year, culminating in that prolonged stay in the hospital, Riley had pretty much become an expert at spotting trouble in her children, and right now, the signs just weren't there. She'd bet money that Miss Watkins and Roxanna were right. Wendy was faking it.

But why would she? She'd claimed to love the day camp.

Riley caught her daughter's chin, making sure they were eye to eye. "Wendy, tell me the truth. *Were* you pretending to be sick?"

"No…" she said, but her gaze slid away.

"Wendy?"

"Will I get in trouble if I say yes?"

"Not as much as if you lie to me."

She frowned a moment, then offered sullenly, "Okay. I did pretend."

"Told you," Roxanna interjected.

Ignoring her, Riley gave Wendy a considering look. What had gotten into this child lately? "Why? Did something happen to make you want to leave? Was there a problem?"

"No, it's lots of fun every day. But…"

"But what?"

"I…I just missed you," her daughter finally said. Then she hopped off the bed and threw her arms around her mother's neck, hugging her so tightly it nearly cut off Riley's air.

Momentarily, Riley was speechless as the small body pressed against her. For the second time that day, her throat felt clogged with emotion, and it surprised her. She hardly ever cried, even over silly, sentimental things the girls did.

"Wendy, honey…"

The child pulled away to stare into her eyes. "Don't make us go back there, Mom. It's fun and everything, but I'd rather be here with you."

"We have to go back," Roxanna told her sister in a peeved tone. "Mom has to make a living. Otherwise the judge will say she can't keep us, and strangers will be our new parents and make us be their slaves."

Riley stared at Roxanna. "Who told you that?"

"I heard it on television."

"I definitely need to cut back your TV time." She drew Roxanna closer. When the twins were side-by-side, she smiled at them. "Girls, I think we need to have another little talk." She lowered her head to give Wendy a meaningful look. "Especially you, young lady."

BY TEN-THIRTY THAT EVENING, the twins were sound asleep. Riley had cleaned up the mess she and the girls had made baking a cherry pie, fixed up the sofa bed and taken her own bath. Now she was sitting at the dining-room table in shorts and a T-shirt, trying unsuccessfully to keep her eyes open while she struggled to get on the internet again.

She was so tired, both physically and mentally. Working in the hot sun this morning had drained her energy. Then there had been the tense, unexpected conversation with Quintin that had left her head spinning. The frantic dash to the day camp and worry over Wendy. Finally, her concern about what Quintin would say when she had to tell him that in spite of her best efforts to make alternate arrangements, she'd blown the meeting with the irrigation company.

Resting her chin on her palm, she stared down at the motionless hourglass on her screen, the symbol she'd taken to calling the timekeeper of death.

"Do something," she growled at it.

While the computer thought about the advisability of letting her go online, she clicked over to her photo album program. Looking at pictures of the girls always made her feel better.

After the serious talk they'd had, Riley had tried to make it a fun evening, but the twins knew that, come tomorrow morning, they'd have to troop back into the day camp. As if they were returning to prison. As if their mother couldn't get them out of her hair fast enough.

God, could she feel any guiltier? Didn't they know how much she missed having them around?

Brad had wanted her to keep their ranch running while he worked for the Bar Seven, and that had been fine with her once the girls came along. She had tried to explain to Roxanna and Wendy that she'd been lucky to be a stay-at-home mom for as long as she had. But it was past time they learned things couldn't always be the way they wanted them to be.

That hadn't made this afternoon's talk with them any easier.

What she wouldn't give to have a few of Quintin's compliments to make her feel better right about now.

Or maybe not, she thought wryly.

That was just one more thing she could fail miserably at. In spite of what she'd said to him this afternoon about remaining friendly, how was she supposed to find a way to negotiate the tricky terrain of a platonic male-female relationship? It would be like trying to control lightning.

Well, she had to try, no matter how hard it got. Besides, being married to Brad had cured her of any foolish ideas about romantic commitment.

She glanced down at the screen. The browser was still searching the universe. With an annoyed sigh, she toggled into her album again, this time going further back.

The first thing that popped up was a shot of her and her ex-husband, taken at their wedding. It was a goofy one of Brad nibbling cake icing off the tip of her finger. He looked incredibly handsome in his tux, she looked embarrassingly charmed and they both looked so young. But for just an instant, Riley felt a terrible craving for the girl she'd once been.

She clicked through a few more photos from that time period, ones she'd uploaded onto the computer back when she'd thought their marriage might still have a chance. The Christmas picture in front of the fireplace. The two of them on the dock at Galveston, getting ready to take a ride in their friend's speedboat. She and Brad in her room at the hospital, each holding one of the girls as newborns. They were beaming at one another. They seemed so in love.

So many bits of their lives pieced together to form a history. Now all these pictures were just a decade of disposable moments.

She knew she'd never regret the decision to end her marriage. But when, Riley couldn't help wondering, had they gone from being that close, adoring couple to two miserable, bitter adults warring with one another? Had the transition actually been that subtle? Had she really been blissfully ignorant of Brad's infidelity for so many years?

Unwilling to be brought low by such morose thoughts, she logged out of the photo album program.

Still no luck with her internet connection.

She looked out the window. The main house was in darkness, though when she'd left for the day, Lilianna must have turned on the porch light. Quintin's truck and the two-horse trailer were still missing from the side yard. Maybe he'd stay over in Houston.

Making a sudden decision, Riley switched off her computer and decided to take her boss up on his offer to use his. She was too tired to sleep, too wired by the day's events to even try. Might as well be productive.

She checked on the twins to make sure they were sleeping soundly, and quietly pulled out the baby monitors. Then she grabbed a flashlight and headed over to the house. If Quintin's computer was fast, she could be back in no time. If one of the girls woke, she'd hear it on the receiving monitor.

She used the spare keys he'd given her to unlock the front door. A light in the kitchen had been left on, but the rest of the house was eerily dark. Creepy, too, with all the hulking equipment the renovation crew had left behind. She found the study. As she settled into Quintin's chair, she switched on the desk lamp, set the monitor to one side, then powered up the computer.

The pool of light illuminated the usual things you'd find on any busy ranch owner's desk. She had no intention of moving anything, much less examining it. The fact that Quintin would allow her access to his most-private business was a new level of trust from him she would never abuse. Yet she couldn't help noticing one small mountain of paper that seemed to have been neatly organized, the top page of which was formatted like a job résumé.

Her successors-in-waiting?

Probably.

"But not yet, guys," she said out loud, barely suppressing a yawn.

From the pocket of her shorts she withdrew the log-in and password information Quintin had given her this afternoon before he'd left, as well as the list of things he wanted ordered from Sheplers, one of the biggest ranch supply stores in East Texas.

Once she got to the website she felt better, but they had about a million pieces of ranch and farm equipment and a pretty poor system for locating stuff if you didn't have the item number. With a yawn and a sigh, Riley set the list in front of her and got busy.

SHE FELT A TOUCH along the side of her neck, as gentle as the kiss of a butterfly's wing. It had to be Wendy. She was the only one who ever got up in the middle of the night. Roxanna slept like a rock.

*Oh, Wendy,* Riley thought in weary disappointment. *Bad timing, sweetheart.* Riley had been dreaming. Something lovely that involved Quintin and a beautiful black stallion that could carry both of them on its back.

Unwilling to give up the dream without a fight, she refused to lift her head or open her eyes. "Go back to bed, honey. I'm right here."

"Riley...time to wake up."

"No. Don't make me." She groaned in frustration. "Mommy needs her rest."

Somehow her sleep-fogged brain registered the sound of a soft chuckle. Then the touch was back, sliding down her cheek this time. "I don't doubt it, but you have to wake up now, Riley."

She scowled. Neither of the girls was allowed to call her by her first name. She opened her eyes, blinking against the light. The first thing she saw was a sliver of Quintin's face, looking down at her in concern.

She lifted her head. "What are you doing here?" she asked, surprised and confused to see him in the apartment living room.

She watched his features as they softened. "I live here. And I assume you're here because you were using the computer and fell asleep."

"I did?" The sudden realization of where she was made her sit bolt upright. "I did! I'm sorry. I was just trying to order those things you wanted. What time is it?" She squinted down at her wristwatch and gasped when she saw that it was ten after midnight. "Oh, no! I have to go."

She grabbed the baby monitor. All she heard was Roxanna. Snoring softly, thank goodness. She wheeled back the desk chair so fast that she nearly ran over Quintin in the process.

He steadied her as she tried to make for the

door. "Take it easy, Goldilocks. What's your hurry?"

"I left the girls alone!"

He motioned toward the monitor in her hand. "I thought you could keep track of them with that thing."

"I can. But I don't like to leave them alone more than I have to, especially at night."

She sprinted out of the house and across the dark yard. The distance between Quintin's place and the barn was short, but by the time she rammed the key into the lock, her heart was pounding.

She left the door open as she ran inside. It was only when she reached the bedroom and saw that both girls were still asleep that her pulse settled. She backed out and closed the door again.

Quintin stood in the living room. She gave him an apologetic smile. "Sorry about that."

"Are they all right?" he asked in a low voice.

"They're fine. I just shouldn't have…" She didn't want to talk about her shortcomings as a mother. Instead she said, "You're back late. How did it go?"

"I picked up the cooler. The horse was a bust. It was a Warmblood, but it was a palomino."

"What's wrong with that?"

"Police horses can't be flashy. Too tempting a target for bad guys."

"Oh, of course. I should have thought of that."

Really, it was amazing how many things she didn't know. How to be a good wife. How to raise her kids so they wouldn't hate her. How to do this job. How to deal with an attractive guy like Quintin Avenaco, who, she discovered, was staring at her at that very moment.

"Riley, are you all right?" he asked.

"Sure," she replied, trying to remain upbeat. "It's just that this afternoon didn't work out very well." Time for a confession, one she dreaded having to make. "I'm sorry, but I blew the meeting with the irrigation company."

"Why? What happened?"

"Before they showed up, I got a call from the day camp that Wendy was sick and I had to pick her up. I tried to walk Jim through what you wanted so he could talk to the irrigation company instead, but I rattled it off pretty quickly. When I got back they'd come and gone, and said you'd have to reschedule."

Quintin looked momentarily disappointed, and frankly, she expected him to chew her out. He might be attracted to her, but he was still a man determined to meet a deadline.

Instead, he amazed her. "It's all right," he said. "I'll call them tomorrow." She supposed her surprise couldn't have been more obvious if she'd written it on a sandwich board. He cocked his head. "What's the matter?"

"I thought you'd be angry."

"Naturally I'd like to get them started, but I'll work it out."

"I'm sorry. But the girls have to come first for me."

He didn't even blink. "Of course. So how's Wendy doing?"

"She's fine."

Riley pressed her palms against each temple, trying to stem the headache behind her eyes. She still felt muddled. Almost without thinking she said, "Wendy made up being sick so she could come home and be with me. She's the soft one in the family. So, I had to lecture the both of them about the way things are right now, and that they just can't expect me to stop working so we can have fun. They seemed to accept that, but I felt awful saying it." She realized that she'd shared more than he was probably interested in hearing, and shook her head. "Don't pay any attention to me. I tend to babble when I'm tired."

"You know you're not a bad mother."

The patient understanding in his tone almost undid her. "I don't *think* I am, but I'll bet that's what all the really horrible mothers say."

Quintin's hand closed around one of hers, encircling her fingers and pulling them away from her face so she would look at him. He was smiling at her, but it was an infinitely sad smile. Those dark, beautiful eyes of his were brittle with old pain, and she realized suddenly that she'd been thoughtless to mention her failings as a parent, when he must carry so many memories of his own faults in that department.

"You're doing the best you can, which I'm beginning to think is all people can ask of themselves. And right now, you need some rest."

"I think you're right," she admitted tentatively. "Thank you for understanding."

"Anytime."

"Again, I'm sorry about the mess with the irrigation people," she blurted out.

He grinned. "Go to bed. Things will look better in the morning."

"You're sure?"

He squeezed her hand, then immediately let it go. "I'm sure."

# CHAPTER TWELVE

INSTALLING THE TROUGH COOLER the next day proved to be more difficult than Quintin expected, but at last it was finished.

He had handled the project himself, working with barely a break. Riley didn't know squat about cooling systems, but she seemed determined to assist, so he let her, in spite of the fact that he could probably have done it faster alone. Besides, regardless of the summer heat, she smelled nice, and he liked having her nearby.

When they'd started out this morning, there had been a few awkward moments. He had sort of expected strained politeness to be the order of the day. But he was no good at sulking, and she had a generous enough spirit not to get all prickly over his suggestion yesterday, so the hours had passed as though nothing had happened.

Actually, he thought the two of them had made a pretty good job of installing the cooler, and once fresh cold water started flowing into the big tank, he exchanged a look with her that said as much. She gave him that sweet smile of hers, and he realized he should probably acknowledge her efforts more often.

Three of the horses came up immediately to suck down gallons. Quintin felt some of his worry dissolve. Good. That was money well spent. The time and effort, all that hard work today? It would pay off.

Riley grinned at him. "I think they approve."

"They should," he replied, wiping sweat from his face with one of the ragged towels they kept on the back of the ATV. "They're getting race-horse treatment."

"It will all be worth it come October. I can't wait to see—"

She stopped abruptly and looked away. It didn't take a mind reader to know what she was thinking. Her time at Echo Springs would be over at the end of the month, so it wasn't likely she'd "see" the outcome of anything here. He could admit to feeling bad about that, but it didn't change anything. After she left, he would have a few grueling hot months to pull every-thing together, and if she thought the job was tough now, she had no idea how much he was going to have to ratchet things up.

"I'd better check on the men," she said. She

turned to head toward the back of the pasture, where the cousins were still tearing down and replacing fence.

Quintin caught her arm. "Hold on. My turn to make an executive decision." He cupped his hands around his mouth and shouted out to the Ramseys, "Hey, guys! Pack it in. The sun's whipping our butts today."

They didn't hesitate; in no time they were trudging toward the house. Quintin canted a look at Riley. "Okay with you, boss lady?"

She glanced down at her watch, then frowned. "There's still a couple of hours left before we normally knock off."

"This is enough for today. We can start fresh tomorrow."

Her eyes narrowed on him. "I know what you're doing. You're taking it easy on me because of last night, aren't you? What? Do I look like I'm ready to drop? Because I'm not. I can go for hours yet."

She didn't appear as tired as she had last night. In fact, she looked so good that his body experienced a supernova heat far greater than anything the sun could dish out. But after the agreement they'd reached at lunch, he knew he'd better keep a handle on it. "I'm sure you can. And even if I thought that, you'd probably hang in just to prove me wrong."

"I don't want you making exceptions, changing the work schedule because you think I'm too weak."

"*Weak* is not a word I would ever use to describe you."

She seemed unimpressed by that comment. He worked to keep his gaze steady while she stared at him a few long moments. Finally she began gathering the tools they'd used to install the cooler, placing them in the bed of the ATV.

He joined her. "Ease up, warden," he said. "So the men get to go home a little early. No big deal. The rest of the week's going to be a killer."

She lifted her hands as though surrendering. "All right. It's your call."

"That's better," he told her. "And we're still having pizza tonight. Right?"

"If you think you're up for Palmer pizza and game night."

"Game night?"

"Oh, that's right. Wendy didn't mention that in her invitation, did she?" Riley smiled, and he suspected she enjoyed laying this added surprise on him. "After we eat dinner, we play games. You'd be willing to do that, wouldn't you?"

*I feel like I'm playing one now,* he thought. But he kept his features carefully neutral. "I think that would depend on what kind they were."

"Nothing too girlie, if that's what you're worried about."

"Nothing that involves a Barbie doll?"

She laughed. "Not a one. But it's not too late to back out, I suppose."

He loved pizza. But game night? Not exactly the kind of private time he'd once hoped for—before that damned agreement they'd made yesterday. A quiet dinner at one of Beaumont's better restaurants. Maybe a nice bottle of wine to settle the nerves. But there'd be nothing private about this kind of G-rated evening, with a couple of kids tucked smack up against Mommy's side.

On the other hand… He'd been discovering that any time spent in Riley's company was far more interesting than all the demands and irritations waiting for him on his desk. He didn't want to risk losing a single moment with her, not even when the idea of having to go one-on-one—make that one-on-two—with Riley's twins scared the living hell out of him. Not even when he knew there was no chance of bumping this evening up to an R-rating.

Riley was watching him with a shrewd gaze. "I'm still good with it," he said with a grin. "As long as I can bring anchovies for my side of the pie."

"You're early," she said as she opened the apartment door.

"Traffic was with me," Quintin joked, holding out the small can of anchovies.

She wrinkled her nose and took them as though they were radioactive. "Not a big fan. But I guess you can put anything you want on your slices. Would you like a glass of wine?"

"That would be nice."

He'd thought about bringing over a bottle, but wasn't sure how that would be perceived, and there were the kids to consider. This wasn't a date, but he had to admit he was nervous. Too many years since he'd done this sort of thing.

And then there were the kids. Ah, hell. How was he going to handle them?

The objects of his concern appeared then, trotting up to their mother, displaying identical interest in him. All of it cautious.

"You met Wendy and Roxanna," Riley said, placing her hand on each of the girls' heads as she reintroduced them. Her quick glance said she understood perfectly that he might not remember their names or be able to tell them apart. He was relieved that she hadn't made it even more difficult by doing the matching outfit thing, although they were both dressed in shorts and T-shirts the colors of sherbet and summer roses.

"Girls, while the pizza finishes up, why don't you show Quintin what you did today at camp?"

She left them for the kitchen, reemerged long enough to pass him a glass of red wine, then disappeared again. He stood in the middle of the small living room, feeling big and awkward as two little girls eyed him as if they were cops and he was a felon who might make a break for the hills. He didn't know whether to pray for relief or guidance.

"You can sit down," the one named Roxanna said. "Mom told us to be nice, so we won't bite you."

Yeah, he'd had her pegged right the first time he'd met her. The tough little cookie determined not to be discounted. Like her mom.

He nodded and took a seat on the couch. Immediately, the twins came to stand on either side of him, invading his space. He smiled vaguely. He had no gift for making small talk, and certainly not with children. Even with Tommy, he'd been hopelessly inept.

"So," he said. "What did you make at camp today?"

Wendy ran into the bedroom, but Roxanna's lips curled in disgust.

"We did macaroni pictures," she said. "I made a castle, but it ended up looking like a doghouse, so I'm not showing it to you. Just a waste of macaroni, if you ask me."

The other girl returned, skidding to a comical halt in front of him. She hopped up beside him on the couch and placed a piece of paper across his lap. "I'm going to be a vet, so I always do animals."

She wasn't any better at macaroni art than she was at drawing, but Quintin thought this one was easier to figure out. "So you made another horse."

She frowned. "It's a giraffe."

He was saved by Riley calling from the kitchen, "Two minutes until pizza, everyone!"

Roxanna and Wendy exchanged a look.

"Something I should know?" Quintin asked them.

"Mom's pizza isn't as good as store-bought," Roxanna explained in a low voice. "We just pretend it is."

Wendy leaned closer, and he got a whiff of fruity shampoo. "But don't tell her. It'll hurt her feelings."

He winked at both girls. "Our secret, then."

"Mom said you had one of the men take down all the animals in here."

"Do you miss them? Because I could bring them back...."

"Nooo!" Wendy said quickly, with a nervous

giggle. "I didn't like them at all." She cocked her head at Quintin, and he could suddenly see Riley in her, too. That softer side he occasionally glimpsed. Her lips pursed. "I'm glad I invited you tonight. You're a lot nicer than I first thought."

"Glad you feel that way."

"Mom would never have let you come to dinner if you weren't," Roxanna said. Then she added unexpectedly, "When can we ride the ATV?"

Before he could respond to that question, Wendy asked an equally uncomfortable question. "Are you married?"

Again, the look they gave him was identical— pint-size interrogators from the Spanish Inquisition. He took a quick swallow of his wine. "No, I'm not married."

"So you don't have any kids?" Wendy said.

"No."

"Do you want any?"

"Someday."

"Our mom's divorced."

He suspected where the child was heading with this conversation, and it was nowhere he was interested in going. He found himself nodding once more, pushing down panic and wishing for hard liquor in his glass instead of wine that tasted as potent as grape juice.

"We never get to see our dad anymore," Wendy continued.

As ill at ease as he felt, he couldn't help being moved by the sadness in her voice, or the way her delicate features seemed to sag a little as she stared at him. It was the kind of look that could make a man go soft in the center if he wasn't careful.

"I'm sorry to hear that," he said. "I'm sure there's a good reason."

Roxanna moved restively. "He's got a girl-friend."

Wendy nodded in solemn agreement, then gave him an earnest glance. "If we can't ever get our old dad back, I'd like to have a new one someday."

Caught in midsip, Quintin had to choke back a swallow. The kid was about as subtle as an anvil, and he had no clue how to respond. Luckily, he didn't have to.

"Don't listen to her," Roxanna said. "We don't need a new dad. Everything is okay just the way it is."

"Good to know," he muttered.

Wendy scowled at her sister. "You don't know what Mom needs. She likes kisses and all that mushy stuff. If he's a good kisser, she might like that."

She looked at Quintin speculatively, and he

could see the question coming. He was amused by it, even as he heard himself inwardly asking God to get him out of here.

Then Riley was at the kitchen door, wiping her hands on a dish towel and smiling like his guardian angel. "Pizza's ready," she told them. She nodded toward the twins. "Go wash your hands, you two."

Quintin downed the last of his wine and just sat there, relieved when the kids hurried into the bathroom like gamboling colts.

Riley leaned against the doorjamb. She wore shorts, too. Remembering that first day when he'd seen her in shorty pajamas, he didn't know how he could have forgotten what nice legs she had.

"What were you all talking about?" she asked. She indicated the macaroni giraffe Wendy had left beside him on the couch. "The intricacies of pasta art?"

"Not even close," Quintin said, wondering how he was going to get through the next few hours. "But trust me, you don't want to know."

DEPENDING ON HOW YOU looked at it, the rest of the evening was easier.

The kids seemed to accept his presence, and settled down. At least they stopped asking embarrassing questions. Riley was good at prompting conversation, and he tailored a couple stories for his audience—anecdotes about ornery horses he'd run into over the years. Anything he could think of that they might find entertaining.

It had been years since he'd had to indulge a child's mind, and he'd been dreading any interaction with Riley's daughters. He was afraid they would do nothing but remind him of Tommy, and his mind would end up going to dark places it shouldn't. But surprisingly, he got through it somehow, though at first the words sounded awkward and silly to him, and he was sure he bored them to death.

The twins were right. Their mother's pizza *was* pretty unimpressive, but the anchovies helped. The three females at the table claimed to be grossed out by them, and Quintin played into it until everyone was laughing, including him.

He loved Riley's laugh, the way it flowed and mingled in a natural rhythm. He loved to see the pure joy when she let go. As for the twins… In spite of how their parents' divorce must have affected them, the girls seemed like well-grounded, exuberant children.

Absorbing the sound of their light, lacy laughter, Quintin felt as though a locked place in his mind had been opened.

After dinner, they played Monopoly, a game

he hadn't fooled around with in years. The children were surprisingly savvy and serious about it, and by the time they'd passed Go a couple times, Quintin realized he'd have to pay close attention.

He ended up losing big-time, having to mortgage everything he owned, including the cheap stuff, but he didn't mind. In fact, he was sorry when the evening ended.

The girls didn't seem eager to go to bed, but they wished him good-night and went off to their room. Riley followed them to supervise while Quintin collected tokens and play money from the table and took empty glasses to the kitchen.

The apartment was small, and he couldn't help overhearing the whispers and soft giggles of a bedtime routine, the kind he hadn't been privy to in a decade. Teresa had put Tommy to bed in just this same way, and for a second or two, a pang of sorrow skipped through Quintin as the memories started knocking. Determinedly, he shut them back in their closet. They might be his forever companions, those ghosts. But not tonight, he thought. He wouldn't let them ruin this night.

Finally, as he closed the lid on the game, Riley returned, shutting the bedroom door behind her.

"All tucked in," she said in a low voice as she came to his side. Her pretty mouth looked as if it had been born smiling. "Although they both wanted to stay up and see if they could beat you at something else."

"They probably could have," he admitted. "We didn't play many games when I was a kid."

"Well, thanks for being such a good sport."

"I've never been around twins before and seen the dynamic at work." He gestured toward the Monopoly box in his hand. "You do realize, don't you, that Roxanna was throwing the game so Wendy could win? For all the impatience she shows with her sister, she's very protective of her."

"I know. I have to talk to them. Roxanna needs to play fair, and Wendy needs to toughen up."

"They seem like good kids, though you've obviously got your hands full."

"It's overwhelming sometimes. But I guess I wouldn't have it any other way."

Riley stifled a yawn. "Would you like a cup of coffee?"

He would have liked to stay longer, but he didn't want to wear out his welcome. Besides, after installing the watercooler today, he knew she must be as tired as he was.

He shook his head. "I think I'd better call it a night. Busy day tomorrow."

She followed him out to the front step, leaving the door cracked open so they could talk freely without being overheard, but still keep an ear out.

He turned toward her. Her hair shimmered in the moonlight, making him wonder what it would feel like brushing over his bare chest. Her eyes sparkled, and her skin looked like cream. She glanced up at him, hugging her elbows in her hands as though the night was chilly, when it was anything but. Was she nervous? A rush of tenderness he couldn't seem to control swept over him.

"I hope the girls didn't drive you crazy," she said. "They can be like tag team wrestlers when they decide to gang up on someone."

"I think I held my own." He decided to risk a personal question. "Is their father really out of the picture? They told me they never see him."

"They don't. And that's how it's going to stay."

Before he could think better of it, Quintin heard himself say, "That seems a little harsh. As a father, I—"

"You probably weren't the kind of father my ex was."

He heard the slight catch in her voice as the words came tripping too fast. Her posture was suddenly stiff, almost military straight.

"I think I've touched a nerve," he said in a conciliatory tone, hoping to relieve this unforeseen tension.

Her features relaxed a little. "Sorry. It isn't you. I tend to get defensive when the subject of my ex and his relationship to the girls comes up. He was…" She shook her head, as though clearing her thoughts. "You know what? I don't want to spoil a nice evening by talking about him. Thank you for indulging Wendy. Both of them."

He let her drop the subject because it was really none of his business, and he had enough off-limit topics in his own past to make him respect someone else's. Instead, he leaned one forearm against the wood over her head, so that he could legitimately stand closer. "I had a great time."

She shifted until her back was pressed against the wall. "I did, too."

"We've been going at it pretty hard lately, so it was nice to take a break and have some fun for a change."

She nodded. "I'm looking forward to the weekend. We have that wedding reception to go to. It will be nice to spend some time away with the girls."

"You're going to the reception at the Flying M?"

"Cassie called and invited me yesterday. I told her I'd feel a little awkward, not knowing the bride or groom, but she convinced me that it's really just a big barbecue."

"It will be. Why don't we ride together? No one throws a party like Ethan and Cassie."

"All right. Sounds like fun. I'll look forward to it." She cast a regretful look back to the open door. "Guess I'd better check on the girls." Glancing across the distance between the barn and the main house, she asked in mock concern, "Can you find your way back without a flashlight?"

"You could come with me," he said with a grin. "Make sure I get home safe and sound."

She grimaced. "We both know that's not a good idea. Besides, it's not completely dark. You'll just have to take your chances."

He brought his hand to the side of her face. When she didn't move away, he played with her hair, never taking his eyes from hers. "That's what I feel like I'm doing right now. Taking a chance."

Dropping his head, he caught her lips with his. It was a warm, sweet touch. Quick. Nothing too dramatic. Nothing too dangerous. She didn't seem to mind, not at all, and when he pulled away, she smiled at him.

"That was nice," she said. "You didn't taste like anchovies."

"That *is* high praise," he replied with a soft laugh. "Guess I'm not as rusty at this as I thought." He angled her jaw so that she couldn't escape. "Hold still. I'm going to try to improve my skills."

This time when he kissed her, she was expecting it. Riley's mouth opened in a clear invitation, and he didn't hesitate to respond to it. Their tongues met and tangled in hot, urgent need, and his whole body stirred in pleasure. The warm flesh-and-blood reality of her had been beyond even his ability to fantasize. He groaned silently, already far too aroused for his own peace of mind, and wondering how he was supposed to call a halt to things now. When his mouth finally lifted from hers, he felt momentarily disoriented, as though awakening from a deep sleep.

"That was even better," she said in a voice that wasn't quite steady.

"I'm a quick study."

"I think Roxanna's not the only one who cheats."

"What?"

"We have an agreement, and my common sense says we should stop this right now. But I'm not sure where it is. I think you may be a man who doesn't play fair."

"Who said anything about playing?" he asked gruffly. "Care to renegotiate?"

And then, just about the time he decided to

reach out and pull her into his arms, a loud bang sounded from inside.

"Mom!" a childish voice yelled. "Roxanna won't share the covers!"

He went still, and Riley gave a shaky laugh. "Oh, yeah, *there's* my common sense."

She slipped under his arm before he could stop her.

# CHAPTER THIRTEEN

RILEY DISCOVERED THAT Quintin hadn't exaggerated when he said the rest of the week would be a killer. It was.

Under a branding-iron Texas sun, eight Warmbloods were delivered the next day from a ranch in Amarillo. There were now twenty-seven horses on the property, and he wanted every one of them put through an intensive checklist. Riley had never taken care of a herd that big before, not even close. Quintin laid out a routine of well-orchestrated procedures, and the Ramseys were there to help do the wrangling, but she was still nervous about it.

Record-keeping of prime stock was standard on most ranches, and Quintin insisted that each one have as detailed a written history as possible.

"Listen up, everyone," he told them as they met at the barn the next morning. "There's going to be a lot of activity around here for the next few days. Police mounts do a great deal of crowd control, and as we go along, I want all of you to keep an eye out for any skittish behavior, attempts to bite or kick, sidling to escape, throwing their heads—anything that looks like they don't interact well with people."

"That's asking a lot from them, isn't it?" Steve inquired. "They're in their prime, and I've never seen a decent mount yet that didn't have a tantrum once in a while. Especially with so many others around."

Quintin shook his head. "Any animal with a problem will go over to Horse Sense for behavior modification. So any issues, report them to Riley. She's keeping track. Got it?"

As they neared the end of the week, Riley began to see why Quintin liked the breed so much. The Warmbloods were intelligent, with a calm disposition that made things easier on everyone. Changes to routine upset any horse, but they were better mannered than most, and as a result, no one had gotten kicked, although Steve received a nip on his arm when one of them had objected to having its ears inspected.

The farrier came out to fit or refit shoes. The horses were dewormed and checked for both internal and external parasites.

Like many ranchers, Quintin did most of his own preventive medical treatment, but a vet arrived to give vaccinations for everything from rhino flu to encephalomyelitis to strangles.

Blood and nasal swabs were taken so tests could be run. A handful of the herd had their teeth floated for better digestion.

On Thursday the vet told them that a case of West Nile virus had been found in a mare three counties over. Quintin, looking grim, called them all together.

"I want every inch of the property walked for debris," he told them. "Even a discarded soda bottle can be a breeding ground for mosquitoes."

"You should keep a lookout for dead crows and jays, too," Riley added. "It's a sure sign the disease is traveling."

They set off early the next day and spent hours combing what felt like every blade of grass. The relief when they found nothing was palpable, even in the Ramseys.

By Saturday morning they were done, and though her arms and shoulders ached from trying to hold horses steady or coerce them to lift hooves, Riley was tempted to throw her hands in the air and shout for joy. She'd never been part of such an intense ranch project.

She was glad the week was over. One look at Quintin's face told her he was feeling much the same.

After the morning feeding, and handling a few chores that had been set aside during the week, she wanted nothing more than to relax. Like a mirage in the desert, she envisioned an afternoon spent luxuriating in a hot bath, giving herself a pedicure and a facial, polishing off a pint of ice cream while she watched a sentimental movie in her bathrobe.

She couldn't remember the last time she'd been able to indulge herself that way. Mommy duties made opportunities like that nearly impossible, and today she also had a wedding reception to go to.

She might have decided to send her regrets if not for the fact that the twins were really looking forward to it. And she would be going with Quintin.

There. She could admit it, to herself at least, and she refused to twist her feelings up with recriminations. She just wanted to stay in his orbit, to be stimulated and charmed and intrigued. It had been ages since she'd enjoyed being with anyone so much, and frankly, one look from him and, agreement or not, her body reacted.

That kiss earlier in the week had nearly gotten away from them. It had started out pretty simple. He'd kissed her with an impatient man's passion and a strong man's restraint, but in about a split second, need had stirred inside her, the kind that had been denied for so long—sharp and yet sweet.

She could only imagine what might have happened had Wendy not called out to her from the bedroom.

But since then, things had settled down a little. The work routine with the horses had put her in close proximity with Quintin, but the long hours had been too hectic to allow much time for personal interaction.

And while the thought of attending the reception with Quintin made her whole body tighten and tingle, she suspected today wasn't going to present too much temptation. There would be a lot of people at the Flying M. He would probably do his best to make sure no one got the wrong idea about their business relationship.

That didn't mean she didn't want to look her best. Yesterday, after she'd picked up the girls, they'd gone shopping and she'd lucked out, finding a short summery dress that didn't strain the budget. A gauzy overlay on the skirt in a blue-and-purple swirl pattern made her waist look small and her legs long. She settled for strappy sandals that were hand-me-downs from Jilly, and pinned her hair up, allowing a few curls to spill down her back.

Looking in the mirror just minutes before Quintin was supposed to show up, Riley thought she'd done all right by herself. The twins, at least, were complimentary.

"It's like you're a princess," Wendy proclaimed in an awed voice.

Roxanna, practical as ever, said, "I think it's pretty, but you'll have to be careful not to spill anything on it."

Quintin's reaction was a little closer to what she'd been hoping for.

"You look…terrific," he said, as she watched his gaze slide over her.

Those three words had such power to exhilarate her.

Since it was the four of them, he drove her SUV instead of his truck. Everyone seemed to be in a good mood, even Quintin.

When they turned onto Flying M property, Riley saw right away that Quintin's friend and former partner wasn't a hardscrabble rancher by any means. The grass on either side of the front fencing was as green and smooth as the felt on a pool table. One of the pastures held a small herd of beautiful Arabians. The house came into view, big and impressive in the late afternoon sun, with dozens of cars parked along the drive. A valet dressed in spotless cowboy garb handed Riley out of the car, then took the keys from Quintin. Another attendant guided them to a mulch-covered pathway that led them around the back of the home.

"Are your friends millionaires?" Roxanna asked. "This place is really big!"

Quintin just laughed. "They might be millionaires by now, but I try not to hold that against them."

"I like yours better," Wendy said. "When it gets all fixed up, it's gonna look like a giant dollhouse."

Quintin grimaced, but gave the child a smile. "I'm not sure that's exactly what I'm going for at Echo Springs, but thanks, Wendy."

To take advantage of the coolest part of the day, the party had started at five, and already seemed to be in full swing under a sky tinted with the pink, purple and gold of the coming sunset. It might be an informal Texas barbecue, but clearly, no expense had been spared.

Snowy-white banquet tables were clustered under a huge tent. Bartenders poured drinks, while waiters weaved among the guests, and there was a massive spit turning an entire side of beef over an open fire. A few guests were dancing to live music on a raised wooden platform. Small white bulbs had been draped overhead, and though they would probably not come on for a while yet, it was easy to imagine how romantic the dance floor would be once night fell.

A corner under the trees had been set aside for

the children. Two attendants watched them, and when one of the women spotted Roxanna and Wendy, she immediately headed in their direction. In less than a minute, the girls were running to join the other kids, some of whom Riley recognized from their day camp.

"Wow," she said as she glanced around. She was suddenly glad she'd gone with something a little dressier than jeans. "Half of Texas must be here."

Quintin nodded. "The Flying M has a lot of friends in this state." He indicated a couple standing arm-in-arm near the back of the house. "Come on. I don't see Ethan or Cassie yet, but I'll introduce you to the bride and groom."

His hand touched the small of Riley's back. As he guided her through the crowd, his fingers trailed along her vertebrae lightly, and it felt so warm, so intimate, that her heart gave a little kick.

She met the Wheelers, Josh and Meredith, who apparently had been married in a small private ceremony at the courthouse earlier in the day. Even if she hadn't known they were the newlyweds, Riley could have guessed it. They were so clearly in love.

*I looked like that once,* Riley thought as she watched Meredith lean in closer so she could caress Josh's cheek. They weren't exactly teenagers. Mid- to late-thirties would have been Riley's guess. Quintin had mentioned that they'd both been through divorces, but they obviously hadn't given up on love.

Nice to think that was possible.

Quintin pulled her out of her thoughts by touching her elbow. "Would you like a drink?"

"Not yet," she replied. She saw him exchange a wave with a man standing near one of the open bars. "These are your friends. Why don't you make the rounds? You don't need to babysit me."

"I don't mind keeping the prettiest woman here company."

There was an unholy light in his eyes, and she had to command her heart to slow down. "Please. I'll be fine."

"I hate mingling."

She really didn't want to turn him loose, but she also knew how valuable networking was. "It probably wouldn't hurt. Connections, you know?"

He conceded that point with a frown. "There are a couple of people I probably should talk to." He glanced up at the sky. "Sunset can't be too far away. How about we meet back here when the lights go on? I'll show you the dance steps I've picked up."

"Picked up where?" She realized that she sounded skeptical.

"Why do you look so surprised? I've seen *Dancing with the Stars.* I think I can manage all right."

"I just didn't think we'd… I guess I didn't expect us to actually dance together. Not in front of people."

"Why not?"

"You know. The whole employer-employee thing."

"I think it's acceptable in this century for an employer to be nice to his employees. If I'm too awful, we can make it just one dance. I promise."

He gave her a devilish wink and filtered into the crowd while she stared after him.

Riley wasn't sure how she should feel. Part of her couldn't wait for sunset and the lights to come on, to be nestled against Quintin as the band played some soft, slow tune. But another part of her was scared to death, because anytime she was close enough to touch him she seemed in danger of losing her head entirely.

She wouldn't think about it right now. The girls were busy playing a game with some of the other kids and clearly didn't need her. Picking up a glass of champagne from a passing waiter, she decided she might as well get to know a few of these people, say hello to Cassie Rafferty if she could find her and just have fun. Making connections wouldn't hurt her, either, she decided.

For the next fifteen minutes, she circulated among the crowd, introducing herself and trying to blend in. She lost sight of Quintin rather quickly, but that was all right. Though she hadn't had to do it much in the past few years, she could hold her own at a party.

She was chatting with an elderly gentleman whose white eyebrows seemed intent on escaping his face—growing straight out a good half-inch—when she felt a tug on her arm. Turning, she discovered Cassie Rafferty.

"Hi," Riley said with a welcoming smile.

"Here you are!" the woman said, as though she'd just spent hours tracking her down. "I need to talk to you." She glanced up at the older man. "Will you excuse us, Fred?" Not waiting for a reply, she pulled her away.

"Great party," Riley said.

Cassie looked harried. "You might not think so in a minute."

"What do you mean?" She angled a quick glance past the crowd to find the girls, but they were still playing. "What's wrong?"

At that moment a middle-aged woman with too much makeup joined them. "Cassie! You and Ethan have outdone yourselves. The place looks fabulous."

A flicker of annoyance came and went on Cassie's face as she was drawn into a hug. The woman gave no indication that Riley was even there. Waiting for the newcomer to drift away, Riley listened with half an ear and began to think about excusing herself.

Where was Quintin? she wondered. She missed him already.

Then, just as the newcomer's monologue began to taper off, Riley heard a hearty male laugh come from somewhere behind her, and her breathing stopped. She turned her head, trying to locate the source, and found it easily.

She supposed there were moments in a person's life, times of complete shock, when everything inside you went still and quiet and fragile. She didn't hear the music anymore. The voice of the woman talking to Cassie faded into nothingness.

A number of guests were clustered around a large table where the wedding cake towered. All eyes were focused on the only man in the group. The women looked enthralled by him. One blonde in particular seemed determined to keep his attention, her hand clutching his forearm.

Riley recognized the woman. It was Doug Freeman's daughter, Mitzy.

And the man, that guy with the luscious appeal of a rich candy bar, was Brad.

Her ex-husband.

Riley vaguely became aware that Cassie was speaking to her, though her voice seemed to come from someplace far away. "I'm so sorry, honey. I didn't know he was coming, I swear. Doug Freeman was invited, since he's done business with Josh, and frankly, he's just too prominent to be ignored." The words were spilling out of Cassie, as though she had to get them said quickly. "When he RSVP'd he asked if he could bring his daughter as his guest, and, of course, I said yes. I never dreamed *she'd* bring a guest, too."

"He's her fiancé," Riley heard herself say.

"That's how she introduced him when they showed up. And then Ethan pulled me aside and said that's where he'd heard your last name before. When he saw the engagement announced in the paper. I just put two and two together and figured I'd better warn you he was here. So he's your ex-husband, right?"

Every muscle in Riley's body seemed locked in a protective stance, but somehow she managed to give Cassie a brief smile. "Big emphasis on the ex, thank goodness."

"Does it make you too uncomfortable to have him here? Yes, of course it does."

Her friend looked so miserable that Riley placed a hand on her arm. "Cassie, it's all right."

"But I feel awful about this."

"Don't. Yes, it's uncomfortable. But it's been months since I've seen him. I hardly ever give him a thought, really," she lied. "And he probably doesn't want to talk to me, either. So we'll be fine."

"I'd find that easier to believe if you had any color left in your face."

"It was just the shock of seeing him all of a sudden."

Some of her equilibrium had returned. She could get through this. Lots of divorced women had to manage times like this. She wasn't a child—

She cut a glance in the direction of the children's play area. The girls. She'd have to make sure they were prepared. But too many people stood in the way for her to have a clear view of the twins, and when she tried to relocate Brad, she couldn't find him, either. He and his little group of admirers had disbanded.

She turned back to Cassie. "Just in case the twins spot him, I should probably let them know he's here."

She maneuvered through the crowd and was nearly at the kid area when she saw Wendy and Roxanna, and realized it was too late.

Plastered against Brad as though he were the Pied Piper, looking up at him, they were practically dancing in place. Mitzy Freeman stood nearby. She didn't appear particularly happy.

All four turned toward Riley as she reached them. Brad had a smirk on his face, but she didn't give a damn what kind of message he wanted to send her. Right now, she only had eyes for the twins.

Roxanna looked happier than Riley had seen her in ages. "Mom! Look who's here!" she said excitedly. Beside her, Wendy was still hanging on to Brad as though he would somehow disappear if she turned him loose.

So much for hoping this wasn't going to be difficult.

"I see," Riley said with as much enthusiasm as she could muster, then glanced up at her ex-husband. "Hello, Brad."

"Rile. What a nice surprise."

"Isn't it?"

She had to admit he was as handsome as ever. His blond, all-American boy looks were just getting better with age. There wasn't an ounce of sincerity in his voice, of course. But if he could be decent and civil for the sake of the twins, then so could she. Although her smile felt so phony it was almost embarrassing

He extricated himself from the girls and

caught the woman beside him with one hand, reeling her in. "This is my… You remember Mitzy Freeman, don't you?"

"Of course I do."

Riley had seen Mitzy only on a few occasions. Although she was a lot younger than Brad, she'd had enough sense to keep a low profile after Riley had filed for divorce. She was a gorgeous blonde, Doug Freeman's spoiled little girl, who still probably got whatever she wanted. And what she clearly wanted right now was to ditch this ridiculous family reunion.

She gave Riley a mere twitch of the lips and said, "Brad, I want to dance."

"In a minute, baby," he replied. He'd never been one to jump to any woman's tune. Cocking his head, he gave Riley a narrowed glance. "So what are you doing here?"

"I was invited. I'm working in the area."

"Mom's a ranch manager now," Roxanna interjected. "Just like you, Daddy."

"Really? What outfit?"

"Echo Springs."

His mouth curled. "Never heard of it. Not exactly playing with the big dogs, are you?"

Odd how that scornful tone of his irritated her almost as much as his presence here. She thought of how hard Quintin was working to accomplish his dreams for Echo Springs, how hard they had all worked the past few days to help make them happen. Somehow she kept her tone even. "The owner runs horses, not cattle. And he focuses on quality, not quantity."

Brad's eyebrows rose. "And you're managing it? Out of your area of expertise, aren't you?"

He really was such a jerk. How had she stayed married to him as long as she had? "Not really," she managed to reply. "I was practically running Hollow Creek by myself while you were busy—" she couldn't help tossing a meaningful glance Mitzy's way "—working at the Bar Seven."

Mitzy shifted restlessly. "Brad…"

Brad didn't let his smile slip, but he was radiating the kind of warmth toward Riley that blows in off a glacier. Deliberately, he turned away from her, catching his fiancée's hand. "Tell you what, Mitz. Let's you, me and the kids hit the dance floor."

Riley wanted to say, "No!"

But in the same moment Roxanna said, "Yes! Let's dance!" and Wendy squealed excitedly.

Brad swung back to Riley, and there was a glitter of harsh amusement in his eyes. With the twins practically begging for permission, he knew he had her. "You mind if I show Wendy and Rox a good time for a little while? Maybe teach them how to two-step?"

"Don't say no, Mom," Roxanna pleaded.

"Please let us. Please," Wendy chimed in.

What could she say? She made her smile the same size as Brad's, but it was so tight that her lips hurt. "Sure," she said. "Go have fun."

Their father whooped, and the girls joined in. Only Mitzy didn't look thrilled.

"Come on, my ladies! Daddy's gonna show you how to have some fun."

Roxanna and Wendy were already rushing toward the stage, and hand in hand, Brad and Mitzy were right behind them.

Before they could get away, Riley caught up with her ex and grabbed his arm. "Brad…"

With the girls out of sight, he looked openly annoyed with her for the first time. "Don't start lecturing, Rile. They're still my kids, damn it. You can have them back in an hour, no worse for wear. I know how to take care of them."

She wanted to remind him how completely untrue that statement was, because she knew how careless he could be with their feelings. But she wouldn't make an unpleasant situation worse.

Instead, she watched as the four of them hit the dance floor and formed a small circle, hands linked. The music was rousing, some country music song with a strong beat. Brad set the pace, leading them back and forth, around and around. They ducked under one another, almost as though they were a square-dancing quartet.

The twins were laughing, breathless with delight. For them, an hour with their dad would fly by.

For Riley, every second seemed excruciatingly long. She stood there, feeling as though a hole had been torn right in the middle of her chest.

# CHAPTER FOURTEEN

TEN MINUTES LATER, Quintin stood watching Brad Palmer lead an attractive blonde and Riley's twins around the dance floor.

He knew it was Riley's ex-husband because Ethan had found him moments ago to let him know that the man had shown up as a guest of Doug Freeman. Quintin didn't know where Riley had disappeared to, which concerned him, but he couldn't help admitting that he had some curiosity about the guy who had been married to her.

What he saw didn't impress him.

"So that's the idiot who was stupid enough to let her get away," he muttered, and he was so caught up in observing the man that he nearly forgot Ethan was still beside him.

His friend snorted. "You're not going to deck him, are you? Because I worked too hard getting all these lights strung to have you tear them down like a mad grizzly."

"I'm not going to do a damned thing to him unless he tries to hurt Riley or her kids. Besides, look at him. Can't you tell he's a lover, not a fighter?"

Palmer was beckoning to other dancers now, trying to get everyone to form a conga line behind Mitzy Freeman and his daughters.

"He seems to be having fun with his children," Ethan said.

"He's enjoying being the center of attention. And everyone on the dance floor thinks the bastard's superdaddy."

Ethan turned toward him. "Maybe he really is, Quint. You said yourself that Riley hasn't said much about her marriage. Maybe what she's told you has been a little…colored. You don't know all the facts."

"I know what unhappiness looks like. That's what I see in Riley's eyes every time she mentions him. She's a tough lady, but he obviously hurt her."

Quintin blew out a breath, scanning the crowd once more for some sign of her and coming up empty. Where the hell was she?

"You're really starting to care about this woman, aren't you?" Ethan said.

"I need to find her," Quintin replied, and headed into the crowd.

It took him another five minutes, but he got lucky and spotted a flash of blue-and-purple among the trees rimming the small creek that wound through the Flying M property. Though it wasn't off-limits to the guests, Quintin saw no one else as he made his way down the path. Probably because there was no action to be found here, unless you considered a wooden bench swing fastened to a branch of a massive oak much in the way of action.

Riley didn't look up as he joined her. She was staring out over the creek, her slim form outlined in the pink twilight. Any other time he might have taken the opportunity to drink in the sight of her and find some way to make it last. But he could guess her thoughts right now, and the urge to do something to help her was bridled by the frustrating fact that he had no idea where to begin.

Finally, she moved her head just a fraction in his direction. Her features seemed frozen, her cheeks as pale as moonlight.

"You all right?" he asked, damning himself for not knowing the best way to handle this.

She barely nodded, and studied the creek again.

"The water's not deep enough to drown yourself," he said. "So I assume you're thinking about collecting rocks to throw at the bastard's head."

"It wouldn't do any good," she replied. "Brad's head is like concrete." She turned toward him. "Cassie told you?"

"Ethan."

"So you saw him?"

"Hard to miss the guy, what with him playing Lord of the Dance."

That got him a tight, tiny smile. "He was always a good dancer. Most of the time, he's perfectly happy showing off what he can do without a partner." She seemed to shake herself out of her grim mood and glanced beyond the trees, where the band had just begun a Jimmy Buffett tune. "I should check on the girls."

Quintin brought her up short by catching her arm. "Leave it alone for just a while longer. Your kids were having a ball when I saw them. Pull them away now and they'll only resent it."

"You don't understand." Her eyes, so dark blue with pain just a moment ago, flashed with anger. "You think he gives a damn about his daughters? He doesn't. If he wanted children at all, he wanted boys." The words came in a sharp, hurried torrent. "When I sued for divorce, he was going to fight for them just to make me miserable. He gave up the moment I said I'd give him my share of the ranch. *That's* their loving father."

Quintin didn't know what to say to that. What could he say? He just knew he hated to hear the edge of bitterness that had crept into her tone.

She grimaced and walked away, but not back

toward the party. Instead she went to the swing and sat down.

Quintin joined her. The swing bounced a little as he sat down, but she didn't move. Neither did he. He just stared out across the creek, thinking that sadness didn't stop the sun from setting, or change the sound of the breeze in the trees, or the hunger you felt for something you couldn't even name.

After what seemed like a long time, he asked, "You want to talk about it?"

She shook her head. He wanted to reach out and finger the strands of blond curls that lay against her cheek, but he didn't. He sat there and felt completely useless.

"I was such an idiot to marry him," she muttered unexpectedly. "But I always thought that when you were faced with a hole, you should try to fill it, and Brad Palmer made me believe he was the answer I was looking for. He's always had enough snake-oil charm to get whatever he wants."

"So what kind of snake-oil charm did he use to get you?" Quintin asked gently.

She shrugged, the gesture a feeble version of what he was accustomed to from her. "It was embarrassingly easy. I was in my first year at college. Scraping by on scholarships. My older sister, Jillian, was trying to help financially, but she had her own education to pay for. I was working part-time, trying to stay ahead of tuition. But every semester it got tougher."

"What about your parents? Couldn't they help?"

"They died in a car accident the previous year. The farm was mortgaged up to the hilt. There was a lot of debt. Once we paid that off, there was just enough to take care of some of Jilly's education. We figured we'd worry about my school needs somewhere down the road."

"What about a student loan?"

She shook her head. "I saw what massive debt did to Mom and Dad, and I just didn't want to go that route unless I absolutely had to. So between money issues and adjusting to school and still trying to accept that my old life with Mom and Dad…was really gone for good, I was pretty miserable."

"Until Palmer came along."

"As incredible as that seems to me now, yes. I met him at a party. He'd graduated the year before I arrived, and he still had friends there. We talked most of the night. He was charming and attentive, and I was so lonely and flattered that I just lapped it up like a silly puppy."

"Seeing him in action, I can imagine how appealing he must have been."

"Oh, he knows how to make that charm work

for him. Pretty soon he was coming up to see me regularly. By the end of my second year, he asked me to marry him. He had a small ranch near Cooper and said he could envision the two of us turning it into something big one day. We'd be like pioneers."

"So you left school and got married?"

She straightened. Her profile looked as though it had been carved from marble. "It seemed so perfect. I could always go back later and get my accounting degree. My sister could concentrate on her own life. But mostly, I just wanted to be married to this charismatic, good-looking guy who seemed to think I was pretty special." She grimaced. "Incredibly stupid of me, but I like to believe I was too young to know better."

"You probably were, and it's hard not to be attracted to someone who focuses so much attention on you."

She gave a shaky laugh. "It was only later that I realized Brad treats every woman like that when he's with them. He can't help himself."

Her chest rose as she took a deep breath. A sense of powerlessness gripped Quintin. He had no idea if he was helping or hurting. His experience with this sort of thing—by his own design—was so damned limited.

"In the beginning, it really did feel like the two of us against the world," she said. "Then the girls came along. I was thrilled, but they took up every bit of spare time I had, and a lot of our money. I know Brad felt neglected."

"He doesn't strike me as the kind of guy to tolerate that very well."

"We fought a lot," Riley conceded. "Then the ranch had a couple of bad years, and he found work over at the Bar Seven. We began to see less and less of him, and honestly, I didn't really mind. He was…too hard to be around when he was in a foul mood."

"Was he physically abusive?"

She bit her lip. "He never hit me. But once, Roxanna mouthed off to him—I'm sure by now you know how she can be—and he was really… rough with her. I stepped in before anything serious could happen, but I couldn't help thinking that if I hadn't been there…" Riley shook her head. "I don't know. After that, I just didn't feel comfortable when he was alone with them."

"The son of a bitch. Those kids seem to adore him."

"Isn't it ironic? It was months before they stopped begging me to take him back. I couldn't tell them that he'd already found someone else, that he'd started cheating on me with Mitzy Freeman long before I filed for divorce."

Quintin snorted. "What a great guy."

Riley nodded. "I wasn't completely stupid.

He was making too many excuses not to come home. I caught him in a couple of lies. Someone told me they'd seen him in an out of the way restaurant with Mitzy."

"So you confronted him."

"Yes." She frowned at Quintin. "How did you know that?"

He smiled and brought one finger to the side of her throat, sliding back a curl. "Because you'd never take the easy way out and ignore it, hoping it would go away."

"Well, I did turn a blind eye for a lot longer than I should have. And then about a month after he told me he'd broken off the affair, Wendy got sick. Ended up in the hospital with pneumonia. I was frantic. It was touch and go for a while. The doctor told us…" Her lips kneaded one another for a moment as she struggled for composure. "He told us we…should prepare ourselves."

Quintin knew what that kind of fear could do to a parent. How it could eat you up from the inside out. "It must have been unbearable for you."

He slid one arm around Riley's shoulders and gently tugged her closer until she leaned against him. She didn't stiffen or pull away. His cheek rested against the top of her head. He pressed his lips to her hair, feeling it slide like warm silk against his mouth.

"It was the most terrifying time in my life,"

she replied. "One night Brad was supposed to be watching Roxanna while I stayed at the hospital. Wendy had had a bad day, and I got scared. Really scared. I called him. I just wanted Brad to be there with me, you know? In case… I just needed him to be there." She shook her head. "But I couldn't reach him, and no one knew where he was. And then about midnight he came strolling into the room, acting as if he just couldn't stay away, telling me he'd taken Roxanna over to our neighbor's house so he could be with me and Wendy."

"But you knew he was lying."

She nodded, and her head settled closer against Quintin's chest. "It was almost comical how guilty he looked. He reeked of a perfume that I don't wear, some expensive stuff we could never afford. But even if he hadn't blown it, I already knew. I'd called my neighbor earlier to ask her to go over to the ranch. That's when she told me she'd been babysitting Roxanna since four that afternoon, when Brad had brought her over."

Quintin couldn't help muttering a crude curse. "He's an even bigger bastard than I imagined."

Riley straightened in his arms so she could look at him. If he hadn't already heard the tearful undercurrent in her voice, he could see the pain in her eyes now. "What kind of father chooses to sneak a quickie with his mistress when he has a child in the hospital? A child who could…" She bit her lip again. "I just couldn't stay with him after that. The minute Wendy was better and out of the hospital, I filed for divorce."

She sounded so lost. Quintin reached out to place his hands against both her cheeks. They were wet from her tears, and so warm she could have been running a fever. He shook his head. "I'm so sorry you had to go through that."

Her mouth lifted imperceptively. "I've never told anyone except my sister what happened that night. You're a good listener, Quintin."

"Ah, Riley." He brought his forehead against hers. His mouth hovered over hers, so close that their breaths mingled, and he felt her damp eyelashes brush his cheek. He wanted her to feel the connection, to know he was here for her. He wanted to kiss her, but didn't dare. Right now she needed a friend, not a lover. "I'd give anything to turn back the clock and keep it all from happening. I wish you'd never met him."

"I might not have the girls then," she whispered. "And I'll never regret that."

For a long, long moment, they stayed that way, barely moving, a hairbreadth away from one another. Her mouth ghosted over his, such an elusive touch that he couldn't be sure it happened. His insides seemed drawn as tight as a bow string, ready to snap.

Then she pulled away, sitting up and glancing toward the reception area. He turned his head and realized that the dance floor lights had been turned on. They glittered like diamonds through the lacy network of trees that surrounded them.

"I have to go back," she said, sounding practical, yet somewhat regretful, too. "He's probably had enough of playing daddy."

She stood, and before she could move away, Quintin caught her hand. "Don't go just yet. Not looking the way you do. Don't give him the pleasure of knowing that he's upset you."

"I don't care what he thinks," she said, wiping her free hand across her cheek. "He can't hurt me anymore. But he can hurt the girls. I don't want them to ever find out what he's truly like."

"They probably will one day. You know that, don't you?"

Her mouth went tight with determination. "Not if I can help it."

Not letting go of her hand, Quintin stood. "Then let's go rescue them. And if you want to go home, we'll do that, too."

She couldn't quite hide her relief at that suggestion, but gamely she said, "I think I promised you a dance once the lights came on."

He brought her hand to his mouth, kissing her palm. "Don't worry. I won't forget."

They went back up the path to rejoin the party. With all the mood lighting, the place looked magical, and if anything, it seemed as if even more people had arrived. The evening had started to cool off, and Quintin could tell it was going to be a late night. Ethan and Cassie would keep this thing going until the last guest left.

Threading through the crowd, he and Riley headed toward the dance floor. A few feet in front of it, several tables and chairs had been set up. They found Roxanna and Wendy there, watching their father and Mitzy Freeman slow dance. When Riley put her hands on their shoulders, they turned in unison. Their cheeks were flushed, their blond hair tousled, but no one could deny that they looked happy.

But in the split second it took to read their mother's expression, they must have sensed catastrophe in the air.

Wendy groaned, but Roxanna spoke up right away. "We're just resting. Dad's gonna want us to dance in a minute."

"We have to go," Riley said.

"We don't want to," Wendy complained. "We're having fun."

"We haven't even eaten yet," Roxanna pointed

out, her jaw starting to harden into a solid wall of stubbornness.

Riley shook her head, and Quintin jumped in, hoping to defuse a scene. "Hey, girls, I'm sorry. I forgot to take care of some things at home, so we need to leave a little early. Maybe we could get takeout on the way."

Riley shot him a grateful look for the lie, but the twins pretty much ignored that. Their focus was all on their mother. He could have told them it was no use. Regardless of how hurt Riley had seemed down at the creek, she had her full armor on now.

Brad and Mitzy were coming down the dance floor steps, and both Roxanna and Wendy ran to their father's side.

"Mom says we have to leave," Roxanna told him.

He looked up at Riley. There were a few long seconds where no one said anything, but Quintin thought the silent battle going on between the two of them might actually be visible if you looked hard enough.

Eventually Palmer shrugged and turned toward the twins. "Sorry. Your mom's the boss." He gave each child a quick kiss on the cheek. "Remember Daddy loves you."

The girls looked bereft, but before they could say anything, Riley spoke up. "Go get your things," she told them in a tone that allowed for no further argument.

Anger flashed across Roxanna's features, then she ran toward the children's corner. With a single sound of disgust, Wendy followed more slowly.

They were barely out of earshot when Palmer turned back to Riley. "You really know how to kill a party, you know that?"

"You've had your hour of fun."

"What's the matter, Rile? You afraid I'll let it slip to them what a bitch their mother can be?"

Quintin felt his blood heat up, and came between them. "Whoa. Wait a minute—"

Riley's hand was on his arm. "It's all right," she said in a voice as brittle as glass. "He always turns nasty when he doesn't get his way."

"I was just showing them a good time. Something you never knew how to do."

She glanced toward Quintin. "Let's go, all right?"

Palmer seemed to notice Quintin for the first time. "Who's this?" he asked with a sneer. "You sheet wrestling with someone new already?"

"I think you need to go enjoy the party," Quintin advised in a quiet tone.

"Let me tell you something, friend. You watch yourself. You know what my nickname was for her? Dream Killer. You're dealing with a woman who doesn't know how to have fun anymore. And she can carry on like she wrote the Ten Commandments herself."

THE RIDE HOME WAS ONE OF the longest and most uncomfortable in Quintin's life.

The difference between the way they'd arrived at the reception and the way they left it was so extreme it was almost laughable.

He made a feeble attempt to boost everyone's spirits, but he had darned little to work with. Riley sat in contemplative silence. In the backseat, Roxanna huffed noisily from time to time, and beside her, Wendy sniffed as though holding back tears.

No one seemed at all interested in burgers and shakes. Quintin knew he had no appetite. All he really wanted right now was to get home and have a beer on the back porch. There he could immerse himself in the thorny problems of horses and lowering water tables and the threat of ledger books bleeding red ink. The kind of things he knew he could wade through. Not this quicksand of a fractured family dynamic that looked as if it had the potential to be problematic for years to come.

His marriage to Teresa had been rock solid, but he knew plenty of marriages that weren't, and that infidelity could be like suffering an internal earthquake if you were the wronged spouse. Listening to Riley tell him about her husband's temper, his last betrayal... It had felt as though someone had picked up Quintin's stomach and twisted it. And once he'd actually met the man, his contempt for Palmer had threatened to curdle into rage.

His heart ached for those little girls and their mother. But if he indulged this raw hunger to involve himself in their lives, he had a feeling there would be no turning back.

He definitely didn't like that idea. It had been years since he'd had to worry about anyone but himself, and frankly, he didn't think he knew how to negotiate a relationship anymore.

He was also pretty sure he didn't want to. And not just because he needed to stay focused on his plans for Echo Springs. That would always be an issue. But because, when it came right down to it, there were just too many ways he could mess things up.

They pulled into the side yard, and Quintin killed the engine, then handed the keys to Riley. The girls released their seat belts and jumped out without waiting for their mother, then ran for the apartment door. She sighed and gave him a look that said she thought it might be a long night. He didn't envy her.

"I'm going to check on things in the barn,"

he told her. "Is there anything I can do to help? I'm not sure what the heck that could be, but I'm willing to give it my best shot."

She grimaced. "They're pretty angry. It might be best if I just said good-night now."

"Riley—"

"Before Brad showed up, I really was having a nice time."

He saw that her hands were restless in her lap. Whatever residual anger she had over seeing her ex-husband, she wasn't thinking about him right now. He suspected she was thinking the same thing he was. How nice it would be just to hold on to one another. But tonight that wasn't in the cards. Maybe it never would be.

She got out quickly, as though she might change her mind if she lingered any longer. Maybe it was just the kids waiting impatiently for her. He'd like to think it was more than that.

She bent down so she could see him through the open door. "Thanks for helping me get through it, Quintin. Somehow it was…more manageable, having you there. Good night."

He watched her walk away. There was a three-quarter moon tonight, and the dark shadows made her look as if she was wrapped in silver. He couldn't seem to turn away. For just a mo-ment, at least, he chose to hold on to the promise of her and ignore everything inside him that said he was getting in too deep.

Only when she finally disappeared inside the apartment did he get out of the SUV. It was too early for bed. As was his habit, he liked to make sure all the animals were settled in for the night. A quick check of the barn, and he'd be ready for that beer.

He was almost there when he heard the apartment door open again. He turned and saw Riley in the spill of light coming from inside. Then she was crossing the yard, making a beeline for him in purposeful strides that made him frown with sudden worry.

"Riley?" he said across the distance that separated them. "What's wrong?"

She didn't answer. Instead, she just kept coming, and the moment she reached him, her hands came up and grabbed the collar of his shirt so that he instinctively lowered his head.

Then she kissed him.

Quintin had to admit she surprised him. How many nights had he dreamed about this very thing? Having this woman welcome him, want him, make his heart stumble in his chest. But those had been dreams. This was real. Riley was real.

Her mouth was hot, but her lips were soft and seeking. Her tongue made sensuous forays against his, stroking, teasing. She kissed him with the greedy thoroughness of a woman who'd denied herself too long, and he couldn't help but respond. Need clawed into him until he was powerless to resist.

Somehow she was in his arms, his fingers finding the curve of her spine. Her body pressed warmly against his, arching closer. Her hands dug deep into his shoulders.

He was still trying to sort out what might come next when she lifted her mouth from his. They were both breathless and shaken.

Reluctantly, too close to the edge to risk going over, he drew back a little. "Was that some sort of retaliation against your ex-husband?" he asked, hearing the lingering intimacy in his voice.

"It didn't have anything to do with him," she replied, and she sounded far calmer than he was. "That was because I'm so damned tired of talking myself out of it."

Looking as though she feared her resolve would fall apart if she didn't put some distance between them, she pushed away and hurried back to the apartment.

## CHAPTER FIFTEEN

THE NEXT DAY, Riley got up early, packed a picnic lunch and hustled the girls through breakfast.

They were still sulky from the night before, but she refused to take it to heart. Running into Brad at the reception had been just an unfortunate accident, and in the future she'd be better prepared to manage his visits. Not that there were likely to be many, knowing him as well as she did.

Today she was determined to show the twins a good time. It was Sunday, and she had the entire day off. The perfect opportunity.

When they realized that something was up, Wendy and Rox came around a little, especially once they saw their bathing suits stuffed in a beach bag. Riley refused to give them any hints as to where they were headed. Last night, when they'd returned from the party, they'd been difficult and whiny. But she was fairly certain that by the time she put the twins to bed this evening, things would be back to the way they'd been before Brad had come along and dazzled them with his slick charm.

While the girls brushed their teeth, Riley finished packing the SUV. "I'll be back in a minute," she told them as she scooped up the beach bag. "I'm just going over to the house to talk to Quintin."

"Maybe he can come with us," Wendy suggested around a mouthful of toothpaste.

Riley had considered asking him, but finally decided against the idea. She didn't want anything to take her focus from her daughters today, and Quintin could certainly do that. After the way they'd left things last night, she wasn't sure whether or not she had any willpower left. She might not be any fun—at least, not Brad's definition of it—but evidently she still had that impulsive streak that could get her into major trouble.

She went across the yard and knocked on the front door, then opened it when she thought she heard a response. "Quintin?"

"In the kitchen," he called.

She found him there, standing in front of the coffeemaker. Since this was also Lilianna's day off, he had to manage on his own.

He turned, cup in hand. His welcoming grin brought a smile to her lips. He looked fresh from a shower, with beads of water still clinging to his dark hair. His jeans were slung low on those lean hips, and the blue T-shirt he wore couldn't have defined his muscles any better. The sharp catch in Riley's stomach was hard to ignore.

"You want coffee?" he asked. "It's not as good as Lilianna's, but it's drinkable."

"No, thanks."

Better get right to the point if she was going to make it out of here without doing anything foolish. The temptation to take the cup out of his hand, set it on the counter and then kiss him was pretty powerful. And judging by the expression on his face, Riley didn't think he would mind.

"I just came over to let you know I'll be away for the day. Probably be back late, actually."

"Everything all right?"

"I'm going to take the girls to Galveston. Let them play on the beach. Maybe go to the amusement park if they have any energy left."

His mouth quirked. "Going to prove to them that you do know how to have fun?"

Hard to put anything past this man. "It's my only full day to be with them," she explained. One of his brows rose. She felt her neck growing warm. "Okay, yeah. I admit it. I'm insecure. I want to show them that I'm every bit as much fun as their dancing fool of a father. What's so wrong with that?"

He leaned back against the counter, crossed

his arms and took a sip of coffee. "Nothing. I'm sure your daughters will love the attention."

She'd gone no farther than the kitchen door. The frame had recently been sanded, and to avoid his gaze, she pretended to inspect it. She found a tiny splinter that had missed the sandpaper, and plucked it away. When she'd lingered at the doorway as long as she could and Quintin still hadn't said anything else, she turned back to look at him.

"What Brad said yesterday wasn't true…." She chewed the inside of her mouth. "I'm really not a dream killer."

"No," Quintin said with a soft chuckle. "You definitely are not."

"Quintin…" She moved forward to the edge of the kitchen table. "About that kiss last night…"

"What about it?"

"I got a little carried away."

"I thought it was the perfect way to end the evening. You disagree?"

"No. I…" She didn't want to apologize for something she didn't regret, but she didn't want him to get the wrong idea, either. "But we had an agreement. And I probably—"

"We have an agreement to enjoy one another's company, but not have sex," he stated, sounding as though he didn't need to be reminded. "Did you want to make changes?" he added in a quiet, gentler tone.

She looked away, aware that he watched her closely now. Aware, too, of how badly she wanted to say yes, let's forget about that stupid agreement. Let's take whatever this is between us and find out where it can go. What would he say to that?

Her fingers clutched the edge of the table, as though it was the only thing holding her upright. For the first time she noticed that it was littered with paper. Knowing him, he'd probably been up early, working.

She recognized the haphazard stack of pages from the night she'd been at his desk. Only now she could see that they'd been marked up, with notations made in the corners.

She knew what she was seeing. She wished she didn't. Résumés.

She stood perfectly still, fighting the feeling of disappointment twisting inside her. Her time here was coming to an end soon, and no matter what happened between them, a replacement ranch manager would be found. She mustn't forget that.

She turned back to Quintin, giving him a tight look. "No," she said, shaking her head. "I don't think the agreement should be changed. If anything, I want to assure you that what—" she wet her lips "—what happened last night won't happen again. We'd best leave things the way they were."

His eyes narrowed imperceptively and he stared at her a long while. Finally, he shrugged. "All right," he said in the mildest tone she'd ever heard him use with her. "Have a good day off."

She had the strong urge to take it all back, those words that were completely opposite of how she truly felt. But she couldn't. "Thanks," she said instead. "I'll see you tomorrow."

"Bright and early," he said dryly, and turned back to the coffeemaker.

She fled the house.

Fortunately, the twins were waiting for her in the car, so there were no further delays. The drive to Galveston took longer than she expected, but Wendy and Roxanna were excited, and Riley led them through every silly game and song she could think of. Anything to keep her mind off how horrible she felt, and how hard it would be to get through this last week of her employment at Echo Springs.

Coming home was a different story. They spent a few hours in the cool, calm waters of the Gulf, then hit the boardwalk, where Riley treated them to almost every amusement that touristy area offered. By the time they headed back to the ranch, a day in the hot sun and all that nonstop action had exhausted all three of them. The girls fell asleep in the backseat and left Riley plenty of time to think about her relationship with Quintin.

Over and over again.

At the wedding reception, Brad had been such a jerk, and Quintin had been so kind, so considerate of her feelings. She was sure it was only his quiet strength and compassion down at the creek that had kept her from doing something really stupid and embarrassing.

But even more than that, it had made her realize what a great guy he was. The kind any woman would want to kiss. Including her. So last night in the moonlit yard, she hadn't been able to help herself, and she couldn't be a bit sorry about it.

But today was different. Today, whatever her reasoning had been, whatever momentary lapses in judgment she'd had, the indisputable fact remained that there could be no chance for a deeper relationship between them. The twins were still her top priority. And if those marked-up résumés were any indication, Quintin still had every intention of replacing her. Maybe he'd even spent the day picking out just the right candidate.

She couldn't be angry about that. He'd been up front from the very beginning. She was the one who'd foolishly thought that somewhere along the way she might be able to change his mind.

As she pulled into Echo Springs, Riley tried to tell herself that it was probably just as well. Forget great chemistry and attraction and all those endless nights longing for something more. She didn't need a man right now. She needed to focus on building a new career and making the twins feel safe and secure in the life she was trying to shape for them.

At least today had been a success. As she tucked the twins into bed, they wanted to giggle and rehash all the great things they'd shared. She let them go on awhile, happy to have her sweet, loving daughters back.

When they finally settled down, she sat on the bed, smiling at them as she repositioned the covers. "I love you both very much," she said softly. "You know that, don't you?"

They nodded.

"And we had a good time today. Maybe we'll even do it again soon."

She got identical smiles and more eager nods. Then Roxanna said, "Next time, do you think we could invite Dad?"

Beside her, Wendy gasped in delight. "Could we, Mom? I'll bet he could build the biggest sand castle in the world!"

Riley sat there, stunned. Well. So much for being the *fun* parent.

MONDAY STARTED A NEW WEEK, but by no means a good one. In fact, by the time Wednesday afternoon arrived, Riley was beginning to think the Fates had it in for her.

On a personal level, her relationship with Quintin had suffered a major setback.

He was pleasant toward her, but it was clear he'd decided to keep his distance. There were no quiet, soul-baring conversations, no dinner invitations, no exchanged glances and definitely no kisses in the moonlight. Their dealings with one another were professional, straightforward and courteous, and it only intensified Riley's unhappiness because she missed the Quintin she'd come to know, and hated that he now seemed lost to her.

Unexpected problems on the ranch made things even more difficult and left everyone edgy.

Quintin took a trip to look at Warmbloods, only to return with an empty horse trailer and a grim look that said it had been a complete waste of valuable time. While he was away, the windmill began to squeal again, then shuddered to a halt. This time nothing short of a new motor would fix it.

The irrigation company returned and started work on Tuesday, but somehow ended up cutting a power line that left the ranch without electricity for the rest of the day. With no juice to run the pumps that fed the outlying pastures, water had to be carried in buckets out to the herd, which meant that erecting pole barns in the pasture had to be delayed a day.

On Wednesday, a truckload of hay was delivered, and Riley and the men spent most of the afternoon stacking it in the loft, only to discover that some of the interior hay flakes held mold spores. Every bit would have to be stripped out.

Thursday morning, however, proved to be disastrous. Riley set the Ramseys to work in the barn, hauling down the contaminated hay, but just before lunchtime, Virgil had a diabetic episode, passed out and fell from the loft. Everyone ended up in the waiting room at the hospital, even Quintin, while Virgil was rushed into surgery.

The Ramseys were extremely close, so Riley spent most of that time trying to reassure Jim and Steve that their youngest cousin would be all right, even though she was sure of no such thing. Quintin kept busy with more practical matters—contacting relatives, making sure everyone got fed and maneuvering through the hospital's admitting department so that any question of insurance got resolved and Virgil would be guaranteed a bed.

By late afternoon, tension in the waiting room

seemed thick enough to cut. The surgery was taking much longer than they'd been told. Had the doctors encountered something life-threatening?

Riley glanced down at her watch and realized it was nearly time to pick up the girls. But how could she leave now, not knowing anything definite? As the ranch manager, she felt an obligation to stay. That sweet boy. If something bad happened to him...

Quintin came up to her. "Go pick up your daughters," he told her softly. "I'll stay."

"I can't." She cast a worried glance toward Jim and Steve. "If the news is bad—"

"I'll be here to help get them through it. Go on. I'll see you at the ranch."

He reached down and squeezed her hand, the first real contact she'd had with him in what felt like ages. For a few seconds, the polite stranger had disappeared, and it was awful how much she wished it would stay that way.

"You'll call me when there's news?" she asked.

"Of course."

Then he walked away, heading back to the Ramsey cousins.

Five minutes after leaving the hospital, Jim Ramsey called Riley to say that Virgil was in the recovery room. The surgeon had set his leg— broken in two places—and removed his damaged spleen. His collarbone and two ribs were cracked, as well, but concern over damage to his spine had proved groundless, and the doctor expected him to make a full recovery.

Riley felt so relieved she was practically giddy by the time she pulled into the yard at Echo Springs with the girls. She saw Quintin's truck there, which meant he was already back from the hospital.

Once she had the twins started on their evening routine, she headed for the barn. The ranch truck had been backed close to the entrance and was half-full of the afternoon ration of hay for the herd. As she approached, Quintin appeared, a baling hook in each hand as he wrangled a bale onto the bed of the vehicle.

She was the one who usually handled the afternoon feeding, with an assist from one of the Ramseys. This delivery would be a little behind schedule, but considering today's emergency, she didn't think Quintin would mind. She didn't want him to think she couldn't work around a problem or two.

"I'll take it out," she told him. "The horses are probably wondering where dinner is."

"I can do it. Now that your girls are home—"

"I have the baby monitor. They'll be fine."

He didn't argue.

"No signs of mold in this batch?" she asked.

"Better not be."

A fresh load of hay had been brought in this morning, sweet-smelling, protein-rich alfalfa. Riley knew it had come from a different supplier, and that it had cost more to get such a large delivery on short notice.

She stood near the rear of the cab, waiting while Quintin positioned the hay so that it wouldn't slide around when she hit the pasture's bumps. "How were the Ramseys when you left the hospital?"

"Relieved. They're a close-knit family."

"I think they've gotten even tighter since the economy tanked. The three of them are trying to keep the whole family afloat. Jim says Virgil hasn't had the money to refill his diabetes prescription for two weeks, and he'd just about convinced him to ask for a pay advance when this happened."

After stripping off his work gloves, Quintin pulled the truck keys out of his jeans pocket and dropped them into her outstretched hand. "I'd have given it to him. He's a good kid."

"He was complaining about having bad headaches yesterday, but it didn't occur to me to question him. To see if he was watching his blood sugar."

"He's probably been stretching out the meds. Trying to get by on the cheap."

"Probably," she agreed. Lots of people were looking for ways to cut corners these days. Including her. "But I should have kept a better eye on him," she said, trying to remember if she'd ever given quiet, shy Virgil much notice. "Especially after Cassie told me early on that he was inconsistent about taking his medicine."

There was no response from Quintin, and when Riley looked at him, she saw something in his eyes that unnerved her. Not chastisement, exactly. Disappointment?

He grimaced. "If you're expecting me to let you off the hook and say it wasn't your responsibility, I won't. As the ranch manager, it's your job to make sure no one on the crew is endangered for any reason. Even if they're too bullheaded to watch out for themselves. You dropped the ball."

That comment nearly drew an audible gasp from her. Not because it wasn't true, but because it hurt so much. The crew didn't just look to her for instructions. They needed her guidance. How could she consider herself real ranch-manager material if she couldn't do a better job of watching out for her own men?

Embarrassed, Riley could do nothing more than nod. "I'll get the monitor," she said, and headed quickly to the apartment.

When she returned, Quintin was in the barn,

brushing down his personal mount, Azza. She thought about asking him how he wanted to handle tomorrow. They were going to be a man short, and it was possible Jim and Steve would hang out at the hospital instead of coming to work. Then she decided against it. *She* was the ranch manager—at least until Sunday morning. She'd call Jim later.

She jumped in the truck. Once she entered the pasture, the herd trotted over, ready to be fed. While they jockeyed for position, she cut the bales and pulled apart the sheaves to scatter the hay.

Sunset was still about an hour away. She watched the herd absently, thinking that tonight she would make something simple for dinner if the girls didn't fuss too much. The day might not have been physically difficult, but she sure didn't feel like cooking. Tomorrow there would be a lot of lost time to make up for.

She scanned the pasture, wondering how far the irrigation crew had gotten, and that's when she noticed one of the horses hadn't joined the others. In fact, it was lying on its side, as if completely indifferent to being fed.

Riley frowned. It wasn't unusual for horses to roll on the ground, especially looking for relief from bugs and hot weather. What *was* strange was for any animal to stay down at feeding time.

A bad feeling pooled in her stomach, and she hurried out to the animal.

It was the black mare that Quintin had doctored for a bite mark. Her neck was stretched out as far as it could go, the upper lip curled. Drenched in sweat and breathing shallowly, she was conscious, but just barely. As Riley watched, the mare swung her head around to try and bite her abdomen, then subsided and lay flat again.

Colic. It had to be. In her entire life, Riley had seen a horse with colic only twice, and neither case had been fatal. But she knew the signs. The question was, how long had the animal been suffering?

The mare groaned and looked up almost pleadingly at Riley. The last thing a horse with an intestinal problem needed was to lie flat on the ground. She grabbed the halter and pulled, trying to get the animal on her feet.

"Come on, girl," she coaxed. "Get up. You can do it."

The poor beast made a halfhearted effort to rise, then settled back on her side and began thrashing against the pain, so wildly that Riley barely missed being struck by a hoof.

The animal needed help, and needed it now. Knowing there was no time to lose, Riley ran, desperate to get to the barn and Quintin.

QUINTIN HEARD THE TRUCK brakes squeal, and even before Riley came flying into the barn, he knew there was trouble. The color had drained from her face, and she was breathing as though she'd run a marathon.

"The black mare," she gasped out. "She's down in the pasture. Colic, I think."

His blood went cold, but he struggled to keep calm. Over the years, he'd dealt successfully with colicky horses plenty of times, but he couldn't afford to take any chances with the Warmbloods.

He unhooked his cell phone from his belt and tossed it to Riley as he sprinted toward the tack room. "Dr. Hightower is number three on my speed dial. Ask her to come. If I can get the mare up and walking, I'll bring her back here, so start clearing out the first stall. No hay on the floor. No water. Pull a couple of blankets."

In the tack room he unlocked one of the cabinets and got down his "standing order" kit, the first-aid box approved by his vet. Every rancher kept one on hand for just such emergencies. Inside were prescription medicines for all the usual ailments. He scooped up a lead rope and the keys to the ATV, and in less than thirty seconds was roaring out to the pasture.

When he got there, the mare still lay on her side. Quintin's heart froze when he saw so many deep gouges in the earth, a sign she'd been down and thrashing for a while.

Colic was merely a symptom of a larger intestinal problem, one horses were prone to because of their delicate digestive system. The mare's abdomen was so swollen, Quintin knew what he'd hear when he brought a stethoscope to her belly.

Nothing. Nothing was moving inside.

Taking her vital signs and checking her color only confirmed that she was in real trouble. He grabbed a syringe and a vial of Banamine. The painkiller would take about twenty minutes to work. Injecting her in the neck, Quintin waited ten, then harried the mare to her feet. The sooner he got her walking, the better her chances of survival.

Trying not to stress her out, he led her back to the barn slowly, offering soft encouragement the whole way. Twice she tried to go down on him, but he pulled her up and kept her moving until they reached the barn.

Riley was waiting, her face still pale, dark fear in her eyes. "Dr. Hightower is on the other side of the county," she told him. "But she'll be here as soon as she can. She said you'd know what to do in the meantime."

Quintin nodded and put the mare in the stall. "Do you know where to find the bran mash?"

Riley grabbed up the bucket that sat just outside the stall. "Got it already. And the turkey baster, as well as a gallon of mineral oil."

Thank God she knew the drill for this kind of emergency. "Let's see if we can get some down her."

For the next hour, they worked together to bring relief to the mare, to get whatever had impacted her system to bust loose. It wasn't pretty or neat, and wrangling a thirteen-hundred-pound animal in pain wasn't easy. By the time Dr. Hightower arrived, both Quintin and Riley were dripping with sweat.

While the vet did an examination, Riley hurried to the apartment to check on her daughters. Quintin didn't really expect to see her back, but she returned in less than fifteen minutes with the baby monitor in hand.

Dr. Hightower started the mare on an IV solution of lactated Ringer's to combat dehydration, and every half hour they took turns walking her for fifteen minutes. In between, they let her lie down. Riley pillowed the animal's head on her lap and stroked her neck, crooning to her softly, while Quintin tried to hold down her legs when she thrashed. They continued that routine all through the evening and into the night, hour after hour, stopping only long enough for Quintin to make pots of coffee and Riley to check on her children.

By six in the morning, when the first streaks of golden light were coming over the trees, they had gone through twelve bags of Ringer's. The mare went down as they were walking her in the paddock, and no amount of prodding, begging or pulling could get her on her feet.

Dr. Hightower took Quintin aside. "If it's a blockage, she should have cleared something by now," she told him. "I think the intestine is twisted."

He nodded, having suspected as much for the last hour. "She's worn-out."

"I don't think she can take much more," the vet agreed. She was a smart woman who'd been practicing veterinary medicine for thirty years. Quintin didn't doubt she knew her stuff.

"What about emergency surgery?" Riley asked. She was seated on the ground close to the mare's head, stroking it and dabbing a cloth against the animal's nose. With no place else to go, fluid had begun to seep from the horse's nostrils. "There's an equine hospital just outside of Houston."

Dr. Hightower shook her head. "Too stressful on her. Her heart rate's down to twenty a minute. I don't think she'd make it." She glanced at Quintin. "It's your call, of course."

Quintin knelt beside the mare, running his hand down her sweating neck, trying to decide what to do. Or rather, trying to accept what he already knew had to be done.

These animals weren't family pets. They were a business investment, and the loss of even one would impact the bottom line. But that didn't mean his gut wasn't knotted with sorrow and regret. The three of them had fought so hard to save her, but it just wasn't going to work.

Quintin ground his teeth together. The mare hadn't deserved to suffer like this. He was supposed to be taking care of his animals, keeping them safe. No one could predict when a horse would have a severe intestinal problem, but somehow, he couldn't help feeling as though he'd failed.

Kind of ironic, really. Earlier, he'd told Riley she had dropped the ball with the men, and he'd meant that. But how much better was he? He'd known they were all going to be at the hospital for hours. He should have made arrangements for someone to keep an eye on things here. Now the mare was going to pay for his thoughtless disregard.

He rose and looked at Dr. Hightower. "Put her down."

"No!" Riley cried. "There has to be something else we can do."

He turned and pulled her gently to her feet. "There isn't," he told her. "Your girls should be waking up pretty soon. Get them ready to go to day camp. By the time you get back from town, it'll be over."

"But—"

"Listen to me. I'm glad you were here to help, but we can't do anything more. If you never follow another order from me, I want you to follow this one. Take your daughters to camp, then come back and get some rest. I don't want to see you outside the apartment until you've had at least six hours' sleep."

"I don't need to sleep. I'm—"

He gave her arms a little shake to get her full attention. "You'll be no good to me if you're dead on your feet. Rest. We'll talk this afternoon. Please. Do as I ask."

She looked as if she might argue further. Then suddenly, she nodded and walked away.

He turned back to the vet. "Let's get this over with."

# *CHAPTER SIXTEEN*

RILEY KNEW THAT on any ranch death was a common reality. But that didn't mean she could easily accept the loss of the black mare.

Quintin had insisted she get some rest, but how could she when her mind wouldn't stop trying to second-guess everything they'd done? Had there been some way to save the animal that they hadn't considered? Before the mare had gone down, was there some problem Riley should have seen? But how could there be? They'd recently gone over every inch of every horse with a close eye, and Dr. Hightower had pronounced the mare perfectly fit.

Finally, Riley had to accept that, short of a postmortem exam, they would never fully understand what had gone wrong.

She dozed throughout the day. Occasional glimpses out the window told her that Jim and Steve had shown up for work. She caught sight of Quintin once or twice. A large vehicle rumbled onto the property and she saw a backhoe make its way down the rutted path to the front paddock. Another brutal fact of ranch life. Because of her size, the mare would have to be buried where she'd gone down for the last time.

Somehow the day passed. Riley went to pick up the girls at camp and treated them to an early dinner at McDonalds. If they sensed her mood, they didn't show it. They chattered incessantly and picked on one another until Riley's temper got the better of her, and she hustled them out of the restaurant with a scolding.

When they reached the ranch, she sent them inside with a warning to behave, while she went over to the barn. It was still an hour before sundown. The branches of the trees were casting lacy shadows on the ground, but she didn't want the day to end without finding out how Quintin was.

A slow, deep breath shuddered through her as she reached the stall where the mare had struggled for so long. All the signs of that fight had yet to be cleared away. Blankets. A jumbled supply caddy. The lead rope they'd used to hoist up the IV solutions still dangled from the lowest rafter.

The mare's halter had been slung over one of the stall posts. Riley ran her fingers down the leather. Since most of the Warmbloods would be sold by October, Quintin hadn't seen the need to give them an engraved name plate on the side strap. But there was a plastic identification tag bearing the horse's stock number, and below it was a name.

Baroness.

A sob filled Riley's throat. Why had she not bothered to learn any of their names?

"You were such a brave girl, Baroness," she whispered. "I'm so sorry we couldn't help you."

To keep from crying, she began cleaning up the mess. She was folding the last blanket when she heard the low roar of the ATV. Quintin, probably returning from one last check on the herd after the second feeding. They always parked the ATV in the loafing shed, so it seemed likely he would use the barn as a shortcut to the house. She hoped so. She was eager to see him.

He appeared a few minutes later, looking weary and windblown from his ride out to the horses.

When he saw her, he frowned. "You don't look rested."

"Neither do you." She grimaced. "Guess that's to be expected."

"How are you feeling?" he asked gently as he approached her.

"I forgot how…how awful it feels to lose an animal."

"You can't dwell on it, Riley." His tone carried a throbbing note of deep conviction. "It happened, and it hurts. But thinking back, there's no blame to take on. Not for either one of us."

She nodded, mainly because her throat was too tight to speak. She bit her lip and hugged her arms to her body.

Quintin pulled off one work glove and touched the corner of her mouth with his thumb. The casual affection in that touch made her shiver inside. "If you're ever going to be a real ranch manager, you do realize you'll have to get a lot tougher?"

"Yes." She inhaled slowly, then looked at him with a steady gaze. "Maybe when I leave here, I should go back to accounting work. Calculators never make you cry."

His face went as still as the air in the barn. In that moment, there was no separation between them.

*Tell me I can stay,* she begged silently. *Tell me you want me to stay.*

But his smile was slow, and all the more compelling because it was tinged with sadness. "Riley…"

There was a sudden rustle behind her. She turned her head to see Roxanna coming into the barn. The child looked furious, driving her heels into the ground, her mouth a tight line of anger.

"Mom. Wendy says she's gonna use your special bubble bath. I told her she couldn't and when you're not around I'm in charge, but she won't listen, and she says she's gonna do it, anyway."

Riley stared at her daughter helplessly, trying to formulate sensitive, motherly words to deal with this latest silly dustup. Unfortunately, she was tired and not feeling particularly understanding. When nothing came to her immediately, she settled for pulling rank.

"I've told you how I feel about tattling, Rox. Go back to the apartment."

"But I'm in char—"

"*Now.* I'll be there in a minute to deal with Wendy." Deliberately, she turned back to Quintin, sending the clear message to the child that the discussion was over. She heard her daughter's huff of angry exasperation, then silence. She could envision Rox stomping off. With everything that had happened in the past few days, Riley couldn't find it in herself to feel guilty. Her patience was on its last legs.

She was almost afraid to look at Quintin. When she did, his hard-boned features held nothing but wry humor. "The joys of motherhood, huh?" he said in a dry tone.

She nodded. "I'd better go and referee. I just wanted to see how you were, and find out if you had an update on Virgil."

He seemed perfectly willing to change the subject from her impending departure. The awful truth rolled around inside Riley like liquid mercury. He really might be relieved when she left. Glad, even. No more distractions. No more having to play nursemaid to her weaknesses.

"Jim says he's doing great," Quintin said. "Eager to get out of the hospital and back to work. But realistically, I don't see how we can..."

He stopped, frowning.

She heard it, too. The sound of a motor coming to life. The ATV. But the Ramseys were already gone, so who—?

An icy chill zipped up Riley's back. "Roxanna!"

Quintin must have suspected the same thing, because he had already turned to make a dash for the back door of the barn. Riley dropped the blankets and ran after him.

Surely Rox wouldn't take the ATV, she tried to tell herself. Her daughter knew better. But how often had she begged for a ride? And she'd been so angry just now.

Riley saw her the instant they left the building. Straddling the seat, the child could barely reach the floor pedals. The vehicle jumped forward as she gave it juice, banging against the side wall of the loafing shed and nearly unseating her in the process.

"Rox!" Riley shouted in her toughest tone. "Stop right now!"

Her daughter tossed her a panicked look. She must have realized what a serious infraction this was, but there was a certain mulish determination in her features, as well. As though she'd decided she'd gone too far to turn back now.

With Riley close behind, Quintin's long strides ate up the distance that separated them. When he reached the ATV, he caught the handlebars and made a grab for the keys.

"I just wanted a ride!" Roxanna wailed in hoarse fury.

The ATV lurched forward again like a wild horse, and even Quintin's hold on the vehicle couldn't keep it from ramming into one of the beams that supported the shed's roof. The crack of splintering wood made Riley's heart grip with fear and then absolute horror as the dilapidated building seemed to implode.

She jumped back, tripping over her own feet, and landed hard on the ground. The earth seemed to vibrate with the rumble and roar, the sickening, slithering crash of collapsing timber and concrete. She turned her face away because the air was suddenly thick with dust and debris.

When the noise stopped and she could finally see again, she stumbled upright, coughing. The loafing shed no longer existed. She felt a thin scream rise in her throat, and bit it back. Panic would help no one.

"Roxanna!" she shouted, staggering around sprawling heaps of rubble. "Quintin!"

Then Riley nearly did scream, because she knew there had been no last-minute escape, no miracle. She caught sight of the crumpled fender of the red ATV, buried in rubble. Somewhere beneath that forest of lumber and concrete lay her daughter and the man she had fallen in love with.

And surrounding her, there was only silence.

QUINTIN DIDN'T LOSE consciousness, but it might have been better if he had. He was on his hands and knees in near darkness, choking, he realized dazedly. His head hurt, his neck hurt. His back felt as though someone had taken a baseball bat to it. Something hard and heavy lay across his legs, and when he tried to shift a little, dust and debris rained down on him and he had to squeeze his eyes tight.

He couldn't smell the smoke anymore. Did that mean the fire was out? If he could just get out from under this mess, he could find Teresa and Tommy. Or maybe the firemen had reached them in time, gotten them to safety....

*No, that isn't right, is it?*

He shook his head a little to clear it, and a wave of pain sharpened his thoughts.

He wasn't in the house in Colorado. Now he

remembered. The loafing shed had turned into a pile of Lincoln Logs when the ATV had rammed head-on into a supporting post. He'd made a mad grab for the girl, sweeping her off the seat and tucking her against his body just as hell poured down on them.

*Roxanna.*

He cursed softly.

"That's a bad word," said a small, quavering voice nearby. "If I said that, Mom would be really mad."

He opened his eyes and blinked a few times to clear the grit from them. He could barely make out Riley's daughter lying below him, in between his spread hands. She was on her back, staring up at him, her eyes wide with fear. No blood that he could see, thank God.

"I think you might be too late in the making-Mom-mad department," he said. He tucked his chin, trying to see her lower body. "Are you all right? Does anything hurt?"

"No. Can we get up now? I'm scared."

"Don't move," Quintin told her quickly.

He suspected he'd suddenly become like Atlas holding up the world. His forearms quivered with the weight lying on his back, but the slightest wiggle seemed to send debris sifting down. He and Roxanna might be locked together in this grotesque archway of safety, but nothing seemed very stable.

He heard Riley's voice shouting his name. He had a feeling she'd been calling for a while before his head had cleared enough for him to hear her.

"I'm here," Quintin called out. "I've got Roxanna."

"Is she all right?" She sounded frantic. "Tell me you're both all right."

"I think we're okay. But we're trapped under here." More quietly, he said to Roxanna, "Talk to your mom. Let her know you're all right. But don't move."

"I'm here, Mom."

"I hear you, baby. I love you so much. Just do what Quintin says. Okay?"

"I will. Quintin's holding the stuff off me."

He heard movement to his right. Carefully, he stretched his neck in that direction, but the light was so poor that all he could see was a wall of dusty lumber, lying crisscrossed like pick-up sticks.

"Just lie still," Riley said. "I'll get you out."

He heard the scrape of something being lifted, and another sprinkle of dust fell over him. "No, don't touch anything! This junk is like a house of cards. Move the wrong thing and it'll come down on us. Do you have your cell phone? I can't reach mine."

"It's in the apartment. Hang on. I'll call 911."

"Call them, but see if you can reach Ethan. He's closer."

Silence then, except for the occasional tinkle of some unknown piece of the shed sliding into oblivion. Quintin closed his eyes, fighting against the pain in his back. His heart had begun to thump so hard that he could practically feel the adrenaline surge. Something dripped off his nose—he hoped it was sweat—and he wondered how much longer he could bear up against the crushing weight pressing down on him.

In the dark, fear, like a goblin, began to drift into every crack and crevice. He heard a sob, and for a moment thought it had come from his own throat. Then he opened his eyes and saw the pale oval of Roxanna's face below him, scrunched in misery.

"Don't cry," he told her. "We'll be out of here soon."

That just made her cry harder. "I'm…I'm…sorry," she sobbed. "I didn't mean for this to happen."

"Of course you didn't."

Fumbling her way to an apology in a voice that begged for understanding and forgiveness, she said, "I was just…mad. And you…you and

Mom…promised I could ride the ATV, but we never did, and I…I…I was just going to—" She sniffed loudly. "Can I…can I lift my hand?"

"Yes. But do it slowly."

The girl brought her fingers to her face and wiped away tears. "Are we gonna die?" she asked in a misery-filled whisper.

"God, no," he replied with more confidence than he felt. "Not if I have anything to say about it."

He knew how impossible it was to offer that kind of reassurance. Hadn't he always told Tommy he'd keep him safe? But he hadn't. Quintin's mouth was suddenly bitter with the taste of failure.

He drew a careful, deep breath. He couldn't give in to that line of thinking. He'd made mistakes in his life, huge ones. But right now, this kid depended on him, and he wasn't going to let her down if he could help it.

Roxanna sniffed again. "You're just saying that so I won't be scared."

He forced himself to grin down at her, even though he had trouble holding on to his smile. "Well, you're still crying, so I must not be doing a very good job." He wished he had more than his voice to comfort her, but he didn't dare move a muscle. "Roxanna, listen to me," he said in his most commanding, calm tone. "I know you're scared. But we're going to get out of this. I just need you to be very strong right now so I can concentrate on holding this junk up and not worry about you. Can you do that?"

"I—I guess so."

"Good. Now just lie there and rest. Take some big breaths, nice and slow. In and out."

In the deep, blue-purple shadows he saw her eyes flicker to his hand, which was beside her head. "I think you're bleeding," she whispered, and he suddenly saw the whites of her eyes very clearly.

Aw, shit. His hand was almost black with blood. Where was that coming from? Luckily, there didn't seem to be an endless flow of it.

Roxanna flicked a finger toward his face. "There's more on your head."

Well, that probably explained why his brain felt as if it was being squeezed in a vise. "It's all right. I've cut myself worse when I shave."

He didn't know if she bought that or not. But in the next moment they heard the pounding sound of footsteps approaching, and then Riley's panting breath again.

"Quintin?"

"Still here," he said. He offered Roxanna another smile and added softly, "Not like we can go anywhere, right?"

"Ethan's coming with some men. It won't be long now."

"Good." He took another deep breath. "Good."

"I've brought a couple of flashlights. Is there any way I can pass one to you?"

"Not a chance."

"It'll be dark soon. We should have lights out here. There should be lights." Her voice sounded agonized, as though she was hanging on by a thread. "Can you see anything?"

"Not much. But we'll be fine." He looked down at Roxanna once more. "Your mom's starting to freak a little. Talk to her."

"It's okay, Mom," the child yelled immediately. "It's like a warm cave in here."

That seemed to reassure Riley somewhat. Quintin sensed her sitting on the ground as close as the debris would allow, waiting for help to come. For Roxanna's sake—hell, maybe for all three of them—she began a litany of encouraging comments. Telling them that someone would be there soon, how Wendy was waiting for her in the apartment, how Ethan had men jumping into a truck even before she got off the phone. That it might seem bad, but very soon the pile of rubble would be pulled off them.

She began to engage Roxanna in conversation, trying to bolster her spirits, and he was glad of

that, because frankly, he was about out of help-
ful things to say.

All he could think about was how much he
just wanted to let go. He heard his breath coming
in swift, labored jerks. This was worse than his
most punishing nightmare. He wanted to wrench
free, fight this claustrophobic demon that had
him in its relentless grip, but he knew that one
violent, unwary movement could mean death for
both him and the trusting child beneath him.

*Don't let go, don't let go. You have her. Now
hang on, goddamn you!*

His mind seemed detached from his cramped,
quivering, aching body. It labored with a kind of
desperate, feverish urgency, but just barely.

He must have been quiet too long, because he
heard Riley call out sharply, "Quintin! Are you
listening?"

"I'm right here," he managed to mutter between clenched teeth.

A brief silence, and then her voice came to
them, from so low on the ground that he wondered if she'd pressed her face to the earth. A
flashlight beam bounced around the rafters surrounding them. "I can see your hand," she said,
as though she'd just spotted some wonderful
treasure. "Please. Please hold on."

"I'm not letting go,' he said with fierce determination, and was shocked that his voice

sounded no more than a painful, hoarse whisper. "I'm not going to let anything happen to her. I promise."

"I know you won't," she said, and he could hear the catch of fear in her voice. "But I want both of you out safe and sound. Do you hear me? Roxanna *and* you. You must hold on."

He didn't answer, and realized in sick despair that he was beyond words. His heart felt as though it was bursting with the strain of remaining motionless under his precarious burden. His resistance was draining away like water down a drain.

And then suddenly he heard the dim sound of vehicles in the yard, the squeal of brakes, men shouting. The satisfying clank and scrape of equipment being unloaded.

"They're here! Ethan's here, Quintin!"

It was Riley's voice again, low and faint, as though she was suddenly a long way away.

In the next moment there seemed to be pencil beams of light everywhere, swooping and diving as frantically as strobes in a nightclub, but beautifully bright. The illumination couldn't quite reach the cave he and Roxanna were trapped in, and it made for deep, menacing shadows that revealed an eerie, nightmarish scene of destruction. The light almost seemed more threatening than the darkness had been.

Quintin heard Roxanna gasp, and he looked down at her. "Close your eyes if it scares you," he told her gently. "It won't be long now."

She nodded and did as he suggested.

For what seemed like an eternity he remained quiet while a flurry of activity went on around them. He heard boards being tossed aside, the thunk of cement blocks, but the pressure on his back didn't ease. He lost track of time and concentrated on taking slow, deep breaths. One. Then another. And another.

Finally, he saw a flashlight probe the interior of their prison. All around them it was suddenly very quiet and still.

"Hey, buddy." Ethan's voice came to him. "How you holding up?"

"I'd be a lot better if you'd stop playing around and get this sh—get this stuff off us."

"Almost there, you ingrate. We're getting ready to pull off the main obstruction now, so be prepared for a little debris shifting."

"Ethan…?"

"Yeah."

A kind of tremor was running up his right arm now, like a crack appearing in an overburdened pillar. "Make it soon. My back's breaking. I'm not…Hercules…."

"One minute. Just be ready and hang on."

Quintin trusted his friend, and true to his

word, in no time the pressure began to ease. As Ethan had warned, a small avalanche started to tumble down on them. With an order to Roxanna to lie still, Quintin let his elbows collapse so that his body covered hers as much as possible. He ducked his head against hers as she squealed in fear, but he just pulled her tighter.

And then suddenly they were free and cool air was touching his back. Hands lifted him up, and he saw Riley's white, stricken face as she pulled Roxanna out of his arms and gathered her close. His legs felt as though they'd been filled with sawdust, and his arms hung uselessly at his sides.

A couple men from the Flying M helped him sit on the tailgate of a truck, and he dragged in great gulps of sweet night air. He saw the flashing lights of emergency vehicles pulling into the yard. He saw the twisted pile of wood where the loafing shed had been, and glimpsed the rear end of the ATV peeking out from under it.

Ethan came up to him, grinning, offering a whiskey flask. "It's probably not what the doctor's going to order," he said, "but you look like you could use it."

Dazed, Quintin took it, noting that his hand was shaking as he brought the flask to his lips. The whiskey went down like liquid fire, but immediately kindled warmth inside him. He touched his temple gingerly, and his fingers came away wet and red.

Ethan surveyed Quintin's head. "Might need a few stitches. You'll be damned lucky if that's the worst of it."

"It is," he assured him. "I'm fine." He didn't feel fine, exactly. His back and shoulders throbbed. But he knew he'd suffered worse damage when a bull named Hellraiser had stomped him into the dirt on the rodeo circuit. He handed Ethan back the liquor. "Thanks for riding in to the rescue."

His friend grinned. "Told you this place was gonna be a bitch to pull together. Almost got the best of you tonight."

Quintin glanced toward Roxanna, who was tucked up against her mother, sobbing her heart out. "I just want the kid to be okay."

"She will be. Thanks to you."

## CHAPTER SEVENTEEN

QUINTIN SAT ON THE tailgate of the truck, exhausted, his limbs not yet completely at his command.

It would be impossible to overstate how much he wished everyone would just leave. He wanted to be alone. He needed time to regroup. But everywhere around him were people, and all of them seemed to have a mission.

An EMT had shepherded both Riley and her daughter into the apartment so he could do a more thorough examination. Caught in a sweep of red-and-blue lights, Ethan was talking to Beaumont Emergency Services, helping to fill out reports. The crew from the Flying M was clearing the loafing shed area. Cassie Rafferty stood near the apartment, comforting a wide-eyed, frightened-looking Wendy Palmer. A second EMT was in front of Quintin now, dabbing at a small cut near his temple.

"Sure you don't want to go to the hospital?" the man asked.

Quintin shook his head carefully. He couldn't

stomach hospitals. It had been all he could do to sit in the waiting room when Virgil was injured. With a suit-yourself look, the technician finally closed up his medical kit and trooped back to the waiting ambulance.

It felt to Quintin as though the wheel of time had spun backward. It might as well have been a decade ago, when he'd lost Teresa and Tommy. Except that this time he was still upright and not being carted away on a stretcher to some hospital, where they would be unable to mend anything that really mattered to him.

It was all horribly familiar, and he hated it.

Word must have gotten around the county. Jim and Steve Ramsey showed up to help the work crew. Lilianna came and, after spending a few minutes making a fuss over him, headed into the house to make pots of strong coffee. Even his personal physician, Dr. Kayne, was suddenly there.

"Who the hell called you?" Quintin asked the man, beginning to feel as though he'd lost control on his own spread.

"I did," Ethan said, coming up to join them. "I knew you wouldn't go to the hospital, so the doc's going to give you a thorough exam here."

"I'm fine," Quintin said, for what felt like the hundredth time. He motioned toward the pile of rubble. "I just need to make some sense of this mess."

"Not right now you don't. Let's get you into the house."

"No," Quintin growled. He looked toward the apartment door, wishing Riley would come out, wishing anyone would come out and tell him how Roxanna was. He would have gone over there himself, but his legs were still shaking too badly to support him, and he didn't want to end up looking like a fool.

Ethan must have guessed what was on his mind or seen the direction of his glance. "Cassie just went in to get an update. Roxanna's going to be fine, Quint, and Riley will be out soon. In the meantime, you're coming with us."

"This is my responsibility. I can't leave it to others."

"That's what you have a ranch manager for, remember? Once she knows her kid is all right, she'll be on top of things. I'll help her. Now we're going to the house."

Ethan and the doctor helped ease him off the truck tailgate, and immediately fire went up his legs and almost drove him to his knees. With Ethan supporting him under one arm, somehow he got across the yard, but with every slow, trembling step it felt as though a dozen charley horses were attacking him.

After that, he sort of lost his place in things. He was vaguely aware of getting up the stairs to his bedroom, of Lilianna offering him a huge mug of coffee, of Dr. Kayne stitching the cut on his head and shaking pills for the pain into his hand. Quintin took the hottest shower he could stand, and groaned with pleasure every second of it. Then he was in bed, and the doctor gave him a shot, something to help with the muscle spasms.

Quintin didn't want to sleep. He wanted to talk to Riley. And after the night he'd had, he was afraid his nightmares would show up in full force. He wasn't sure he could handle that. But he couldn't seem to keep his eyes open....

When he woke later, the bedroom lay in near darkness. Someone had left the bathroom light on as a night-light. The curtains were drawn. Beside the bed he saw the outline of a chair, but it was empty.

He wondered how long he'd slept. An hour? Two?

He hadn't had bad dreams, and his head only pounded dully. No longer a full-fledged drum line showing off in there. He felt a little foggy, but not too bad, really.

Gingerly, he sat up and turned on the bed-side lamp. His body protested in about a hundred different ways, but for the most part did as he commanded. Continuing to lie in bed would only make stiff muscles worse, so he decided to rise. He'd get dressed, then find out where things stood downstairs.

He was trying to get his legs into a fresh pair of jeans, and wondering how he was going to manage pulling on a shirt, when the bedroom door opened. He heard a soft gasp behind him and turned slowly to see Riley standing in the doorway.

"You're awake," she said.

He nodded, which sent fresh pain to his head. "I just needed a nap."

"You've nearly slept the clock around. It's Saturday."

That made him blink. He snapped his jeans and went over to his dresser. His watch said it was nearly eight. A little over twenty-four hours since all hell had broken loose. Annoying to have lost so much time, but no help for it, he supposed.

"How's Roxanna?"

"Mortified by all the trouble she caused and eager to apologize, but no worse for wear."

"That's a relief," he said, and inside him, a knot of tension gave way. But Riley's face was white and strained. He frowned at her. "What is it? What's wrong?"

"You. The bruises on your back and shoulders…" She pressed her fingers against her lips. Then she crossed the room to stand in front of him. "They look so horrible."

"Riley…" he said, and stopped, unsure of the right comfort that should follow. He knew his back probably looked worse than it was because he still carried burn scars from the past. But he wasn't willing to talk about them.

She came forward, then just stepped into him. Carefully, she brought her arms around his waist, crushing her face against his chest.

"Okay," he said, placing his fingers against the back of her head. "It's okay." Stupid words, but it was something to say. "I'm all right. No permanent damage done."

She looked up at him. "I'm sorry. I promised myself that I wouldn't be weak and girlie. But Dr. Kayne said we should keep an eye on you in case you had a concussion, and you slept for such a long, long time that I really started to worry."

He wasn't so tired and achy that he wasn't completely aware of how close Riley stood, of the tickle of her hair against his bare chest, the softness of her body pressed against his. He wanted to pull her even nearer, but didn't dare. It took gut-wrenching effort to step back and then let her go. Still, he managed it. It was either that or make love to her, with no thought of agreements and tomorrows.

"You can stop fretting," he assured her. "Tell me what's been going on while I've been sawing logs. Is Ethan still here?"

She shook her head. "He spent the night, but he left this morning."

That explained the chair by his bed. "Is he the one who was always waking me up, asking me my name? Pissed me off, I can tell you."

"Yes, all night. Lilianna watched after you today, but she's gone, too. This is supposed to be my shift."

"God. Make me feel like an invalid, why don't you?"

"Just following Dr. Kayne's orders." Riley walked over to the bedside table and picked up a small bottle of pills. "He wanted you to take one of these when you woke up. Muscle relaxers, I think."

"I don't need it."

"Ethan said you might say that, and if you did, I should call him."

"Why? I don't take orders from Ethan."

"No," she agreed with a small smile. "But he said he'd come over and help me hold you down."

Quintin frowned, but allowed her to shake a pill into his hand, because frankly, every part of his body felt like a sledgehammer had been taken to it. She poured water from a carafe, and he took the glass from her fingers. "Your bedside manner stinks," he told her, but swallowed the medicine down. The water took away some of the fuzziness that seemed to be coating his tongue. "I'm losing valuable time. There are things that need to be done."

"No, there aren't. What do you think I've been doing all day?"

"If it's Saturday, there's no day camp. So I assumed you were with your kids."

"Cassie offered to take the girls over to the Flying M for the night. I think Roxanna was relieved to go, since she's expecting me to lock her up and throw away the key anytime now."

"Don't be too hard on her. I suspect she'll be much tougher on herself than you'll ever be."

"Hmm. We'll see."

"So. Tell me where we stand."

"Well, let's see…." She lifted her hand to count items off on her fingers. "Jim and Steve and I were like well-oiled machines today. We put a new motor in the windmill. You know those pole barns you wanted in the pastures? We're almost finished with the first one. We hauled the last of the debris from the loafing shed to the dump. The herd's had both feedings." Her mouth twisted as she struggled to remember everything. Then she brightened. "Oh, and the irrigation crew tried to say they'd feel better holding off on the next step until you were back up and around—"

"What? Did they think I was going to croak and not pay them?" Quintin muttered.

"They're just lazy. So I pitched a fit until they gave in." She grimaced. "I think I scared them, but it got their attention." She pushed her hands into the back pockets of her jeans and straightened with a challenge in her gaze. "So what did we miss that can't wait until tomorrow?"

For the first time since that damned shed had collapsed, he felt his lips tilt into a grin. Riley Palmer wasn't like any woman he'd ever met. She might have a few quirks and weaknesses, but damn, she was amazing. Did it matter that she wasn't a bona fide ranch manager with a long list of credentials? Did it really?

"Would you like something to eat?" she asked. "I'm willing to add feeding you to my job description. Just this once."

Even though he'd had nothing to eat since yesterday's lunch, surprisingly, he wasn't hungry. If anything, his stomach felt a little queasy. "I'll pass for now."

"All right." She pointed toward his head. "But your bandage needs changing. The doctor left supplies on the kitchen table. I'll get them and be right back."

When she left, he went into the bathroom,

took care of business and brushed his teeth to clear the cottony feel out of his mouth. There was a small bandage at his temple, and the flesh around it was somewhat swollen, but it didn't look too bad. Riley had been right, though, he acknowledged as he checked himself in the mirror. The bruises on his back and shoulders were pretty wicked.

By the time he got back to the bed, he was shaking a little. Maybe it was the pill, but reality seemed just warped enough to leave him feeling off-kilter. He hated it, but supposed he'd just have to wait it out.

Riley returned with supplies—scissors, tape and gauze, a tube of ointment. She went into the bathroom and reappeared a minute later with a basin of fresh water, which she placed on the chair near his bed.

She sat down beside him. Her nearness brought her scent to him, that soap-clean fragrance tempered by a whiff of warm woman that had been with him for days. He breathed it in before he could stop himself, and the involuntary tightening of his body was inconvenient, but no real surprise. Around her, he always seemed to be in a state of semi-arousal.

When she lifted her hands to pry away the bandage, he moved the bedcovers over his crotch.

She frowned as she surveyed the wound.

"Tell me you can't see my brain poking through," he said.

"No. But it's not pretty. Does it hurt?"

He wanted to say, "Only when I breathe," but one look at Riley's face, and the joke never left his mouth. Her face was paper-white except for two bright spots of color on her cheeks. When they'd tried every unpleasant thing they could think of to save the black mare, she'd been a real trouper, so he was thrown by how stricken she looked. He felt her cool fingers again his brow. Was he just imagining that they trembled?

He scowled. "What is it? What's the matter?"

She bit her lip. "Nothing."

"Tell me. I was joking about my brains falling out, but—"

"All I can really think about right now is how lucky I am. I could have lost my little girl, Quintin. But I didn't. Because you put your own life in danger. What can I ever say or do to thank you enough for that miracle?"

"It wasn't—"

She stilled him by placing her hand on his arm. "I mean it. You didn't just save Roxanna's life. You saved mine, as well, because if I'd lost her…" She looked him directly in the eyes. "You have more courage than anyone I know."

Surprise and embarrassment held him silent

for a moment. He wished his tongue didn't feel so lazy, that he could find words to keep this conversation from going any further. He shifted. "You're making too big a deal of it. I was under there, too, you know? And I wasn't ready to pack it in."

"Yes, but I could hear the strain in your voice. I know how terribly hard it was. Even Ethan said he was afraid you might not be able to last until they could get to you." She squeezed his arm, and there was more comfort in the feel of her fingers on his skin than he would have believed possible. "But you didn't let go," she said softly.

"You'd have haunted me forever if I did," he said lightly, because he felt so uncomfortable. But it came out all wrong.

Her eyes were darker than the deepest blue sea he could imagine. "Like your family haunts you?"

*This is why it isn't a good idea to let anyone get too close,* he thought. People always asked more of you than you wanted to give. "Riley…"

"It's all right," she said with a slight smile, and withdrew her hand. "You don't have to say anything about that time in your life. I just want you to know that telling me what happened to your wife and son, what made you so determined to save Roxanna…that isn't like putting a weapon in my hands, Quintin. I'd never hurt or judge you. I'm too thankful you were there when she needed you."

The last thing he wanted was Riley's gratitude. What he did want was her hands on him again, touching more than his head or his arm, bringing him the contentment that so often seemed just beyond his grasp.

There was an awkward silence then, but neither of them seemed compelled to fill it. He never talked about the past with anyone if he could help it. His reluctance was bone-deep. But he suddenly felt a real need to try and explain things to Riley. Maybe because she didn't have any preconceived notions. Maybe it was just the drugs in his system, loosening his tongue in a way that he'd regret tomorrow. But tonight, he found himself staring at her, wanting the connection.

"Teresa was a teacher on the Arapaho reservation where my grandfather lived," he said. "Everyone loved her. She had a way about her. She made people feel special, particularly the kids. After I met her, I knew there was no one else for me. I'd been kind of a hell-raiser when I was young, but she had such a quiet patience with people. She made me believe I could be… better than I was."

"She sounds like a wonderful woman."

"She was. We had a great marriage. Even better once Tommy came along. I don't know if you've ever spent much time around an Indian reservation, but they can be grim, hard places to raise children. I was never happier than when we were able to buy a small ranch away from all that. It was a real fixer-upper, but we didn't mind."

"So you've always been the kind of guy who likes a challenge."

He grimaced, remembering just how big a challenge that ranch had turned out to be. "I suppose so. I just knew I wanted something more for my wife and son. And for a while, it looked like we could have it. Teresa and I used to lie in bed at night, talking about all the things we were going to do to the place." He exhaled heavily through his nose. "Funny how that works. When you're lying side by side in the dark, you can almost have the life you long for."

His voice died in his throat as he heard what he'd just said. He never talked this way. Never wanted to. Damn. The drugs were making him stupid. He needed to stop talking. Right now.

He felt Riley's fingers slip around his, and it was amazing how nice that felt. Like an anchor. "Tell me what your ranch was like," she said gently. "Did you run cattle?"

He found himself telling her. His thoughts were too tangled to remember all the details, but most of it was indelibly etched in his mind, and even after all these years, the words just came. He didn't know if she was really interested or just being kind, but it felt astonishingly good to revisit that part of his life, before everything had gone so horribly wrong.

"We were struggling," he said at last. "But it was manageable. Then the winter Tommy turned five, the furnace started acting up. Fine one day, down the next, but I was sure I could baby it through the hard months. Cattle prices were in the basement that year, so I didn't want to shell out the money until we had to. Teresa was tired of waking up to a cold house, but I just kept tinkering with it." He scrubbed a hand over his face, then winced when his fingers scraped his tender temple. "I wish to God that I'd listened to her."

"Lots of people try to avoid making large purchases until they have to. You couldn't have known—"

"I know that in my head," he acknowledged roughly, "but somehow…" He frowned and looked at Riley. "Am I making any sense? Everything feels so…muddled."

"You're doing fine. Go on."

"We had a bad snowstorm one night. In the morning, the house was freezing, and Tommy ended up in our bed, snuggling under the covers with us."

Riley smiled. "I can imagine how nice that must have been."

"Yeah, it was," Quintin agreed, remembering. "But I had to get up and make sure I hadn't lost any cattle. That's all that mattered to me. So I left Teresa and Tommy in bed. They were going to go back to sleep."

He shifted uneasily, because this was the part that always got to him, that last image of his family, the last moments he'd held them. Teresa, looking all sleep-mussed and smelling like warm spices. Tommy, curled and giggling against his mother's side, so innocent and trusting.

"The last thing Teresa said to me was that she wasn't spending another night in that house if I didn't do something. I just laughed and kissed them both. And that was the last time I saw them alive."

Riley's fingers twitched in his. He looked over at her, but her gaze was lowered, as though she was fascinated by the hand resting in her lap.

"The furnace started the fire," he went on. "By the time I got back to the house... I tried to get to the bedroom and ended up under a bunch of beams when the roof collapsed. The fire department came. Pulled me out. I was taken to the hospital. But they couldn't reach Teresa and Tommy in time. They found them still in the bed."

"Oh, God."

"The fire marshal said the smoke got to them before the fire could, so maybe it wasn't…it wasn't as painful. I like to think so, anyway."

"Quintin…" He could barely hear her speak his name. When she went on, after a long moment of silence, Riley's voice was low and not quite steady. "Cassie told me you'd lost your family, and I tried to imagine your pain. But I don't think I can. Those days in the hospital with Wendy… I thought I'd lose my mind. But this… I think there are places a person just can't get to unless they experience them. I'm so sorry this happened to you."

"No. You're right. You can't know." He shook his head. "The guilt you carry. People try to tell you that it's not really your fault. Accidents happen. But it…it breaks you down. Sometimes I see their faces that morning. The love and trust any man would treasure. I try to imagine what I'd have done to any bastard who put my family at risk the way I did, and I just can't…let myself off the hook."

She lifted her chin to look at him. "You can't change what happened," she said, her voice no more than a ragged rasp, but still determined. "Eventually, you'll have to move past that kind of guilt, or you'll go crazy. You must want that for yourself, or you wouldn't be doing what you're doing here now. Trying to rebuild. Trying to put meaning in your life again."

"I don't know. Sometimes I wonder why…"

"I know it's difficult, but I think I know you well enough now to say that you'll never break. That's not who you are. So I have to believe that you *will* move past it one day. And your family loved you. They'd want happiness for you, too. I just feel that in my heart."

Her eyes were huge in her pale face. He could feel the tremors in her hand. Sharing his dismal history with her affected him as nothing else would have, and it was all he could do not to lean over and place his lips against hers.

"I want to believe that, too," he said. "But I don't want to talk about it anymore. I can't."

"Then we won't," she told him gently. "Let me finish changing your bandage, all right?"

He turned toward her, allowing silence to stand as his answer. His lashes came down, and he rested his gaze on the roll of gauze in her lap. Her rib cage moved with each breath, so close. He wanted to slide his fingers under the soft cotton of her blouse. To cup her breast and put the pad of his thumb right on the spot where her heart pounded. The drugs were in his system, making him feel sluggish, but not so much that he didn't know how wonderful that would have been, just to feel her flesh against his hand.

She fussed over him, taking so much time with the bandage that he began to think he would explode if she didn't stop touching him.

At last she seemed satisfied. "All done," she said, giving him a smile as though he was a nursing home inmate. "Do you want to rest awhile?"

She patted the bandage lightly, then nudged the hair back from his brow. Before he could think twice about it, he caught her fingers, stilling them in a grip meant to get her attention, but not to bruise. "I don't want any more babysitting," he said softly. "I want you to let me make love to you."

Her eyes widened slightly, almost seeming to glitter, but she kept her body still, didn't try to escape or pull away. Held his gaze.

"I'm not so drugged that I don't know what I'm saying," he told her. "Stay with me, Riley. Please."

## CHAPTER EIGHTEEN

RILEY DIDN'T INTEND to move. There was no recognizable command from her brain. One moment she was sitting beside Quintin, doing her best to show nothing more than calm concern, and the next she leaned forward and kissed him gently on the lips.

There was no single moment when she said to herself, *This is what I want. This is what I'm going to do.* It just felt like a compulsion, a need she couldn't ignore.

She knew very well that any more time spent in Quintin's bedroom meant acceptance of whatever might come later. She didn't care. She loved this man.

Quintin was everything she'd ever wanted in a mate. Strong and decent. Caring and honorable. She was drawn to him in some deep, visceral way she couldn't explain. And right now, she just knew it felt right. No matter what came tomorrow. Tonight, she decided, she would make every minute count.

He made a low, hungry sound in his throat as

her mouth grazed his. He responded by deepening the connection, and there was discovery for Riley in the warmth of his lips, in the way they molded to hers. Then a quiet surprise and comprehension. With the drugs in his system, she hadn't expected him to be so responsive. To react with such strength.

She broke away and turned her face into the curve of his neck. With her lips against the salt-flavored velvet of his skin, she whispered, "Are you sure you can do this? That pill…"

He chuckled and wrapped his arms around her. "Let me worry about that. I think I'm up to it."

Pulling her closer, he rubbed against her. She felt the heat of his pulsing arousal. His body was so hot where it met hers, even through his jeans, and the contact was so exciting that an involuntary shiver ran through her.

"It would seem so," she said.

Refusing to wait another moment, Riley pushed Quintin backward on the bed. Her hands went quickly to his waistband, finding the button of his jeans, then the zipper. She began yanking them down his legs. "Lift your hips."

He smiled up at the ceiling, but did as she said. "Do you know how many times I've dreamed about this?" he asked. He made an attempt to rise, but fell back.

"Probably no more than I have."

With an embarrassing lack of finesse, she got his pants off and tossed them over the chair. She'd never seen his bare legs before, but they were as long and muscular as she expected. She pushed away the thought of how good they'd feel wrapped around her body.

First things first. She tapped his thigh. "Now the boxers, cowboy."

"Whatever the lady says," he said in his most agreeable tone, and while he pulled them off, she stripped out of her own jeans and flung them aside.

When he was naked at last, he just lay there, not a bit bashful about his body. She stared down at him, and her blood suddenly felt as though it might burst in her veins. A craving to capture him in her hands, to explore every rippling inch of him, drove her. She couldn't have said where this boldness came from. She'd never been particularly aggressive in a sexual sense. But whatever accounted for it didn't matter to her right now. Not one bit. It shocked her how little conflict there was inside her.

She reached down to take him.

He caught her hand, making her look up. "Uh-uh," he said, grinning at her. "Your turn."

He pulled her farther onto the bed, so that she was forced to go down on her knees. She sat back on her heels, facing him, while he did the same. She saw something come into his eyes, some vivid emotion that drove out the shadows and erased much of the tiredness lining his face. It was longing. So potent and sexual that heat shot through her again.

He ran a finger along the collar of her blouse. "This is pretty," he said. "Matches your eyes. Now let's take it off."

He began unbuttoning, and anticipation fluttered through her, following the path of his touch until her body was quivering with eagerness. He slid the shirt from her shoulders, then did the same with her bra.

He looked at her for what seemed like forever, and she felt color come to her cheeks. Riley wasn't used to this kind of blatant exposure. She'd had children. She wasn't a teenager anymore. She wanted so badly to please him, but insecurity made it impossible for her to resist the temptation to cover her exposed breasts.

"Don't," he murmured, capturing her wrist and anchoring it gently behind her so that her chest thrust even farther up and outward. "Don't you know how beautiful you are to me?"

A small gasp escaped her when he brought his free hand to her throat, then trailed it slowly down to a nipple, rubbing it with his thumb, tugging lightly until one, then the other, responded with embarrassing ease, and pleasure moved through her in waves.

He planted kisses on every part of her that came into range. Fierce, hungry kisses that felt so different from the gentle touch she had experienced from him before. She loved it.

He brought his mouth to her breasts, working her nipples with a tongue still wet and warm from a kiss. His lips moved over her in a lazy, possessive way that made her skin tingle and heat.

When she moaned, he pulled back. "I don't want to hurt you," he said. "If I am…tell me. Just tell me want you want."

"I want…" She swallowed hard. "I want… more."

She heard his rumbling chuckle, and then he showed her how much more there could be.

Eventually, his hand slid down her waist to slip inside her panties. There was no barrier between his warm fingers and her skin, and when he pressed deeper, stroking the sensitive flesh between her inner thighs, she groaned and arched against him. Under the spell of his heavenly charm, she was lost.

"Easy," he whispered against her ear. "It's all right. I've got you, and I won't let go."

Before Riley could say anything, they both heard his stomach growl loudly.

He swore and she couldn't help a weak laugh as she dropped her head forward against his shoulder. "Oh, God, Quintin," she gasped. "If we stop now because you have to have something to eat, I'll go mad."

"My stomach," he said with a smile in his voice, "hasn't been waiting for food as long as I've been waiting for this. Ignore it. I intend to."

And then he was skimming the silken wisp of her underwear down her thighs and away, bringing her under him in a sweet, stage-by-stage embrace. Engulfed with wanting, she lifted her arms around his back, feeling the shifting patterns of his smooth muscles beneath her palms. She had the hazy thought that she might hurt him—those bruises had been ugly—but he seemed to take no notice, and when she felt his breath on her throat like a nectar bath, his kiss against her collarbone, she forgot about it, too.

Her breathing became rapid, and so did his as they grew more and more fluent with each other's bodies. Time seemed to slow, stretching to accommodate them. With murmured words and encouraging hands, they searched for perfect delight. Every taste, every moist curve and silken hollow explored brought them closer to that exquisite, ancient threshold.

By the time Quintin placed his hands on her hips, holding her steady as she writhed beneath him, Riley knew she could take no more. She needed to be closer, needed to be a part of him and he a part of her. She quivered with eagerness as he thrust a finger inside her, then a second, stroking her into readiness, though it was hard to imagine how she could be any more so. His warm touch worked a wicked magic on her, making her mind spin until she moaned again.

"Quintin. Please…"

Her gaze connected with his. He gave her a tender half smile, and he seemed so incredibly beautiful to her in that moment. With her control stretched whisper thin, she spread her legs wider. She was trembling now. Panting. Her body begged for release from this aching, wonderful anguish.

His mouth invaded hers again, and at the same time she felt the powerful warmth of him slide into her, then sink deeper. She surged against him, feeling the need to merge with him, to absorb his strength. He began to move faster, and she met that primitive rhythm, unwilling to wait any longer, and feeling as though she was coming alive again after so very, very long.

A wildness overcame her then, primitive and almost brutal. There were no sighs now, no murmurs, only hissing breaths and thundering pulses. Beyond all reason, she bucked against him, and he thrust hard, angling her rocking hips so that he could immerse himself into her deeper and deeper.

"Quintin!"

The gasping sound of his name was at once a plea and a promise. Her vision grayed. She couldn't catch her breath. She was *with* him, but she couldn't hold on any longer.

Ecstasy bubbled up within her, filling her to the point of sweet pain. Pleasure burst inside her suddenly and she shuddered and called his name again, realizing that Quintin's own control was slipping away. For a moment his eyes searched hers as though they were looking for something to hold on to. Then he exploded into her, tumbling into a realm beyond time and place.

Afterward, wrapped in a warm, wonderful lethargy, he lay on top of her. She cushioned his head on her breast, her fingers slowly easing sweat-damp hair away from his brow. His eyes were closed, his breathing ragged.

Eventually he raised his head and searched her face. "I thought I'd have more control than that," he muttered. "I'm sorry."

Riley smiled, her mind and her body deliciously drugged by the savage wonder of their lovemaking. "I'm not."

"How do you feel?"

"Like I've been floating and floating, and have just now come back down to earth."

He pushed upward and dropped a light kiss on her lips. "I think we should both rest."

She nodded. He eased his weight to one side, turned off the bedside lamp and pulled her against him, as though he didn't want them separated, even in sleep. She curled beside him like a kitten, loving the warmth of his body next to hers in the dark, comforted by the sound of his heart beating so close to her ear. She could hear his breathing start to settle, softer, gentle now as he began to drop into sleep.

She disappeared into that moment. Tomorrow would be here soon enough. She loved Quintin, but had absolutely no reason to think he felt the same way toward her. Nothing had changed, really. They had different lives, with problems and duties that love would only complicate.

It was going to be so hard to leave him.

What had he said earlier? That in the dark, you could believe all the things you longed for were possible. There was truth in that. Tonight, she was here. And she was his.

PAIN TUGGING AT THE BACK of her neck woke Riley. Her eyes snapped open. It took her only a moment to realize where she was, and when she did, she smiled.

She was still nestled against Quintin. Her head lay on his shoulder, one of his hands cupped her breast loosely. Sometime during the night, his legs had tangled with hers, but she didn't mind sharing that space. Her hair, however, was trapped under his arm, which explained what had pulled her out of the wonderful dream she'd been having about the two of them. Slowly, careful not to wake him, she moved until the strands he'd trapped were free.

Tilting her head, she glanced up at him. He looked boyishly handsome in sleep, and yet so magnificently male. So alive. It seemed right to be here like this. To hold him and sleep with him and wake with him. She longed to stroke him awake and make love. It was downright pathetic the way her heart took off racing, and her body quickened at the thought of feeling his power inside her once more.

What would he do if she kissed him? If she reached beneath the sheets and took him gently in her hand? She grinned in the darkness, just thinking about it.

Quintin mumbled something in his sleep. Raising one hand, Riley brushed her thumb against his lower lip. "Come back to me," she whispered, her voice thick with a longing she couldn't hide anymore. "Come love me."

He responded by turning his head, nuzzling his cheek deeper into the pillow.

She started to reach for him again, then fought

off the urge. In the past forty-eight hours he'd been through so much. Dealing with the mare's death. The shed accident. Even though he'd seemed perfectly capable of doing any number of wonderful things to her body last night, his must have limits. He needed rest. She didn't have the heart to wake him.

Beyond the curtains, it was still dark, but her internal clock told her that it must be around five in the morning. If this was a normal workday, she would be up in another hour, getting the girls ready for breakfast and then day camp. She'd be in the pasture by seven, seeing to it that the herd was fed.

But this wasn't a normal day. It was Sunday. The twins were at the Raffertys' place, and she lay here in the arms of a man she'd come to love with all her heart.

And along with that knowledge came the instant reminder that Sunday was also her last day at Echo Springs. The end of the arrangement.

*Why am I suddenly so scared?* she thought anxiously. *From the very beginning, I knew this day was coming. I knew I was going to be unemployed again.*

*Because,* came the faint answer, *you're losing this job* and *Quintin, and that's more than you can bear.*

Riley's mouth went dry and she felt sick inside, just thinking about that.

The impulsive side of her quickly offered up possibilities. She could tell Quintin that she loved him. She could take the biggest gamble of her life and just lay it all out there, see what he said. She knew he desired her. Last night they had proved they had chemistry together. Suppose she tried to explain all the ways he'd made her fall in love with him? His kindness. His strength. All the things that made him so uniquely Quintin Avenaco.

*Think you can talk him into loving you back, Riley?*

Quintin had joined his body to hers with an almost desperate passion, but he'd said nothing of love. The night had been about pleasure. She knew enough about men to be certain of that. But what would this day bring? And the next day? Where could the relationship go if it was entirely one-sided?

Something stirred inside her, something that felt like a terrible sadness. In her dreams they were perfect for one another. In her dreams they could build a life together here. But only in her dreams.

Grief for a lost illusion held her still for a long time. A chill spread over her heart until she was cold through and through. It was time to go.

Desperate not to wake him, she slid from beneath the sheets. His fingers flexed as though to pull her back, but he didn't wake. She took one last look at his profile in the predawn light, then silently made for the door, grabbing up her clothes as she went.

Finally, she took several deep breaths and slipped out of the bedroom.

## CHAPTER NINETEEN

BACK IN THE APARTMENT, she ran a shower and laid out fresh clothes. She would pick up the girls at nine, then head out of town. Back to Jilly's for the time being, she supposed.

She knew she couldn't leave without saying goodbye to Quintin, but she wanted to keep it brief and as painless as possible, although the thought came to her that it was already too late for that.

In the bathroom, the hot water had steamed up the mirror. She wiped her hand over the glass. Her mouth was rosy and slightly swollen from Quintin's kisses. There was a bloom in her cheeks. Was it just her imagination that her eyes were soft and lustrous with a sensuous glow that hadn't been there yesterday?

No, she wasn't being fanciful. But there was no point tormenting herself about how foolish she'd been, either. She wiped her image away and stepped into the shower.

When she emerged, she threw on a T-shirt and shorts, then pulled out suitcases and began packing. The supply boxes she'd never gotten rid of were still in the closet. She hauled them out and worked nonstop, filling them with canned goods from the pantry, towels, toys, her laptop. In surprisingly little time the apartment looked as though the Palmer family had never been there.

The sun came up, promising another hot day. As she settled one of the supply boxes into the back of her SUV, she heard a soft whinny. One of Quintin's two mounts calling for breakfast. Azza, probably, who always seemed ready to eat. Riley went into the barn, and as expected, the horse swung its head over the stall door in eager anticipation.

Riley glanced at her watch. Still early yet to say goodbye and pick up the girls at the Flying M. She decided to feed Azza and Sandy, the mare that occupied the stall next door. There wasn't enough time to haul hay out to the pasture for the herd, but this could be her last official duty as ranch manager.

She tipped grain into their feed bins, then took a moment to stroke Azza's head. Was this the animal Quintin had ridden on that awful day when he'd desperately raced to save his family from the fire? She supposed that, like so many things about him, she'd never find out.

"Take care of him, you hay burner," she said softly to the horse.

She turned and took a long look around her. The fancy stalls she and the Ramseys had somehow managed to piece together. The siding that had been replaced and sweated over. The crummy little tack room that looked professional now. She had done a hell of a job here, she thought with grim pride. Maybe she wasn't a ranch manager wunderkind, but she had nothing to be embarrassed about.

Lifting the latch to the rear doors, she walked from the barn and squinted out at the back pastures. She could just make out the sleek, dark shapes of the herd as they grazed.

They were such a beautiful, impressive lot, and before the summer was over, more would join them. In October many would be going to new homes, their destiny linked to men who would keep the public safe, and maybe do a better job of it because they had the right partner.

She remembered the day Quintin had hired her, when they'd sat in his study and he'd explained what he wanted to accomplish. He'd told her about an incident that had happened up north somewhere last Fourth of July. Firecrackers had been set off near a mounted police officer. The horse had panicked, and before it was over, three people had been sent to the hospital, including the cop.

"Senseless. Stupid," Quintin had told her. "The right breed of horse, trained properly, and it should never have happened."

He had looked so determined that day, so passionate. Was that the moment she had begun to fall in love with him?

She stood staring at the Warmbloods, and after a while realized that she was beginning to feel slightly resentful. Damn it! She had worked hard to look after those horses, to meet every one of Quintin's demands, to make herself invaluable to him. She deserved to see the fruits of all that labor.

All right, so she wasn't perfect for what he had in mind for Echo Springs. So she was a distraction. And she had only to glance over to where the loafing shed had stood to know he had a point about the danger of kids being on a ranch. But lots of working properties in Texas had children on them.

Where was the fighting spirit she'd had on the day she'd met him, looking like an idiot in her bathrobe and unlaced sneakers? Hadn't she managed to reinvent herself as a ranch manager out of pure grit and determination not to give in to fear?

And the love she held for Quintin in her heart?

Was she really such a coward that she would slink away from Echo Springs without telling him how she felt? If she told him, it would be like risking everything on one throw of the dice, but she was already standing on the ragged edge of misery just thinking about leaving.

Wouldn't it be worth it to take one last chance?

Before she lost her nerve, she swung around and went back through the barn and out the other side. She marched across the yard and let herself into the house. As she started to head up the stairs to Quintin's bedroom, she heard his voice in the study.

She realized he was on the phone. Very clearly she heard him say, "…appreciate it. I know I said you could start tomorrow, but I really need you to come today. We have a lot of things to discuss, and I've gotten a little off schedule lately."

The shock of those words, and their meaning, was enough to halt Riley in her tracks. But not soon enough. She hit the study door, her mind numb, but her feet carrying her forward.

*Her replacement.* She wasn't even off the property yet, and Quintin was making sure the new ranch manager was ready to start.

He was seated behind his desk. He still had the bandage at his temple, but he seemed in good shape, fresh from a shower and rested. Spotting her, he motioned her forward as he listened to the person on the other end of the line.

She took a slow, deep breath and moved into the room, pushing back her shoulders and trying to fend off the hurt and anxiety tumbling through her. All right. Not the way she had wanted to start, but there still had to be hope for them. Didn't there?

"Right," Quintin said into his mobile phone. "If you take I-10, it ought to bring you here by noon."

She couldn't look at him. Her eyes fastened on his free hand, which lay on the desk. That hand had played her body in such wonderful ways last—

And then it hit her like a one-two punch, and anguish poured into every cell in her body. Beneath Quintin's palm lay the framed picture she'd seen that first day. The one of him and his family.

It hadn't been on the desk last night. She distinctly remembered Dr. Kayne sitting there, writing out a prescription for pills, handing the paper to her over an uncluttered blotter. But it was there now.

Riley envisioned Quintin waking up this morning, smiling a little because sex between them had been so damn good. Maybe even hoping for an encore. But the sex had just been fun, he'd probably told himself. Like make-believe.

As clearly as if she'd been in the room with him, she pictured him sitting here, looking down into the faces of his wife and child, filled with love for them. Filled with unbearable longing. The memory of the life they'd shared was trapped in his mind and heart as surely as their images were trapped behind that glass.

Riley could fight for this job. She could fight for love. But she couldn't fight the past. The past was real. The past was powerful. And it had a hold on Quintin she knew she couldn't break.

Smothering waves of sorrow washed through Riley, but somehow she managed to reach across and pick up a pen and paper. She jotted down a message, then put the pad on his desk. Still unable to look at him, she turned and walked out.

Like a woman in a trance, she went across the yard and into the apartment. She was trembling, and didn't think she had ever felt more alone. Tears stung her eyes, but she would not cry. She wouldn't. In another half hour she'd have the girls with her, and she mustn't let them see how upset she was. They were already unnerved by what had happened with the collapse of the shed.

Placing the apartment keys on the dining-room table along with the others she'd been given, Riley hefted the last box of supplies and went outside. *Get out of here,* her brain shouted. *Just go.*

She rounded the corner and saw Quintin leaning against the driver's door of the SUV, his arms crossed over his chest.

She felt the blood drain from her face. The last thing she wanted right now was a scene. And then immediately she thought, *Why should there be one?* Wasn't this exactly what he'd wanted from the very beginning?

Her feet didn't falter as she walked past him, though she couldn't look up. She opened the hatch and placed the box inside. When she closed it and came back to the driver's door, the note she'd left him was caught between two of his fingers, standing upright like a flag.

"*This* is how you leave?" He opened the note and read it aloud. "'Azza and Sandy have been fed, but not the herd. Best of luck to you, R.'" He wadded it up and threw it on the ground. "Kind of abrupt, don't you think?"

"I didn't see any reason to drag things out. What would be the point? Isn't this where we've been heading since the day I got here?"

"So you've packed up, and now you're just going to jump in the car and go."

"Yes, if you'll please get out of the way."

His voice, though quiet, was startling in the silence. "What about last night?"

Her heart pounded furiously, but she refused to be swayed. "Oh, last night," she said, waving off the subject as if it hardly warranted a discussion. "That was lovely, wasn't it? I'm sorry I took such advantage of you when you weren't feeling one-hundred percent, but it couldn't be helped, really. We've been dancing around one another forever, and it just…" She shrugged. "It just finally happened. I'm not a bit sorry our agreement got blasted to smithereens, but here we are, back in the real world, and it's over now."

"Is it?"

"Of course."

"It doesn't have to be."

She bit her lip, then turned toward the car, because she couldn't bear it if he saw how difficult this conversation was for her. She rested her arms against the back window, intending to offer something light and wry, but at the last minute she heard herself say in the most miserable voice, "Oh, God, Quintin. If you ask me to stay here and be your live-in lover until we've both had our fill, I really will be sick."

He moved then, straightening to cross the short distance that separated them. He didn't touch her, thank God. She didn't know what she would have done if he had. It felt as though she was about to shatter into a million pieces.

He snorted out a disgusted sound. "Do you

honestly believe I'd suggest something like that? That I'd hurt you or your girls by treating you like some easy lay I could throw away whenever I got tired of you? Is that how you see me?"

She turned her head to look at him, and felt the delicate shift of his mood. No longer just curious, but a little hurt, as well.

"Truthfully, no," she admitted. "You have a disgustingly honorable streak in you. But if I'm not going to work for you, and I'm not going to be your lover, that doesn't leave a lot of options. Not for remaining at Echo Springs."

"Sure it does. I thought you were so…innovative. There was a line on the résumé you sent me. Excellent at thinking outside the box, it said. Now suddenly you can't come up with answers?"

"No, I'm fresh out." She rapped her knuckles against her head. "Oatmeal up here at the moment."

"I'm not buying that."

"Okay, how about this? I *lied* to you. I put everything down on my résumé that I thought you'd like to hear because I knew I had to reinvent myself. And it worked. At least for a little while. But the truth is, I'm not an out-of-the-box thinker. Not on my best day. And definitely not today."

His eyebrows skipped upward in mocking disbelief. "You know, I might buy that if I hadn't worked with you the past three weeks and seen what an amazing woman you are."

Now he was just making her mad. "And yet you still don't think I can do this damn job permanently!" she snapped. "You ass. Let me by."

She tried to push past him, but he caught her arms in his hands. Bitterly hurt, she struggled briefly, but he wasn't going to let her go. She looked up at him, mortified that she might not get away from Quintin before real waterworks started.

"Riley," he said patiently. "You're not listening. I don't want you to be my ranch manager. I don't want you as a friend with benefits. I want you to be my wife."

"I— What?"

After an aching moment of silence he said, "I want you to marry me."

She was so stunned she just stared at him. She shook her head again in abstract denial, and at last her power of speech returned. "You don't mean that."

"I do."

"Well, it's insane. You don't love me."

"I'm afraid you're wrong."

"I'm not."

His head tilted and he frowned. "Why would you say that?"

"Because I know— You're just not."

"Are you going to be this difficult once we're married? I suppose I'll get used to it. I'll have to, because I love you too much to let it stand in the way. In fact, your contrary attitude may be one of the things I find most charming about you."

"Quintin, please don't joke…"

He shook her a little. "Then give me an honest reason why we shouldn't get married."

"Because you're still in love with your dead wife!"

His head jerked back. He looked as stunned as she felt. "What?"

"You still love Teresa. Did you think I wasn't listening last night when you told me what happened? Do you think I didn't hear how much grief there is in you?"

"Grief isn't—"

"You love her, and I understand that. I do. Your wife, your son. They were your whole world. And it must be so horrible that they can't be here with you, and you can't turn back the clock and be with them. So now you're…you're stuck somewhere in between. Some limbo that you can't escape, even if you wanted to."

He let her go and crossed his arms again. She couldn't tell how her words affected him. If he was angry. Sad. Accepting. But what he said was, "It sounds like you've given this theory a lot of thought."

"I didn't have to. I saw it. A little while ago, when I came into your office and you had that picture of them right in front of you. It was so clear to me then. You'll never be able to move beyond your past."

"You honestly believe that, don't you?"

"Before that phone call… Are you going to tell me that you weren't sitting there thinking about Teresa and Tommy?"

"No," he admitted, and even though she'd known it was true, it still hurt to hear him say it. "You're right, I was. Thinking about how much I loved them. About how much I've missed them. And how much I always will."

"Of course you will—"

He brought up his hand to halt her words. "No, stop. Just listen to me." He sighed heavily and ran his fingers through his hair as though he wasn't sure how to begin. Finally, he said, "I was thinking about how I've let ten years of grief and guilt keep me from happiness. After they died, I walled myself in and threw away the key because it was so much easier than facing my fear. I've never wanted to leave myself open to that kind of hurt again." He shifted and stared down at his hands for a moment. Then he raised his head and his eyes met hers, dark and direct. "But what you said last night… That neither one of them would want me to continue living this…

this half life. It's true. So yeah, I was looking at their faces. And all I thought was how happy I was in that picture, and how I haven't ever felt that way again." He reached out to cup her shoulders. "Until the day you walked into my life."

Tears came to Riley's eyes in a sudden rush. "It could never work, Quintin. I love you. I think I would try to be anyone to make you love me back. Anyone. But not her. I can't be *her.*"

"I don't want you to be Teresa. I want you to be you. The woman I fell in love with."

"The woman you had sex with."

"No," he said softly, yet with surprising firmness. "The woman I fell in love with. The one who tries to slay stuffed monsters for her kids, and who doesn't want to admit she hurts even when her hands are covered with blisters. The one who can gentle a fifteen-hundred-pound animal with just her voice, and who's willing to turn herself into someone else if it means she can put food on the table for her family. That's not a memory or a dream. That woman is real. And she's someone I want to spend the rest of my life with. She's you."

He placed his hand against the side of her face, slipping his fingers into her hair again so that she had to look up. His thumb slid to her cheek to wipe away the wetness of her tears. "What do

I have to say to make you believe me?" he asked in a low, soothing voice.

"I want to believe you," she said. "I do. But…"

"You think what? That we had such mind-blowing sex last night that I'm just confusing love and lust? All right, yes, the sex was terrific, and I can't wait to repeat it. But asking you to marry me isn't just a whim that suddenly popped into my head."

"It's not?"

"Hell, no." He gave her a smile of breathtaking charm. "I think it's been rattling around in my subconscious for quite a while. Fear made it possible for me to ignore it most of the time. But the subconscious doesn't lie or just go away, and the idea kept pushing and pushing, and every so often I'd get this vision that would snap open like a shutter. You and me, making a life together." A wicked glint came into his eyes. "So this morning, I just woke up and decided to stop fighting it and propose."

"You're serious."

"I need you, Riley. I can make this place work, but I can't be happy if you're not sharing it with me. I don't want to be that man stuck behind the glass anymore. I want to be out here in the real world. With you. Because you make me feel alive for the first time in so long."

He drew her to him for a kiss that carried

so much feeling it left Riley gasping. When he pulled back, his eyes were shimmering with a depth of emotion that should have scared her. Instead, it made her heart begin to soar. "Say you'll marry me," he said hoarsely. "I love you. Let me show you how much."

Joy was exploding inside her, sending fiery excitement through her blood, and Riley had to swallow twice before she could find her voice. "Yes," she said in a barely-audible breath, then her voice grew stronger. "I love you, Quintin. I wanted to tell you last night, but I was so afraid. And then this morning, I thought I'd just do it, but I lost my nerve when I came into your study."

He grinned. "You don't have to tell me. I see it in your face. I feel it in your heart, in the way it pounds when I touch you." His hand pressed against her T-shirt, and a moment later a teasing glint came into his eyes. "You're not wearing a bra, are you?"

"No. I was in a rush to get out of here and just threw this on."

He laughed and pulled her close again. "God, I'm going to love being married to you."

She abandoned herself to his touch then. Slow, languorous kisses that left her knees weak and her breath in tatters. She was so happy she thought she could laugh and cry and shout all at once. How could she have been so foolishly timid this morning? How could she—?

Riley lifted her head as a sudden thought occurred to her. "Wait a minute…"

"Oh, God," Quintin said, having to draw in his own share of morning air. "Save me from a woman who asks so many questions at the worst possible moments."

She ignored that. "A little while ago, I heard you on the phone. Asking someone to come today instead of tomorrow. Are you telling me you weren't talking to my replacement?"

"Sweetheart. There's no one who can replace you."

She punched him playfully on the arm. "I'm serious, Quintin. I know what I heard, and it wasn't much of a leap to figure it out. That person—a man, I'll bet—applied for the ranch management position, and you hired him."

Quintin was hardly paying attention to her. He seemed fascinated by her hair, rubbing the strands between his fingers again and again. "You have the most beautiful curls—like a thousand different threads of gold. You can't imagine how many times—"

"Quintin."

"I did hire someone," he admitted absently. "He starts today."

"As the ranch manager."

"As your assistant. I figure with Virgil out of the picture, and the two of us trying to make a go of things here, you'd need the help. If you don't like him, you can choose someone else, but I insist that you have the help."

"Oh. An assistant ranch manager. I guess that's all right, then."

"Anything else before I kiss you again?"

She sobered a little as one more worry came to her. "There's something I have to ask you, and please tell me the truth. I know you loved your son, and he can never be replaced. But I'm still young enough… What I'm trying to say is…I want—"

She broke off as he suddenly gripped her face between his hands. "I will always love Tommy and want to honor his memory," Quintin said, his voice thick. "But I can love more than one child. I'm going to love being a father to Wendy and Roxanna, but I want more."

"You do? Because I do, too."

"Yes. I've been thinking we need at least two."

"Two?"

"Well, Wendy's a soft touch, and someone's got to protect us from Roxanna."

Suddenly they were both laughing and kissing. Quintin locked his arms around her and made a low, deep sound as he tried to pull her closer still.

"Can we go back to bed now?" he said, his breath a feathery delight against her throat. "I'm dying to make love to you again."

"I can't."

He lifted his head and frowned. "Why not?"

"I haven't fed the horses yet," she said with a grin as she motioned toward the far pastures. "And my boss is kind of a stickler for schedules."

"Then we'll do it together. And when we finish, something tells me we'll be able to renegotiate your employment contract."

"I want a good benefits package," she teased.

"You'll get it. I'll give you all the benefits you want." He pulled her against his side. "In every room in the house."

\* \* \* \* \*

The series you love are now available in

# LARGER PRINT!

The books are complete and unabridged—
printed in a larger type size to make it
easier on your eyes.